A TIMELESS Romance ANTHOLOGY

SUMMER IN NEW YORK COLLECTION

A TIMELESS *Romance* ANTHOLOGY

SUMMER IN NEW YORK COLLECTION

Six Romance Novellas

Janette Rallison

Heather B. Moore

Luisa Perkins

Sarah M. Eden

Annette Lyon

Lisa Mangum

Mirror Press

Interior Design by Rachael Anderson
Edited by Annette Lyon and Kelsey Allan
Cover image # 144800323, Shutterstock.com
Cover design by Mirror Press, LLC

Published by Mirror Press, LLC
TimelessRomanceAnthologies.blogspot.com

ISBN-10: 1-941145-74-4
ISBN-13: 978-1-941145-74-6

TABLE OF CONTENTS

MORE TIMELESS ROMANCE ANTHOLOGIES

Winter Collection
Spring Vacation Collection
Summer Wedding Collection
Autumn Collection
European Collection
Love Letter Collection
Old West Collection
All Regency Collection
Silver Bells Collection
California Dreamin' Collection
Annette Lyon Collection
All Hallows' Eve Collection
Sarah M. Eden British Isles Collection
Mail Order Bride Collection
Road Trip Collection
Blind Date Collection

JOB HAZARDS

Janette Rallison

OTHER WORKS BY JANETTE RALLISON

Masquerade
All's Fair in Love, War, and High School
Son of War, Daughter of Chaos
My Fair Godmother
My Fairly Dangerous Godmother
My Unfair Godmother
My Double Life
Blue Eyes and Other Teenage Hazards
Just One Wish

ONE

Fighting crime wasn't supposed to involve wearing a leopard-print miniskirt, a silky halter top, and stiletto heels. Not once while Lydia Robinson was in the police academy a year ago had she envisioned that the job would land her on a seedy New York street posing as a hooker. But as Lieutenant Miner had told her a week ago after he called her into his office, "You're a natural."

A natural hooker? "Is that supposed to be a compliment?" she asked.

He held up his hands to stop her protest and nodded at the glass window of his office. Outside, two other female officers were talking about a case. Officer Loomis was fifty-two and had more wrinkles than a pile of forgotten laundry. Officer Dustin was seven months pregnant. "I just meant," Lieutenant Miner said, "that you're the best one in the department for the sting."

So now Lydia stood on a dimly lit corner next to a row of bars and strip clubs. She wore so much makeup that she looked like she was part of a Broadway play. Her usually long, brown hair had been curled, teased and poofed. It was magazine-girl, *notice-me* hair. Half-a-bottle-of-hairspray hair.

For the last four nights, Lydia had staked out different corners as part of the district's anti-prostitution sweep. She was the subject of catcalls and leers from men, and disapproving glances from other women who drove by. She was also cold, bored, and her feet hurt. Really, whose great fashion idea had it been to create heels so high that you felt like you were tip-toeing from place to place?

"My career is taking off," she muttered. Hooker humor. It helped ease the boredom.

Into her earpiece, Thompson, the head officer of the backup team, said, "You're doing great. We've had more busts with you as bait than we've had in years."

"Yeah, well, I'm a natural."

"Your mother would be proud."

Actually, her mother would be worried. Lydia had told her mom that her police job mostly involved paperwork. Office stuff. Safe stuff.

Strictly speaking, this gig *was* safer than most of the domestic-violence calls officers were called to. She'd never had a john fly into a rage and throw a chair at her.

"You gotta work on your strut," Thompson said, teasing her. "You're too *I'm-about-to-slap-handcuffs-on-you* and not enough *come-hither*."

"I can't do *come hither* in these heels. I only want to go thither and soak my feet."

"On second thought, Carey says your *I'm-about-to-slap-handcuffs-on-you* strut works. I'll take a vote and see what the rest of the guys in the van think."

Lydia leaned against a lamppost, trying to take some of the weight off her feet. "Don't make me mad, or you'll be the one out here in heels and a miniskirt."

"That would be one way to stop prostitution on this street corner."

Thompson's voice was light. A stark contrast to the graffiti and litter around them. It was easier to joke about the situation than to keep thinking about it. Young girls were often the ones out on this corner. Runaways. Drug addicts. Prostitution was filled with girls who'd been abused. The guys hiring them should know better. Half of the johns were middle-aged, educated businessmen. Yesterday she'd arrested a high school history teacher. Married with kids, at that.

A black BMW pulled up to her corner. A nice car for this part of the city. Lydia left her lamppost, swaggered over to the car, and put on an alluring smile. Two things needed to happen before she could say the words that would bring in the backup team. The guy needed to ask for an elicit act, and he needed to offer her money.

The tinted window rolled down. Lydia leaned toward it. "Looking for some fun, handsome?"

She called everyone *handsome*. She might have to act like a hooker, but at least she could be polite about it. As soon as the words left Lydia's mouth, she realized she hadn't misspoken. The man sitting behind the wheel was drop-dead gorgeous. She'd always thought so. Especially while dating him in high school.

Harrison Aldridge's sandy-blond hair was short and smooth, less tousled than it had been six years ago. The blue eyes were the same. Pale, like sunlight shining through water. His shoulders were broader. He'd grown into his height.

Lydia stared at him, incredulous. Of all of the places she

could have run into Harrison, he had to pull up to her corner while she was pretending to be a prostitute.

In that one moment, her mind flashed back to her senior year, to the time he'd given her a heart-pendant necklace for Valentine's Day. He'd shown up so many times at the grocery store where she worked as a clerk that her boss finally said that Harrison either had to stop coming to see her or start helping her shelf things. They spent many an evening restocking the snack aisle. On prom night, Harrison said he loved her.

And then a week later, he broke up with her. The memories about him always ended there—on the day, and the night before it, when she realized love hadn't meant much to him.

She and Harrison had been sitting on his apartment balcony, the lights of New York spread out in front of them like a constellation that had fallen to earth. Sitting on Harrison's balcony made her feel like she was soaring above the city, that all of her problems could be as easily overlooked as the dirt on the streets below them.

"So what's your good news?" she asked.

Earlier, he'd texted that they would be celebrating. Harrison had brought two wine glasses and a bottle of sparkling apple cider—underage champagne—with him to the balcony. He poured the cider into the glasses and handed her one.

"The good news is that you're looking at a Harvard freshman." He clinked his glass against hers in a toast. "Or at least I will be in September."

She had the grace to not drop her glass. She was even able to force a smile. "Congratulations!"

She wrapped her free arm around him in a hug. If they were hugging, he couldn't see her face, and he wouldn't be able to read the raw despair in her eyes. She had a moment to mask it, time to calm her shaking. "Wow, Harvard. That's great." When she pulled away from him, she was composed.

Lydia couldn't protest that going to Harvard would mean that the two of them wouldn't be together at CUNY. Harrison's parents had planned for him to go to Harvard since he was born. His father and grandfather had gone there. It was as much a part of the Aldridge tradition as running their family's property management business.

Lydia took a sip of the apple cider. The bubbles felt sharp inside her mouth, bitter. Harrison went on telling her about getting the letter today, how his parents had made a big deal about not opening it until they were together at dinner. "All I could think was, *If I don't get in, the rest of dinner will be really awkward.*" Harrison tilted his head back and laughed. He was all ambition and possibility. The happiness lit up his features, making him even more handsome. "Dinner crisis averted."

"That's the important thing." She laughed along with him, but even to her ear the laugh sounded strained. Hadn't he thought of her—even a little—while he'd held that envelope? Hadn't the miles that stretched between Massachusetts and New York made the paper a little heavier?

She took another drink and tried to push those thoughts away. She was being selfish. Attending Harvard was a huge accomplishment. Harrison couldn't change the fact that Lydia didn't have the money to go to a university like that. She was only at their private school on scholarship. Besides, people managed long-distance relationships all the time. Love knew no distance. They could overcome this.

Harrison went on, telling her how beautiful the school was, how rich with history. It was the oldest university in the country. John and Samuel Adams both went there. It was filled with pomp, ceremony, and trees that dripped red leaves in the fall.

Anxiety made Lydia grip her glass. "Will you come home on the weekends?" She didn't mean every weekend. Just sometimes. A lot of sometimes. She wanted some sign that he would miss her, and that he would make an effort to keep their relationship alive.

Harrison let out a scoffing sound that already sounded infused with elitism. "It's Harvard, Lydia. I'll be studying on weekends."

A piece of her heart broke right then, cracked and shivered. He wasn't thinking about her at all. Which only meant one thing; he didn't care that much about her. It was easy for him to leave. He was here celebrating it.

The lights around them seemed dimmer, both the ones in the sky and the ones in the landscape. "I'll miss you," she said.

"We'll still talk on the phone."

As though that could be enough. But then, maybe it was for him.

She nodded as he went on, knowing that she was being unusually quiet. He didn't notice. He was already gone, far away in a land with red-brick buildings, white-tipped towers, and the ghost of John Adams.

The next day at school, Lydia was a bundle of emotion. The hallways seemed too noisy, the classrooms too crowded. One moment she was devastated, the next angry, and the next resigned. She hoped that resignation would be the prevailing emotion during lunch when she and Harrison sat together. At the very least, she hoped she could fake some sort of bland happiness. But by third period, her emotions had swung toward angry. It was all she could do to hold herself together.

She texted Harrison that she had to go somewhere at lunch, so he didn't need to wait for her, then shoved her phone into her book bag. If he was so eager to do without her, he could start now. He might as well get used to it. They both should.

She made an excuse to her teacher and left the class five minutes early. Less chance of running into anyone in the hallways who wanted to talk to her. Feeling claustrophobic, she hurried outside. She would walk somewhere, get lunch from a street vendor, feed the pigeons, maybe skip out from the rest of school.

The air was warm today, reminding her that school was almost over. Her childhood was almost gone. Everything she'd known—over. *Don't think about it*, she told herself. *Don't think about any of it*. The last thing she wanted was to start crying before she was off school grounds. She walked with her head down, staring at the speckled remains of flattened gum on the sidewalk. She didn't see Brett Nicholson coming the other way until she nearly ran into him. Which was even more awkward because it was just the two of them on the sidewalk.

Brett was Harrison's friend, and thus her friend too. He was the school's quarterback and all-around sports darling. That alone would have been enough to make him popular, but Brett was also tall, dark, and too handsome for his own good. He never stayed with one girl long. Flirting, for him, was as much a sport as football.

Lydia plastered on a smile. This sort of run-in required a greeting. "Late for school?" she asked.

He shrugged and gave her his all-star grin. "School is overrated."

It was today. Well, enough talk. It was time to go feed pigeons. That was what lonely people did, wasn't it? Today she was getting a jump on her true calling.

"I heard the latest Harrison update," Brett went on, oblivious to her dark mood. "Harvard. Pretty great, huh?"

And then all of Lydia's holding it together fell apart. There on the sidewalk, she burst into tears. It wasn't subtle or delicate. She put her head in her hands and cried.

The next moment, Brett's arms were around her, comforting her. "Hey, he's going to Harvard, not dying."

She didn't answer, but her mind began a list of differences. Dying is less expensive than going to Harvard. And not nearly as exclusive. And if it were death, she could look forward to joining him one day.

"It's going to be okay," Brett whispered. His voice held a sort of panicked awkwardness. He didn't know what to do with a crying girl. "There, there," he murmured. "There, there."

"Exactly. Harrison's going there. There."

Brett ran his hand over her hair, soothing. Soft. "Hey, I'm trying to think of something to make you feel better."

"Try harder. 'There, there' isn't working."

"Okay, how's this: you don't have to worry about Harrison cheating on you, because everyone knows that really smart chicks are ugly."

"Have I ever mentioned I'm a straight-A student?"

"Seriously? Well, you wouldn't know it to look at you."

She half laughed, half cried. "You suck at this, Brett."

"It's only four years."

Four years. She felt like she would hyperventilate. "You're still sucking."

"Okay, I'll stop talking and let you finish crying." He kept stroking her hair. He was so understanding, so attentive. Everything Harrison hadn't been last night.

She put her head against his chest and cried. Her tears only lasted a minute longer. Then she felt embarrassed to have made such a scene. She didn't move because she didn't want to have to look at Brett. She didn't want to admit that she was a selfish girlfriend who cared more about spending time with Harrison than being happy he'd gotten the future he wanted.

That's when she heard Harrison's voice behind her—cold and biting. "Well, it looks like you won't miss me that much after all."

Lydia jumped, startled. She knew how this must look—standing there with Brett's arms wrapped around her. At the same time, certainly Harrison could see that she was upset. Surely he'd realize that Brett was just comforting her.

Brett stepped away from her guiltily, hands held in the air as if he were surrendering. "That isn't what happened."

Lydia repeated the assertion in a way that actually made sense. "Nothing was going on between us."

Harrison glared at them both, his blue eyes blazing with anger. "You have an interesting definition of *nothing*." Without another word, he turned and strode back toward the school, fast-paced, fists clenched, each step an accusation.

She went after him, hurrying to catch up. "Harrison, wait!"

He walked on without pausing, strident in his indictment.

Didn't he even want to hear her explanation? Didn't he at least owe her the chance to defend herself? In a few moments, she caught up with him, walked beside him so he had to listen to her. "Look, I was upset about you leaving and Brett was trying to make me feel better. Nothing else happened."

He stared straight ahead. "Yeah, you were really upset about me leaving. I could tell by the way you were all over each other."

"All over each other? He was just—"

Harrison stopped then and turned to face her. The eyes that she loved, the ones more familiar than her own, were looking at her with disdain. "I know what Brett was doing. He's told me how he can get any girl he wants to do anything he wants. I told him he was wrong about you. I guess I don't know you as well as I thought I did."

The words hit her like a slap. "I guess you don't, not if you think I would cheat on you." After all, she was the one whose heart was in shreds. He was fine being without her.

His eyes narrowed. "Don't lie to me."

Lie? She had never lied to him, not about anything.

She saw for the first time what this argument was about. It was an excuse for him to break up with her. He'd never cared enough about her to want a long-distance relationship, and now he'd found a reason to end things. Fine. Let him go off and find some blueblood princess; Lydia wouldn't prolong this moment by groveling and telling him how much she loved him, not when he didn't feel the same way.

"Goodbye," he said. The phrase had a permanence, like a door being slammed. He headed back to the school, leaving her standing there on the sidewalk.

They'd never spoken again. Not really. Ironically, it was Brett who had apologized again and again about that day. He said he'd tried talking to Harrison, who wouldn't listen. Par for the course.

"Lydia?" Harrison asked, jerking her back to the present. His voice was deep and rich. Concerned. He leaned closer to her window. "It is you, isn't it?"

She wanted to run, to sink into the sidewalk. She wanted to blurt out that she was an undercover officer. But she couldn't break her cover even for the sake of an old acquaintance. That would be showing preferential treatment.

A panicked solution bubbled inside her. Maybe Harrison wasn't certain it was her. He hadn't seen her for six years, and she was wearing hooker makeup and poofed hair. It was a thin hope, but she grabbed hold of it.

"The name's Trixie," she said in a low, seductive voice. "But I could be Lydia if the price is right."

Harrison dipped his chin. "I recognize you, Lyd. What are you doing on this street corner?"

"What are *you* doing on this street corner?" She never thought Harrison would be the street-corner sort. He'd been so proper and upstanding in high school. He didn't even cheat on tests, let alone break the law. And heaven knew a guy with his looks had more than enough attention from women. Underneath his jacket, she could make out his still-fit physique. Football-star physique. Stealing-kisses-under-the-bleachers physique.

Still, Harrison's good looks didn't make him immune to the seedy side of life. Men didn't hire hookers because they couldn't get a date. They did it for the thrill. They did it so they could have a woman whose only requirement was a few twenties.

If Harrison wanted to break the law, Lydia would be more than happy to bust him along with everybody else who pulled up tonight. Maybe even happier. Her eyes flicked to his left hand. No wedding ring. At least Lydia wouldn't have to deal with his distraught wife later at the station.

Lydia laid her arms against the open window and leaned toward Harrison, a move that usually made men gulp in anticipation. "So, what'll it be, sugar?"

Harrison kept staring at her. At her face, not at the cleavage her halter top revealed. "What happened to you, Lyd?"

She rolled her eyes. "Oh, I don't know. I guess after you

dumped me, I gave up on love. Street corners were all that was left to me."

"I'm serious. You need help."

She winked at him. "My help costs sixty dollars for a half an hour. Are you interested or not?" It would feel so good to see him dragged out of his shiny black BMW and cuffed. *Go ahead and look down on me,* she thought. *I'm not the one who'll be spending time in jail.*

"Do you need money?" His blue eyes were serious, intent. "Get in the car. I'll help you out."

Getting in the car wasn't part of the normal routine. She was supposed to work out the deal, give the code words, *Let's party*, then stand back while the van down the street pulled up. Four guys in uniforms would pour out and swarm the car.

Lydia pushed a strand of hair behind her ear in her best starlet fashion. "Before I get in the car, tell me what you want."

It was either time to prove he wasn't a slime ball so she could calmly explain the situation and redeem her reputation, or time he showed his true colors so she could introduce him to four of her colleagues.

He pulled his wallet from his pocket. Supple black leather. New. She'd gotten good at judging men by their wallets. The beat-up ones belonged to guys whose lives were much the same. The bulging ones were owned by men who carried bits of disorganization around with them. The cheap wallets were Father's Day presents. Harrison's wallet said money, orderliness, and style. He casually opened it, and his gaze returned to her.

"When Rochelle said she saw you here, I didn't believe it. I still can't believe it, and I'm looking at you."

Lydia blinked. "Wait, Rochelle? Rochelle Ingleside?"

Rochelle had been the school's head cheerleader. The sort of girl who smiled at you while retrieving the proverbial back-stabbing knife from her pompoms.

Harrison flipped through some bills and pulled out three, each a twenty. "Yeah. She texted your profession to our entire class."

"What?" Lydia hadn't given a second thought to chasing down an armed robber two weeks ago. She hadn't flinched while tracking down a notorious gang leader. But now her voice spiraled upward in alarm. "Rochelle texted people that I'm a hooker?"

"Sent a picture, too."

Lydia ran her hand through her hair in aggravation. Her aggravation grew when her hand got stuck in a tangle of hair-sprayed, teased, poofed hair. "Great. That's going to make our ten-year reunion fun."

"Get in the car," Harrison said gently. He held the money toward her. "We'll go somewhere and talk."

Lydia put her hand to the bridge of her nose. "My mom is going to kill me." It wouldn't take long for her old schoolmates to spread the news to their parents—her mother's friends.

"Your mother loves you," Harrison's voice was soothing. "I'm sure that will never change."

In her earpiece, Lydia heard Officer Thompson's voice. "Look, I hate to break up your stroll down memory lane, but you've either got to close this deal or have lover boy move out so you can concentrate on paying customers."

Harrison put the car in park and reached toward her. He took one of Lydia's hands and put three twenties into it. His fingers curled around hers. They felt warm, strong. She couldn't help but remember the other times he'd held her hand, how it had felt so natural to slip her fingers into his hand.

"You want me to pay for your time?" he said. "Here's sixty." He cracked open the passenger-side door. "I'll give you more after you get in the car."

She did what she always did with the money, tucked it into the pocket of her mini skirt. It was evidence.

Harrison took two fifties from his wallet, held them out for her to see, and opened the door further so she could get in.

She cocked her head. "Why do I suddenly feel like a stray cat you're luring inside with a can of tuna?"

He took out another twenty. "Here kitty, kitty."

Did he always carry around this much cash, or had he stopped at an ATM for lure-the-hooker-into-the-car money?

Harrison held up the bills to her, gesturing with them for her to come closer. She wasn't supposed to get into a john's car. It could be dangerous. On the other hand, Harrison would get suspicious if she refused to climb in his car. Besides, she didn't have to worry about Harrison hurting her.

"I'm paying your price," Harrison reminded her. "That means you owe me an hour and a half."

He hadn't suggested doing anything illegal for the money. She couldn't arrest him, but she couldn't send him on his way either. If she let him off the hook before it was absolutely clear that he wasn't soliciting, the team would think she was cutting Harrison a break due to high-school nepotism.

Lydia sighed. "Fine. I'll get in, but you can't drive anywhere." She slipped into the car. The seats were soft with luxury.

"Why can't I drive anywhere?" he asked.

Her skirt had ridden up when she sat down. She tugged it so it covered more of her legs. She was suddenly self-conscious of all the skin she was showing. "I have a place I can take you. My, um, boss doesn't like me to go too far out of his sight."

"Your boss? Your pimp, you mean." Harrison's jaw tightened. "Lydia, you're better than this."

She held out her hand, palm up. "In that case, it's one hundred dollars for a half an hour."

A muscle pulsed in Harrison's jaw. His gaze went to the road in front of them, and he put the car in gear. "We're leaving."

Before Lydia could protest, he gunned the BMW down the road, weaving around the car in front of him in a way that would have made New York City cabbies proud. Lydia automatically turned in her seat, looking for the police van. "I told you I couldn't go anywhere. You can't just drive away."

"I'm paying for your time. That's all that matters, isn't it? Don't you want to go someplace better than here?"

Lydia inwardly groaned. The other officers weren't going to be happy about this. She would undoubtedly be in for a long lecture about following procedure. "Harrison, you need to stop the car and let me out."

He didn't respond to that, didn't even act like he'd heard her. Outside, an assortment of rundown buildings flashed by.

"Listen," Lydia said for the team's benefit. "I know you, Harrison. I know you're the type of guy who would never hurt anyone . . ." She glanced out the back window. The van had peeled out of the parking lot and was speeding down the street in an attempt to catch them. "You would especially never hurt *me*, so there's no reason for anyone to do anything drastic like try to shoot out your tires."

"What are you talking about?" Harrison cut her a glance. "You're strung out, aren't you?"

"I don't use drugs." She couldn't hide the indignation in her voice. "You shouldn't jump to conclusions." She turned back around and folded her arms. "That was always your problem."

"We're talking about *my* problems now?"

"Yeah. Speaking of which, I didn't do anything with Brett, but would you believe me? No."

Harrison rolled his eyes, and kept driving too fast. "Sorry for jumping to the conclusion that you're taking drugs. I just can't see a lot of other reasons you would sell your body to strangers."

"And that's another thing. Rochelle Ingleside said I'm a hooker, and you immediately believed her."

"No, I believed you were a hooker after you came to my car window and told me your prices."

Lydia couldn't argue with that. She tapped her foot against the car floor. It was spotless, but then, Harrison had always been the clean type. His locker was more organized than an office-supply store. She ached to tell him that she was really an undercover police officer. The words were on the tip of her tongue, but technically Harrison hadn't made it clear that he didn't expect services for his money. For all the guys in the van knew, he was just taking her to a location he deemed more suitable.

"Where are we going?" she asked. They zoomed around the corner. He was going fast. Racecar-driver fast.

Harrison's eyes flicked to the rearview mirror. "I haven't decided. As far away from your boss as I can get you. Is that him in the blue van?"

She couldn't concentrate on his question. Officer Thompson was talking in the earpiece, calling for backup to intercept the BMW. "I'm fine," she told the team. "This is probably just a misunderstanding that we'll all laugh about one day." Some of the guys would undoubtedly laugh more than others.

Harrison let a scoff. "I'm not laughing yet."

"So you only want to talk to me, right?" she asked him. "Nothing else?"

"Oh, there's a lot else."

She straightened. Maybe this case wasn't closed. "*A lot else* meaning what?"

Harrison weaved around the car in front of them, going up on the curb to get ahead of it. "Really Lydia, I don't know whether to lecture you or to strangle you. Right now I'm leaning toward strangling."

"That's a hyperbole," Lydia clarified for the listening team. "No need to shoot anyone."

"How could you do this to yourself?" Harrison asked.

This had gone on long enough. She opened her mouth to tell him the truth. But the words "Why do you care what I've done to myself?" came out instead. "You didn't care what happened to me when you broke up with me and moved to Harvard. You never cared enough about me to call or visit when you came home for vacation. Why all the concern about me now?"

He remained silent for a moment, hands tense. "I don't deserve that."

The light ahead was red. Instead of waiting behind two other cars, he cut through the gas station parking lot on the corner to make a sharp right onto that street. "Just because I broke up with you doesn't mean I don't care what happens to you."

"Yes, it does." She held onto the armrest, swaying with the turn. "That's exactly what not calling and not visiting mean. That's pretty much the definition of not caring."

"I was angry about Brett. Can you blame me?"

"Yes, because Brett and I were never together. He told you that. *I* told you that. And you called me a liar." She folded her arms, staring at a rundown pawn shop they passed. "And by the way, I'm an undercover police officer, so you really need to pull over and let me out."

He shook his head, eyes on the road. "You've got chutzpah. I'll give you that. You tell me your prices then deny being a hooker, just like you were all over Brett and then told me nothing happened."

"Nothing *did* happen."

"I saw him with his arms wrapped around you and your head on his chest."

"That's called a hug, not an affair. It happens. Brett explained everything to you."

Harrison raised an eyebrow at her in disbelief.

"He *told* me that he explained everything to you," Lydia repeated.

Harrison rolled his eyes. Apparently whatever had gone on between him and Brett hadn't been pleasant.

The light ahead of them turned from yellow to red. He revved the car through the intersection anyway.

She watched the oncoming traffic, wincing. "That is *so* illegal. I can't believe you did that after I just told you I'm a police officer. Do you have any idea what a ticket runs these days?"

He checked his rearview mirror. "I think I lost your boss."

She reached into her pocket, took out her badge, and held it out to him as proof. "Before you put us in mortal danger again, look at this."

He gave her a quick unimpressed glance. "Nice. Do you have a set of handcuffs too? I bet your customers love that."

She slapped the badge down on the seat between them.

"This is exactly what I was talking about. You're too suspicious and judgmental."

"Right, Trixie."

She thought about pulling out her earpiece and the wire tap and showing those to Harrison too. But if he hadn't believed the badge, why would he believe her when she showed him a couple of electronics?

Harrison pulled his cell phone from his breast pocket, glancing at a message. "I asked my secretary to check out some treatment facilities for you. There's some nice rehab places around. Think of it as an all-paid vacation."

Lydia lifted her hands then let them fall back at her side. "You are impossible. And by the way, checking your phone while driving is also illegal."

Harrison slipped his phone back into his pocket. "I blame myself for the thing with Brett. He used to brag about how he could take any girl away from any guy in the school. I should have warned you what he was like, but I never thought you'd be taken in by him."

It was then that the police cars came into view, blue and red lights pulsing, sirens shrieking. Three of them screeched to a stop, blocking the road ahead.

Lydia put her badge back into her pocket. "Do yourself a favor and listen to me for once. Stop the car, get out slowly, and keep your hands where they can be seen. I'll tell the officers you were trying to save me from a life of crime."

Harrison stared at the lights with shocked realization. As he braked, he turned to Lydia, really seeing her now. "Those are for us?"

"And the badge is legit too." Into her earpiece she said, "Everything is fine, guys."

Unfortunately, she had no way of communicating with the officers in the patrol cars in front of them. And *they* apparently didn't think everything was fine. When a guy abducted an officer and sped off, it tended to make other officers edgy.

As soon as Harrison cut the engine, officers poured from their cars, guns drawn.

Harrison watched them and swore.

Lydia cleared her throat. "This would be a good time to put your hands up."

TWO

If you had told Lydia at high school graduation that one day she would see Harrison slammed up against his car by angry police officers—and that it would bring her no pleasure—she wouldn't have believed it. In fact, she wouldn't have believed it half an hour ago. But seeing Harrison treated like a criminal *didn't* make her happy.

Okay, so he'd been a jerk in high school, and granted, he'd been a little too willing to believe she was a crack ho, but he'd cared about her enough to have his secretary look up treatment facilities. He'd gone over a sidewalk and through a red light to free her from the clutches of her supposed pimp. When was the last time a guy did anything like that for her? Usually they just brought flowers.

So Lydia did her best to explain the situation to the arresting officers. She didn't know any of them—different precinct—and while she spoke, they barked out things about reckless driving and attempted kidnapping.

"I didn't kidnap her," Harrison said. Or at least that's what Lydia thought he said. His face was being pushed into the side of his car while the officers cuffed him, so it was hard to tell.

"It was all a misunderstanding," Lydia emphasized. "I was never in any danger." Except possibly when Harrison ran the red light. But she didn't bring that up.

The officer nodded to let her know he'd heard her, but didn't uncuff Harrison. "Sir, I'm going to ask you to sit in the back of my car while I run a few checks on you."

Lydia couldn't argue with that. She didn't know whether Harrison had any outstanding warrants and doing that kind of check was protocol.

As the officer led Harrison across the street, she called out to him, "Hey, it was good to see you again! Say hi to your mom for me!"

In her earpiece, Officer Thompson muttered, "That is just cold, Trixie."

"I meant it," Lydia said, watching Harrison walk stiffly to the squad car. "His mom always liked me."

"Yeah, well, the next time you want to reconnect with an old flame, make it easy on the rest of us and use Facebook."

A few moments later, the unmarked van rounded a corner and pulled up to Lydia. Officer Thompson rolled down his window and grinned. "You can run, but you can't get out of work that easy. You're only halfway done with your shift."

He was right. She shut her eyes and inwardly sighed. It was going to be a long night.

The next evening, Lydia stood outside an upscale apartment in Manhattan. If the BMW hadn't told her that Harrison had done well for himself, the apartment where he lived would. Ornate stone banisters led to large curved doors decorated with all sorts of intricacies. No doubt the place had doormen, an oversized crystal chandelier hanging in the lobby, and spa services tucked away somewhere.

Technically Lydia shouldn't have looked at Harrison's records to see his address. Although if asked, she could claim she got it off the Internet. Nobody's address was safe from the Internet.

Lydia had come here to return Harrison's money. In the excitement of last night, she'd forgotten about the bills in her pocket until after her shift was over and she was changing out of her hooker clothes. The money had fallen out of her pocket and stared up at her like an accusation. *Not only did you nearly get your ex-boyfriend arrested, you took his cash too.*

Now that Lydia was outside his building, she had second thoughts. He hadn't wanted to talk to her back in high school when he thought she'd cheated on him. So he probably wouldn't want to talk to her after burly officers had shoved him against his vehicle and then dragged him to a squad car.

But she needed to give him his money back. And apologize for everything he'd gone through last night. After all, he'd only been trying to help her. But then again, she'd only been doing her job. Should she have to put up with his anger when she'd just been trying to rid the world of crime?

Decisions, decisions. She looked up at the windows of the building as if they would tell her what to do.

She was still looking up when Harrison's BMW pulled up next to her. The tinted window rolled down. He wore a suit and tie, but otherwise looked like he had last night. Broad-shouldered, blond, and gorgeous. He looked less worried for her soul now: more guarded. And slightly ticked off.

"Hey Trixie, hanging out on another street corner?"

It was embarrassing to be caught loitering in front of his building. Sort of stalkerish. "Oh, hi." She couldn't think of anything else to say, so she took the stack of bills from her purse. "I came to return your money."

He didn't say anything, just stared at her appraisingly.

"From last night," she added.

"Yeah, I remember last night. In fact, the events are permanently seared into my memory."

He was still appraising her, and she was glad she'd taken extra time getting ready. Her makeup was soft now, emphasizing the green in her hazel eyes. Her long hair hung loose around her shoulders, its natural wave giving it bounce.

She held the bills out to him. "Here kitty, kitty. I won't bite."

He tilted his chin down. "As I recall, you were supposed to give me an hour and a half of your time for those. I had what, ten minutes? And then I was frisked, cuffed, and put in a squad car."

"Yeah, about that . . . Sorry." Her apology didn't come out nearly as heartfelt as she had planned.

"Did I mention I was handcuffed?"

"I was there for it."

"Yes, you were."

She put one hand on her hip. "It could have been worse, you know. Rochelle Ingleside could have taken a picture of the event and sent it to our high school classmates."

Harrison nodded. "Well, there's always a silver lining, isn't there?'

Lydia leaned into his car window, holding out the money. "So anyway, sorry again about everything, and here's your money."

"Get in the car," he said. "I don't want the money. I want to talk to you for an hour and a half."

Her insides tugged between aggravation and happiness. He wanted to talk to her. Maybe he had changed since high school. Happiness won.

"All right. I guess I have the time." Her next shift didn't start until later that night. One of the benefits of being a faux streetwalker. She climbed into the BMW and shut the door. The car had that new smell to it. She hadn't noticed that detail last night while they were fleeing from the police van.

Harrison pulled into traffic. "Where do you want to go?" He momentarily let his blue eyes drift to her.

"I've got one hundred and eighty dollars. I could buy you dinner."

"Hmm. Someplace good then. I want my money's worth."

It suddenly felt like high school again, pre-Brett. Comfortable. Easy.

"By the way," Harrison added, "my mom says to tell you hi back."

Lydia turned to better see his expression. "You actually told her about last night?"

"Yeah. She called me this morning. One of her friends forwarded Rochelle's picture to her. She was worried about you."

Lydia let her head thunk backward against the headrest. "Great. The news is already reaching the older generation." She supposed that any time now, her own mother would call, worried and demanding answers. Yeah, Lydia should have told her mother that she was more than a desk clerk. But really, undercover work was pretty safe. Last night was the first time someone had tried to abscond with her.

"My mom was relieved you're still an upstanding citizen," Harrison went on. "And she suggested arresting Rochelle for slander. I explained the laws regarding slander, so then my mom just wished a lot of bad karma on her."

Lydia looked upward, considering. "The problem with karma is that it takes too long to work. Last time it took six years."

"I'm going to pretend that I don't know what you're referring to."

"Rochelle's picture wasn't *all* bad," Lydia admitted. "Three more guys from our class stopped by my corner last night. Unfortunately, their intentions weren't nearly as noble as yours." She smiled at the memory of the guys' wide eyes as their cars were surrounded by police officers. "Who knew so many men would pay money to spend time with me?"

"I did," Harrison said as though it proved his point. "Who got arrested?"

She hesitated. "Are you going to gloat if I tell you one of the guys was Brett?"

"Yes."

"Then I don't think I should tell you."

Harrison smirked. Gloatingly. "So who else showed up besides Brett?"

She told him the names. They were people she had known but never talked much to in school. "You can see their photos online. That's part of the anti-prostitution sweep. We're posting the offenders' pictures." She relaxed against the seat in satisfaction. "I forwarded the link to Rochelle."

"Brutal."

"Yeah. I think word will get around pretty quickly that I'm actually an undercover cop."

Harrison's eyes slid to hers again. "What else are you?"

"What else?"

He shrugged. "Are you married, do you have a family, are you happy?"

"Not married, no family, but yes, I'm happy."

"Good." He smiled. "I mean, I'm glad you're happy."

She could still read him. He was glad for more than her happiness. "How about you?" she asked.

"I've been too busy with school and work to have much of a social life. So I'm not married, no family, and I'm a lot happier now than I was last night."

"Yeah, people usually aren't too happy when we cuff them. Go figure."

He sent her a look laced with meaning. "I meant I'm happy you're not some down-and-out streetwalker."

"Oh, that. Me too. Being a police officer is much better. At least most days."

He grinned, just like he had when they used to talk in high school. "I know a great place for dinner."

THREE

Harrison took Lydia to a restaurant she'd never heard of, a place where the staff knew him by sight.

The maître d' smiled broadly when they walked in. "So good to see you again, Mr. Aldridge. Would you like your usual table?"

His usual table, it turned out, overlooked the city. French art hung on the wall. Glowing candles sat on the table, and soft violin music drifted into the room.

Harrison was charming at dinner, smiling easily, letting his gaze rest on her so often that she began to feel her pulse quicken every time his eyes went to hers. He asked how she ended up in police work when she'd started college as a secondary education major.

"You were going to save underprivileged teens with the power of education," he said. "What happened?"

At first she teased him with different versions of the story of her career change. In one she was a reformed cat-burglar who'd made a deal with the DA. In another, she'd been saved from criminals by a daring cop and had joined the force to repay society.

"I'm not going to let you leave until you tell me the truth," Harrison said. "My mom will want details."

Lydia finished off a bite of sautéed duck. "The real story isn't that interesting. I didn't like teaching as much as I thought I would, and I realized I didn't want to spend my life grading poorly written essays on *The Scarlet Letter*. Putting criminals away seemed like a more immediate way to save the world."

Harrison nodded. "As long as the world gets saved somehow."

"Right. And compared to dealing with surly hormonal teenagers all day, facing criminals is easy."

In some ways, the dinner seemed surreal. It felt like she'd stepped back in time, like this was just one more date with Harrison, and that when they walked out of the restaurant, they would find themselves in high school again. In other ways, it seemed all too real. The way his eyes rested on her, the curve of his jaw, everything about his presence made it hard to think about anything else.

When they'd both finished their meals, he asked, "Do you have a boyfriend?" His eyes were back on her, watching her expression.

"I go out every once in a while, but the pool of available guys becomes much smaller when they know you can run background checks on them."

"Only if you're into the criminal element."

"Well, I always had a thing for bad boys." She said it jokingly. Harrison had been the farthest thing possible from a bad boy.

He took a sip from his glass. “That would explain Brett.”

“There is no explaining Brett.” She meant that there was nothing to explain where he was concerned, but Harrison didn’t catch her meaning.

“So true,” he said, and put down his glass.

The waiter came in then, asking if they wanted dessert.

“I’d better not,” Lydia said, irritated. Despite Harrison’s flirting at dinner, he still refused to believe her. “I need to be able to fit into my hooker clothes.” She forced a smile. “It’s a tough business. I don’t want to lose clients.”

The waiter raised his eyebrows in surprise. Good. Let the staff wonder who Mr. Aldridge had brought to his usual table.

Harrison pulled his wallet from his pocket and took out a credit card. “She’s an undercover officer,” he told the waiter.

The waiter nodded as he took the card. “Yes, sir.” He probably would have used the same agreeable tone if Harrison had said, “She’s a mermaid.”

As soon as the waiter left, Lydia remembered that she was supposed to pay for the meal. She pulled the money from her purse and held it out to Harrison.

“I’m paying this bill,” he said. “I want to cash in my time with you later.”

What did he mean by that? The edge to his voice didn’t sound like he wanted time happily reminiscing about the good old days. Maybe he wanted an hour and a half to yell at her for compromising his reputation at his restaurant. And okay, she probably shouldn’t have done that, but she wasn’t going to apologize unless he apologized for the Brett comment.

“Are you free tomorrow night?” he asked. “We could walk around Central Park.”

Central Park had been her favorite place back when they were in high school. Still was. "Okay," she said.

Was he asking her out on a date? It seemed improbable. Guys in Harrison's tax bracket didn't date cops. They went out with high-powered businesswomen, heiresses, or Broadway starlets.

After they left the restaurant, Harrison drove Lydia to her apartment in Queens. His voice was neutral as he asked questions about her family and work, but she could feel an undercurrent there. He wanted to talk about something else.

Her apartment building was much less impressive than his. It was a four-story brick building older than her grandparents and just as quirky. The bay windows and woodwork were charming, the lack of an elevator less so.

Harrison insisted on seeing her to her door, even though it required a three-story hike. That was another thing about him that she remembered from high school: he was a gentleman.

They reached her door. He didn't make a move to leave, and she didn't pull her apartment key from her purse. He was staring at her as if she was a memory from long ago. But then, she supposed that's what she was.

"So, Officer Robinson," he said slowly, putting his hands in his pockets. "You have a thing for bad boys?"

She made a small, indignant sound. "Nothing happened between me and Brett. Didn't he explain that to you?"

Harrison looked upward, remembering. "I think *rub it in* would be a better descriptive term for what Brett did."

Lydia inwardly groaned. "He told me he explained everything."

Harrison was still gazing upward. "I also recall shoving him against a wall and exchanging a few swearwords. Then he shoved me and said he could do whatever he wanted.

There might have been some punches thrown." Harrison returned his gaze to hers. "Fun times."

"Sorry," she said, sighing. "I thought he made things clear. But even if he didn't, you still had *my* word that nothing went on."

Harrison cocked his head. "Why weren't you this insistent back in high school? You never even tried to talk to me after I ran into you and Brett on the sidewalk."

"Because our breakup wasn't about Brett. It was about you going off to Harvard and not caring about leaving me behind."

One of Harrison's eyebrows went up. "I don't remember it being about that."

"That's because you never talked to me about it." She fingered a knick in her doorframe, feeling suddenly like that vulnerable eighteen-year-old again. "You never acted like you were going to miss me."

Harrison let out a slow breath. "That's ironic. Because I missed you like crazy." He took a step closer. He smelled of cologne and summer nights. It brought back memories of the times he'd held her close and she'd rested her head against his shoulder. "At college, I kept thinking of things I wanted to tell you, and then I remembered we weren't speaking anymore."

She paused, pulled herself away from memories. "You knew my number. You could have called."

"You wouldn't have answered."

"Yes, I would have."

He pulled his phone out of his pocket, pushed a button, and her phone rang in her purse. "You still have the same number," he said, surprised.

"You didn't take me off your contacts?" she asked, just as surprised.

"I didn't take you off my speed dial."

"Ah," she said. "I would think that's sweet, except that knowing you, you were too busy studying to take the time to delete it."

He still held his phone to his ear. "You said you would answer. You're not."

She reached into her purse, pulled out her phone, and held it to her ear. "Hello?"

"Hi, Lydia." His gaze stayed on hers. "I called to tell you I'm sorry for not trusting you in high school." His voice grew softer. "And I'm sorry you got the impression that I wouldn't miss you. Nothing was farther from the truth."

It was ridiculous standing here talking to each other on the phone while they stood inches apart, but she didn't feel like laughing. Her heart was racing. The heat of possibilities warmed a trail through her. She recognized that look in Harrison's eyes, that *I want to kiss you* look.

She shouldn't kiss him. Their relationship was water under the bridge. You couldn't bring back the past. You shouldn't try. He stepped toward her.

Water under the bridge, she told herself.

He leaned in, and his lips came down on hers. Softly, questioningly. It was a question she gladly answered. Her hands made their way up his chest, feeling the muscles underneath his tailored shirt. He was warm, familiar, and kissing him was as easy as talking to him had been. Their relationship was water under the bridge, and right now that water felt like it was a torrent. Strong and fast and easily able to pull her under.

"I did miss you," he murmured into her ear before letting his lips brush against her lobe. "The most important thing I learned at Harvard is how rare someone like you is. I should have fought for you." His lips moved to the skin beneath her ear. "When I saw that picture of you, when I thought the Lydia I knew was trapped in that sort of life . . ." He stopped kissing her and raised his head. "I don't want to lose you again."

She ran her hand through the blond hair at his temples. Her voice came out throatier than she expected. "Do you think we can give this another shot, or is that living in the past?"

"Try me." He dropped another kiss on her lips. "I'll listen this time. Say whatever you wanted to say to me back then."

She leaned away from him because his kisses were making her knees week. What had she wanted to say to him back at the end of high school? It was hard to think clearly. "Um, I would have said that I was going to miss you like crazy."

Harrison didn't let go of her. He kissed the corner of her mouth. "I completely believe you."

"I was crying with Brett because you were going away, and he was comforting me. That's all that happened."

"I'm sorry I didn't believe you." He kissed the other corner of her mouth. "See how well this is going?" He drew her closer and kissed her bottom lip. "What else did you want to say that I should have listened to?"

She wrapped her arms back around his neck. "I don't want you to go off to Massachusetts where I won't be able to see you."

"Okay," he said. "I'll stay here."

She smiled lazily, letting her fingers tousle the hair at his nape. "You wouldn't have said that."

"But I just did. I'm not going anywhere."

"Living in the present has its benefits," she mused.

"Lots of benefits," he said, and then neither of them spoke again for a long time.

ABOUT JANETTE RALLISON

Janette Rallison (who is also sometimes C. J. Hill when the mood strikes her) writes books because writing is much more fun than cleaning bathrooms. Her avoidance of housework has led her to writing 21 novels which have sold over 1,000,000 copies and made her a *USA Today* bestseller. Her books have been on the IRA Young Adults' Choices lists, Popular Picks, and many state reading lists. Most of her books are romantic comedies or urban fantasies (with romance) because hey, there is enough angst in real life, but there's a drastic shortage of fantasy, humor and hot guys who want to kiss you. She lives in Arizona with her husband, kids, and enough cats to classify her as eccentric.

Visit Janette's website here: JanetteRallison.com

Follow her on Twitter: @JanetteRallison

A TASTE OF SUN

Heather B. Moore

OTHER WORKS BY HEATHER B. MOORE

Esther the Queen
Finding Sheba
Lost King
Slave Queen
The Aliso Creek Series
Heart of the Ocean
The Newport Ladies Book Club Series
The Fortune Café
The Boardwalk Antiques Shop

ONE

Winona Grant climbed out of the taxi, stepped over a rain puddle, and craned her neck to look at the apartment building where she'd be living for the summer. New York City. It couldn't be more different from the California city of Irvine, where she'd grown up. The sun and sand had been replaced by rain and cement.

The taxi driver unloaded her two suitcases and carried them to the steps beneath the awning of the front entrance, getting them out of the rain quickly. The sixty-something doorman stepped forward, eyeing Winona.

"You're Ms. Grant's niece?" he asked as she joined him beneath the awning.

"Yes," Winona said. She brushed the raindrops from her jacket and tried not to stare at the doorman. He wore a uniform, and he was expecting her. This was so not home.

"Do you need anything else, miss?" the taxi driver asked.

Winona could swear that the doorman had scrunched his nose, but then his expression was placid again. "I'll assist Miss Grant," he said with a pointed look at the taxi driver.

Winona turned to the driver and paid him the fare. "Thank you so much."

Apparently there was some sort of unspoken protocol Winona would have to learn; taxi drivers weren't let inside exclusive Manhattan apartment buildings, apparently. Winona shouldn't have been totally surprised. Aunt Genevieve never went by a nickname; it was always the full *Genevieve.* This summer, Winona was housesitting for her aunt while she worked in Europe, launching a new fashion designer. Genevieve Grant was the one of the top publicists in the fashion industry, and if she said something was gold, it turned platinum.

By the time her aunt returned, the new designer would surely be featured in every top fashion magazine and booked for a year's worth of shows.

The doorman started to wheel her suitcases, and Winona winced a bit, knowing they were awkwardly large. She followed him inside the plush lobby, which sported marble pillars and a thick Turkish rug. She wanted to stop and stare; instead, she followed the doorman to the elevator.

Inside, she had a chance to read his nametag. "I really appreciate your help, Mr. Johnson."

He nodded and gave her a brief smile then was back to business, pressing the button for the eighth floor. Winona leaned against the wall and let a small sigh escape. It had been a whirlwind getting everything organized so she could spend the summer in New York. Her boss at Meyer Graphics & Design had been great about her working remotely for a few months, but it would hurt her chances at getting promoted when the vice president went on maternity leave in a week. Rumors were that Stacy wouldn't return, and when she made the official announcement, her job would open up.

Working remotely would put Winona at a disadvantage; most likely, one of her coworkers would get the promotion. No way could Winona assume the VP job while in New York. A VP had to be hands-on with their Irvine clients. But Aunt Genevieve had asked for this favor, and Winona really owed the aunt who'd put her through college after her parents had split and her father had decided that his new wife was more important than his daughter.

The elevator chimed and stopped on the fourth floor, pulling Winona's thoughts back to the present. As the door slid open, Winona heard a woman shouting.

A man hurried into the elevator then pressed the close button over and over.

The woman's voice drew closer. "You'll pay for this, Steve! You two-timing jerk—"

The doors slid shut, and the elevator jolted upward again. Winona dared sneak a couple glances at the man standing in front of her, who was taking deep breaths now. He stood a couple of inches taller than she, with dark hair that curled above his collared shirt, which looked like it had been hastily pulled on. Must have had a lovers' quarrel. Maybe his girlfriend had caught him with another woman.

Before Winona could look away, the man turned. Warmth flooded her face as his deep blue eyes held hers. His skin was olive and his hair dark, a bit wavy with that messy look some men could pull off.

"Sorry about that," he said. He looked anything but sorry to have fled from his girlfriend's rants. The doorman gave a short nod and pursed his lips.

"Are you moving in?" the man asked, his gaze still on her.

Winona's thoughts scrambled at the man's gall. He'd been kicked out by his girlfriend moments ago, and he now wanted to chitchat?

"Sorry," he said. "I should introduce myself. Steve Monti. Ninth floor." He stuck out his hand.

She had nowhere to escape, so she shook his hand, letting go quickly. "Winona Grant," she barely managed to get out.

If possible, his eyes turned bluer. "Oh, you're Genevieve's niece. Welcome to Manhattan." And he grinned.

At that moment, Winona realized two things. First, she was stunned that this man could be so cheerful after his girlfriend's tirade. Second, heat had rushed through her whole body at his smile, which meant that she was attracted to her new neighbor, who also happened to be a "two-timing jerk."

She would have to start taking the stairs. She'd had enough of two-timing jerks in her life.

TWO

Steve Monti exhaled in frustration as he stepped out of the elevator and started down the hall toward his apartment. Nothing was going right today. First, his brand new gallery had had a cancellation. Second, somehow Leisa had found out about it. He would have loved to book her a spot, but the truth was, she wasn't a big enough name yet. As much as he recognized her talent, his business plan didn't include debut artists. Especially a debut artist who was also a trust fund baby with too much time on her hands, which amounted to her pestering him every chance she got.

At least he still had the anchor artists for the show, but how was he supposed to come up with another name when the gallery opening was less than a month away? Steve unlocked the door to his apartment and stepped into the cool, welcoming interior. Here, away from the bustle of the city, he'd be able to strategize how to entice one of the bigger artists in New York to display at his new gallery.

He'd probably have to lower his commission. Promise a ton of publicity. His grand opening had to be stellar to hit all the papers and media outlets. Monti Gallery couldn't fail. Steve had put every resource he had into it, both personally and professionally. But now he had to find a new artist.

His cell phone beeped, and it looked like he'd missed a call. Probably while in the elevator and the coverage had been lost for a couple of moments. He typed in his passcode then listened to the message while grabbing a water bottle out of the fridge.

Genevieve Grant's voice came loud and clear—a bit bossy—but that's what Steve loved about her. She'd been a generous donor to his projects over the years, and Monti Gallery was no exception.

"Steve, dear," Genevieve said from his voice mail. "I was hoping you could show my niece around the city. She hasn't been here since she was a teenager, and I can't do it myself. I trust you, and besides, I think you two will get along great. She's a sweet and beautiful girl."

He winced. Genevieve had set him up with a few women over the years—mostly artists and designers—thinking they'd have something in common because of the art industry. Since everyone knew everyone else, even if it was three times removed, anyone he dated ended up as fodder for gossip. Eventually Steve had sworn off dating any woman tied to the art world. The business was too cutthroat, and Steve had made promises that he hadn't been able to keep due to the nature of the business.

Case in point—Leisa. He'd never promised to debut her art, yet because they were friends, and she'd spilled her hour-long sob story a few months ago, she felt that he owed her now. What would it have been like if they *had* been dating?

Genevieve's message ended, and he realized he hadn't heard the last part. He pressed the number one to replay it. The ending wasn't at all what he expected.

"I need someone I can trust to show Winona around, but someone who won't take advantage of her—and especially someone who will *not* fall in love with her. She's been through some hard things the last few months. She needs a break from men and heartache. That's the real reason I asked her to come to New York. She couldn't get a breath of fresh air in California with all the memories of her ex-boyfriend. She's a bit of a workaholic, and if someone doesn't knock on her door, she'll probably stay in my apartment, working on her laptop, until August."

Steve sat on one of his barstools and continued to listen, becoming more and more intrigued by the minute.

"Thanks, honey," Genevieve said. "I owe you big for this favor. Winona is absolutely precious to me, and I wouldn't trust her with anyone else. Love and kisses!"

After the message ended, Steve set the phone down, then took a long drink from his water bottle.

The Winona in the elevator had been a bit wide-eyed, although she was definitely a pretty girl. Her hazel eyes had complimented her dark-blonde hair in a simple way. Maybe it was the lack of the kind of dramatic makeup, opposite of what he was used to seeing among the women he worked with. They treated their faces like canvases. Steve guessed Winona to be twenty-seven or twenty-eight, probably too young for his thirty-five. Besides, he had spent plenty of time with pretty women yet had never fallen in love, so he certainly wasn't worried about whether he could honor Genevieve's request. The only problem was that this month was perhaps the worst to play tour guide to anyone. It wasn't that he didn't have the time, but the gallery opening was taking his stress level to an all-time high.

Steve rose from the barstool and crossed to the living room windows, then pushed back the vertical blinds. It was still raining—not a good day to go out anyway. Yet he had to help out Genevieve. He couldn't leave her niece hanging. He exhaled, thinking her message over again. It was soon apparent that his mind wouldn't get the notion out of his head until he made an appointment with Genevieve's niece. Then he could get back to finding that artist.

THREE

The apartment was gorgeous. Absolutely gorgeous. Winona felt like she'd walked into a French Baroque museum, yet it was even better than that because she could touch everything. Before she did so, she took a shower and changed into bona fide lounge pants. She'd bought four pairs, intending to take a break from public interaction. She'd been looking forward to completely letting go since her aunt had called three weeks before.

Winona wandered through the apartment and determined that Genevieve must have a professional cleaning service, as there wasn't a bit of dust on any of the priceless antiques. A small misgiving grew in her chest. She wasn't the tidiest person in the world, and even though Genevieve wouldn't be home until August, Winona would have to keep the place up.

After familiarizing herself with the layout, she crossed to the living room windows. Rain was still coming down, but it created a cozy, peaceful feeling. Winona was tempted to curl up on the couch and nap with her head on a brocade pillow. Although she'd barely slept the night before, napping wasn't an option. If she didn't push through several hours of work, she'd be too stressed to sleep tonight.

She powered on her laptop, and while she waited for her graphic design programs to load, she found tea packets in the kitchen cupboard. New York was already proving to be heavenly. Just her, the rain, her laptop, and a cup of tea . . . divine.

Winona logged onto her email as the tea bag steeped. She was scanning the revision requests from a client when someone knocked on the door. The last thing she'd expected was company. Maybe it was the cleaning service? Winona didn't move, hoping they'd go away, but when the person knocked again, she reluctantly rose and crossed the room.

A check of the peephole told her it was the man from the elevator. Steve—the "two-timing jerk."

Had she made any noise he could have heard? Maybe, if they ever crossed paths again, she could pretend she'd been asleep. She turned away and crept back to the couch.

"Winona?" his voice came through the door. "Your aunt called me."

Winona stopped her tiptoeing. Why hadn't Genevieve called *her*? She'd better find out what was going on. With a sigh, she turned around and opened the door.

His eyes were bluer than she remembered, and his hair darker. She didn't know why she even noticed. Paul had been blond, and she'd never really been attracted to dark-haired men. Until this one. She mentally shook her head before she could analyze the butterflies in her stomach, and said, "What did Genevieve say?" Maybe she'd called her neighbor over watering the plants or picking up her mail. But that didn't make sense; Winona already knew those details.

Steve leaned against the doorframe. Winona supposed it would be the polite thing to invite him in. She didn't.

He had a slight smile on his face, and Winona suddenly realized what she was wearing. She sidled a bit behind the door to hide her holey t-shirt and lounge pants. At least the pants were new, but she was also barefoot and her hair was still damp. Not to mention that she didn't have a speck of makeup on.

He continued to smile. "Genevieve wants me to show you around the city—you know, Statue of Liberty, Central Park, the best pizza joints . . . all that good stuff."

Winona exhaled, her embarrassment at what she must look like making her warm all the way to her toes. This guy was way too cheerful and confident. He must be an expert heartbreaker with those looks. She couldn't even bring herself to smile back. He was like the rest of the men she'd ever dated: charming on the outside, insincere on the inside. Like Paul, who'd told her he loved her then broke her heart.

Besides, didn't Steve have a job? What was he doing here in the middle of the day at her door? She was through dating men with too much time on their hands. At first with Paul, she'd thought it was fascinating that he'd sold his successful business and was financially stable, but she'd soon learned that he intended on living off that wealth for a long time and had no ambitions to do anything else but live off his money and focus on himself.

"I didn't come to New York to sightsee," she said, keeping her tone even. She'd let her anger at Paul creep back, making her want to slam the door in the unsuspecting Steve's face.

He laughed. *Laughed!*

"Yeah, I get that. Genevieve said as much. But she's commissioned me to show you around." He raised his hands. "Not right now, of course. Maybe we can go out tomorrow for a couple of hours. Knock a few things off your list."

His blue eyes would be the death of her, but the Winona-visiting-New-York was not the pushover-Winona-of-Irvine. She would not be charmed or played.

"I don't have a list, Mr. Monti. And I didn't come to New York for a vacation, so please don't bother me again. I have a lot to do."

FOUR

Steve stared at the closed door after a puff of wind that had blown in his face when Winona Grant had shut it on him. Not only had she been rude, but she'd completely turned him away. It was as if she hated him. But that was impossible; she didn't even know him.

He might never, never understand women. His rational side said that that wasn't true, that women were humans too. He felt anything but rational right now.

First the artist's cancellation, then Leisa's fury, then Genevieve's completely inconvenient request, and now—a door slammed in his face.

He leveled his gaze at the peephole. Now that he thought about what had just happened, it was a miracle Miss Winona Fancy-Grant had opened the door and graced him with her presence at all.

Steve started for the elevator, then paused and turned back. He refused to let Winona stand in the way of helping Genevieve. He returned and knocked again, waiting a moment until he was sure Winona was either at the peephole or at least listening. "Look, Miss Grant. I have a busy week too, but your aunt asked me to show you around New York, and I can't tell her I failed. She's much too dear to me. I'll be in the lobby at 10:00 tomorrow morning to take you on a tour through Central Park. If you're there, then great. If you don't show up, at least I did my duty."

Without waiting to see if she'd open the door or speak to him through it, he turned and strode to the elevator. Then he opted to take the flight of steps to his apartment level. He was half-tempted to jump rope or pound on the floor so she'd hear it below. Instead, he sat at the desk in his office and began to search for an artist he could feature in his gallery.

Better than dwelling on Winona's hazel eyes and scrubbed-clean face, which made her even prettier. Steve pushed out a frustrated breath. He'd been around plenty of beautiful women—models, actresses, artists . . . What was so different about Winona? He couldn't figure it out, and he didn't have time to spend on a stubborn woman.

That was it. He leaned back in his chair and laughed. She was just like her aunt: stubborn, feisty, adorable. Steve leaned forward and propped his elbows on the desk, scrubbing his hands through his hair.

Winona was right. They shouldn't be touring the city together. But he still hated to disappoint Genevieve.

FIVE

The morning sun made the city sparkle, and Winona was missing out. As tempted as she was to go take a walk—maybe even find a fabulous bakery—she didn't want to run into Steve. From the safety of the balcony, she'd seen him leave the building about fifteen minutes after ten.

As he'd reached the end of the block, he'd looked toward her. Of course, it was impossible for him to have seen her. Genevieve had more plants on her balcony than a full-sized atrium; it was practically an exotic jungle in the middle of the never-ending sounds of Manhattan traffic.

Winona had no idea when Steve would return, so it wasn't a good idea to venture out until she was sure she wouldn't run into him. Even as the thought crossed her mind, though, she knew she was being ridiculous to be avoiding a man she didn't even know.

Her phone buzzed, and she groaned when she saw the text message.

Darling, I hope you're having a wonderful time. My neighbor Steve Monti said he'd show you around the city since I can't do the honors. Let me know how it goes. Xoxo

Winona shoved away her guilt, but it crept right back in. She decided to let the text sit for a while so she could decide how to best respond. If she pretended that Steve had taken her around, she'd need to get him to agree with the cover-up.

She buried herself in her work, creating an ad campaign for a Napa Valley vineyard. This was a regular client; every six months, she refreshed their advertising strategy. While she browsed the images of vines and fruit that her contact had emailed her, someone knocked on her door.

Startled, Winona checked the time. It was nearly one; she hadn't looked up from her computer in almost two hours. Standing, she stretched, then walked to the door. When she saw Steve on the other side, she let out a sigh.

Really? What does he want now?

Then she reconsidered. Maybe she could reach an agreement with him.

She cracked the door open just as his hand was poised to knock again. His perfectly dark eyebrows lifted when he saw her. "Since I don't have your number, I have to give you an update in person."

Winona folded her arms. "About what?" She couldn't help it; rudeness just came out around him. This guy was like Paul—a two-timer—and the less she was around Steve, the better.

"About what we did today." Steve took a step closer, smiling again as if there were nothing wrong with him invading her space. As if he didn't have an angry girlfriend a few floors below. He had to be the cockiest man alive.

"Central Park was perfect," he continued in that smooth, happy tone. "The day after a rainstorm, all of the flowers come alive, and everything smells earthy and fresh. There was a funny incident, though, when—"

"Wait." Winona held up her hand. "What are you talking about?"

"You know, our sightseeing excursion that I went on by myself. I'm filling you in so we have the same story to tell your aunt."

Winona gaped at him. That very thing had been *her* idea—collaborating on a scheme to keep her aunt happy. She didn't know whether to be impressed or annoyed.

"I figure if we have our stories straight, your aunt will think I'm keeping my promise." He winked. "What do you think?"

She couldn't deny the appeal of the plan. "Sounds great to me. I've got a ton to do, so even a couple of hours away will put me behind."

"What kind of work do you do?"

Winona let herself relax a touch. If Steve was willing to let her off the hook about touring the city, she could at least have a decent conversation with him. "I do graphic design for an advertising firm."

"So you're one of those artists who turned to graphic design?"

Winona's face heated up. "Pretty much. Isn't that the fate of all art majors? Paint for fun, but get a real job to pay the rent? I mean . . ." She looked down at her gray t-shirt and navy lounge pants. "I'm far from the artsy type anyway, and I never fit in my college classes. As you can see, I have no sense of style, something that's pretty much a prerequisite in the art world."

Her face warmed even more as Steve's gaze followed the

length of her body. "You were put together well when you arrived." His eyes widened as if he'd realized what he'd implied. "I mean, not that you don't look great now."

Winona smiled. "Please. Don't even worry about it. I know what I look like."

"No, you look great," he rushed to say. "Not many women are comfortable dressing down." His face pinked. "I—I should shut up now."

She laughed. "I know what you mean—don't worry."

"Really, though," Steve said. "Tell me about your art."

Winona exhaled and met his gaze. Was he serious? She hadn't thought of herself as an artist for a long time, not since getting hired at the firm. Sure, she'd continued to dabble in digital art, but she'd long since put away her oils. "I haven't done anything serious for years."

"Did you sculpt? Paint? Watercolor?"

"Oils, but now I mostly photograph and digitally enhance the pictures." She couldn't believe she was telling him all of this. She'd told no one. The work she'd loaded onto the digital art sites were all under a pseudonym.

"Do you have a website or something with your portfolio?" he asked.

He couldn't really be so interested, Winona decided. "I've loaded my stuff onto a few sites, but nothing major," she hedged.

"I guess I need to Google your name to see your stuff."

"You won't find anything under my name."

"Oh?" He was watching her closely.

Winona just smiled. "I'll let you know if I decide to share it with you."

He staggered backward as if she'd struck him. "Ouch." Then he was smiling again. "I'll get it out of you somehow. Tomorrow, meet me at the same time in the lobby. We'll go see the big one."

"What's that?"

"Lady Liberty, of course."

Winona's stomach twisted. Steve was growing on her. This was too much, too fast. She had to put a stop to it. *Remember his girlfriend's accusation.* "I really can't—"

"It's okay," he said, cutting her off. "Then I'll report back. Our stories have to match." He saluted her. "Later, Miss Grant."

And then he was walking down the hall, and Winona found herself staring after him.

SIX

Steve had just spent thirty minutes talking to Winona at her door, who turned out to be an artist, of all things. Had he flirted with her? He reviewed their conversation in his head. Damn. He *had* been flirting. Although he wasn't sure if she'd flirted back. Genevieve had been right about Winona—her ex must have done a number on her. How recent was the breakup? Something was preventing her from relaxing around him, and he was chalking it up to her recent break-up and he decided not to take it personally.

He wished he weren't so curious about her. He'd promised himself to never date another artist. Steve exhaled. Now he was thinking about *dating* her? He had to pull his thoughts together and not dwell on her hazel eyes and the sound of her laughter when he'd utterly failed at telling her she was pretty.

He fished his cell from his pocket and mindlessly scrolled through a series of texts as he sat on his balcony in the afternoon sun. Three people had gotten back to him—other gallery owners—but only one with a lead. He pulled up the number of the recommended artist and called her—Jeanmarie Hobby. He'd met her the year before. Her blown glass art had been steadily growing in popularity, but with only a few weeks until his launch, transportation for her pieces from her Boston studio might be hard to arrange.

The phone rang until it went to voicemail, so he left a message. He saved her number in his contacts so he'd know right away when she called back. He doubted that she could bring in the same draw that the previous artist would have, but she was better than having a gap in his show.

A text came from Genevieve. *How has it been going with Winona? Where have you taken her so far?*

The woman was persistent to say the least. He was about to reply with made-up details about Central Park when someone knocked at the door. His heart skipped a beat as he went back inside to open it, thinking it might be Winona. Maybe she was warming up to him. When he saw Leisa standing there, he regretted not looking through the peephole. She was fully made up from her bombshell curls to a silky wraparound dress that hugged her ample curves.

"I'm *so* sorry, Steve," she said, wrapping her arms around his neck and kissing his cheek. Apparently, she'd completely forgiven him.

He stepped back, trying not to inhale what must be a dozen spritzes of perfume. "I still can't give you the spot."

Her full lips curved upward. "You found someone? Wonderful!"

"I haven't confirmed it yet, but I'm close."

Her hand slipped into his. "I could still fill in if you need me to." She blinked her green eyes at him. She had inched closer, moving her body against his. Leisa had a boyfriend, but they had a fairly open relationship, and she wouldn't think twice about using her body to encourage him to agree with her.

He pulled his hand away and put some distance between them, but then she entered his apartment.

"In another couple of years, I'd love to put you in my gallery," he said, closing the door after her.

The pouty lips were back, but then she smiled wide. "All right, babe. I can live with that." She crossed to his kitchen. "I really need a drink. Do you have anything good?"

She knew he didn't drink—and that he hated it when she brought it up. She pulled open the refrigerator and started browsing as if she lived there. "Water? Really, Steve, you can be so boring sometimes."

The back of his neck bristled, but he walked to the counter and settled on a barstool. "I may have some sports drinks on the bottom shelf."

"Even worse," Leisa pronounced, pulling out a water bottle and twisting the cap off. After taking a long drink, she smiled. "Let's go clubbing tonight. Jens is out of town."

Apparently, when the boyfriend was away, Leisa wanted to play. "You know I hate bars."

"Come on." Leisa sauntered over and looped her arm around his shoulders. "I'll keep you safe. I won't let you touch a drop."

It was hard enough to watch everyone else with their champagne at gallery events. But being surrounded by it at a bar? "I don't think so."

She dragged her fingers across his neck. "How about a quiet night at home with the two of us?" Her lips were dangerously close to his.

Yet he felt nothing. Wanted nothing. Leisa was a beautiful woman who had become a friend, but when she was like this, he wanted nothing to do with her.

He rose to his feet. "I've got an appointment at the gallery in a few minutes. You're welcome to help yourself to anything here, but I won't be back until late."

She dropped her arms in defeat. "Fine. I just wanted to relax with a friend. I was up half the night painting—hoping that I'd have someplace to show my new pieces."

And just like that, they were back to square one.

SEVEN

From her balcony, Winona watched Steve walk down the block. Again he had waited fifteen minutes, and she had again ditched him. This time she'd been tempted to join him. He stopped at the corner and looked up at the balcony; she smiled. He couldn't see her, but he must have guessed she was watching. It was like they had a secret code between them.

He smiled too.

Winona wanted to laugh. So maybe he wasn't exactly like Paul. He was still a heartbreaker. She could easily see women falling at Steve's feet, with the end result, of course, being disastrous. What was his story? What was his job? Had he lived in New York his whole life? She watched him cross the street, then hail a taxi.

Was he really going to the Statue of Liberty alone? He'd

probably visited her a dozen times. Or was it the sort of thing that New Yorkers didn't do—instead, leaving the excursion to the tourists?

She wasn't really counting the hours or watching the time, but by the time he knocked on her door at three that afternoon, she'd imagined that he'd gotten hit by a taxi or had fallen down one of those open sewer holes she'd seen in movies.

After Winona hurried to the door and flung it open, she remembered—too late—that she probably shouldn't being acting so enthusiastic.

Steve grinned. "Waiting for me?"

"I—uh . . ."

He laughed. "It was great. The weather perfect—maybe a little too warm, but that makes the hot dogs taste better. Ellis Island was crowded with summer tourists. You know how they are."

Winona smiled and leaned against the doorframe, as he told her about how he rescued a little girl's cotton candy before it could blow away in the wind. "It had a few specks of dirt in it when I handed it back, but that didn't bother her much."

She laughed. "Sugar is sugar."

"Right," he said, his eyes warm. "So how'd *your* day go?"

"Not as exciting as yours." Winona wanted to invite him in, but something held her back.

"I see you're actually dressed."

She looked down at her jeans and blouse. "I was expecting company."

"Oh? Who?" Steve asked. "Sorry. It's really none of my business."

Winona lifted a brow and said in a teasing tone, "*You*, of course. You think I'd ditch you day after day then have a secret alliance in my apartment? No, you're my only expected company, and I'm just a regular, boring workaholic. Something I'm sure my aunt informed you about."

"She did, actually," Steve said. "She has a lot more faith in me than I do. Yet she apparently thinks I can get you out of the apartment."

"Maybe you still can."

His eyes lit up, so Winona quickly backtracked. "I almost came today, but I had to redo a campaign, and then another job came in that will keep me busy for the rest of the week."

"*Almost* is good," he said.

"What about you?" Winona cut in. "Where do you find the time to take around a phantom tourist? Are you between jobs?" She sincerely hoped he wasn't about to confess that he had no job.

"I'm trying to salvage my gallery opening. So my current job is to make sure that what I've already set up doesn't fall apart. And that amounts to a lot of sitting around and stressing."

"Gallery? As in an art gallery?"

"Yeah. I've spent months putting it all together, from leasing the space to lining up the artists." He ran a hand through his hair, his gaze somber, and it was the first time Winona had seen him look anything but upbeat.

He wasn't an unemployed waif. She felt a bit guilty as relief shot through her. Not that she had anything against a man between jobs, but Paul had taken that lifestyle to the extreme. "You are seriously off the hook, Steve Monti. Don't even think about scheduling another minute with me."

"I'll admit, the request from your aunt put a bit of pressure on me at first, but . . ." He paused. "It's actually helping me get away from the stress for a couple of hours a day. Besides, I'd do anything for Genevieve." He was staring at her, and she couldn't look away.

In the depth of his eyes, she caught a glimpse of how much he cared for her aunt. It was sweet. "My aunt is way too fussy about me. I'll be fine. Please, don't go out of your way for me."

He leaned in, and instinct made her want to move back, but she didn't. She could smell his skin—like sunshine and faint cologne.

"I think she's watching out for both of us," he said in a quiet voice. "You may as well know that I'm a recovering alcoholic. Stress over the gallery opening makes it crazy hard to keep my thoughts focused. Touring the city the past two days has helped a lot. So, really, I owe your aunt."

"I—I guess that's good, then," Winona said, feeling completely lame that she couldn't come up with something better to say.

"Don't worry; I've been clean six years."

Steve's smile returned, and Winona found herself very relieved at that.

"So, about tomorrow . . ." he continued. "We're going on a ferry ride."

"*We* are, are we?"

"Ten o'clock." He winked and took a step backward. "Hope to see you, but if not, I'll be back to report on what a great time we had."

EIGHT

The following morning, Winona rushed out of her apartment. It was eleven minutes past ten; she'd overslept, which was a miracle in and of itself. But she didn't have time to dwell on that. She had to get down to the lobby before she could talk herself out of going to meet Steve.

She dashed down the stairs, not wanting to wait for the notoriously slow elevator. After bursting into the lobby, she stopped. Steve was just heading out the door, and her commotion made him turn around.

"Well, well," he said.

Winona flushed, but she put a smile on her face, and she kept walking toward Steve. She tried not to notice how his gaze seemed to be assessing her, as if he was trying to determine if her smile was genuine.

"Don't worry," she said as she reached him. "I'm here of my own free will."

"Your aunt didn't threaten you?" He slid his hands into his pockets, watching her.

"No. She'll think this is excursion number three."

"Then we'd better make the most of it," Steve said with a laugh.

That laugh did something funny to Winona's breathing.

He pushed through the door and held it for her.

Winona walked past him and stepped outside. The sun was partially hidden behind a cloud; otherwise it was going to be a warm day. As they walked to a waiting taxi, the scent of exhaust and spicy cooking assailed her.

They climbed in the back seat and the taxi jolted forward, pulling into traffic.

During the ride, Steve glanced over at her a few times, smiling.

"What? You don't think I'm really sightseeing with you?" she asked.

"Just checking." He brushed his fingers against her arm. "You do feel pretty real."

Winona laughed, hoping to cover up the fact that goose bumps had broken out on her arm at his touch. "I'm not that horrible, am I? I mean, I get caught up in my work, but my aunt never demanded that I tour the city with her neighbor as some ploy to get me outside."

"Are you sure about that?" Steve said as the taxi pulled over and let them out. "I haven't seen you outside since you arrived."

Winona raised her eyebrows.

He lifted his hands. "Not that I've been stalking you or anything."

"Sure you haven't." She climbed out of the taxi, letting him take her hand and help her out. She tried to keep a smile off her face.

"This way," Steve said, letting go of her hand and motioning toward a traffic light. "We're only a couple of blocks away."

They walked to the corner and stopped, then Steve sidled up next to her. "What do you do for fun back home? Southern California, right?"

Pretty pathetic that Winona had to rack her brain to come up with something. When she was dating Paul, it had been everything Paul. After him . . . well, there had just been work. "Driving along the PCH is always great. Tons of shops and art galleries to explore."

"Do you have a favorite artist?"

"I've liked Monet since I was a kid. My mom had a bunch of his framed prints around our house. And of course Van Gogh." The light turned green, and they crossed the street together.

"*The Starry Night*?"

"Definitely." She cast a sideways glance at him. "That painting was kind of my inspiration for getting into digital art."

He nodded. "I can see what you mean. So, are you ever going to show me your work?"

She lifted a shoulder. "Maybe."

"Don't go all out for me," he said, making her laugh.

As they walked, he pointed out a few things, like his favorite hole-in-the-wall Italian café and a place where one could buy vintage records.

"Do you have a record player then?" she asked. It was interesting seeing the shops through his eyes, it was like seeing a whole new city. When she'd arrived in the taxi, everything had been a rainy blur.

"I do," he said. "There's nothing purer than vinyl." He started singing a Journey song—way off-key.

"I get the idea," she said, motioning for him to stop. "What?" He widened his eyes. "You don't like my singing?"

She hid a smile. "I'm hoping you have other talents."

"I have many talents." He nodded to the record store as they passed. "We can stop in on our way back, and I'll dazzle you with my vast knowledge of music."

"We'll see what time it is. I can't take a whole day off of work."

"You're killing me, Winona."

She laughed. "Tell me more about your gallery."

So he did. Winona had always loved art, but hearing about that world from a different perspective was fascinating. He explained how most of the business was about networking, who you knew and who they knew. "So you're basically a brownnoser?"

He chuckled. "Exactly. I brownnose the artists, then the buyers, then the public, and it all starts over again with the next showing." He slowed his step as they reached the final intersection before the ferry launch.

They crossed together and barely made the 10:30 a.m. ferry.

"This thing is huge," Winona said, as they walked along one of the outer decks. She glanced at a brochure on the history of the ferry. Reading it would be a good way to keep her from watching Steve too much. His eyes were almost the exact shade of the shirt he wore. "Did you know that twenty million people ride this every year?"

"And you just increased that number by one."

"Genevieve will be so pleased." Winona looked back down at the brochure as Steve leaned against the rail and gazed out over the water. "Did you know that in 1926, the city's original white color scheme was eliminated in favor of a red-maroon? That was changed to municipal orange later so that the ferries could be seen in heavy fog and snow."

Steve didn't answer, so she looked up to him watching her. He was smiling.

"What?" she said. "You knew that already? Or you think it's funny that they changed the ferry colors?"

"I've never had anyone read a brochure to me," he said.

She leaned against the rail. "Really? You didn't go to museums with your parents and listen to them as they droned on and on reading the brochure and every plaque?"

"Not exactly." His voice went quiet. "Never knew my mom, and my dad tried his best, but it didn't quite work out. I left home at seventeen. Genevieve is the closest thing I've ever had to a mom; she's saved me more than she knows."

His tone wasn't particularly sad, just matter-of-fact. Had his childhood contributed to his alcoholism? Or was it something else entirely?

"Then my aunt saved us both," Winona said. "My parents divorced when I was seventeen, and my mom was faced with paying bills while working as a waitress. Genevieve paid for college. My dad's still pretty much out of the picture, living happily with his new wife and kids."

Steve's eyebrows rose. "So your life turned upside down at seventeen too, huh?"

"We have something in common," Winona said.

He nudged her shoulder. "It appears we do."

"Sad stories and Genevieve."

His smile was back, and relief shot all the way to Winona's toes. She liked the smiling Steve much better than the quiet one.

He reached over and took the brochure. "Did you know that on February 8, 1958, the *Dongan Hills* was hit by the Norwegian tanker Tynefield and fifteen passengers were injured?"

Winona tugged the brochure out of his hands and read, "Did you know that in 1978, the American Legion crashed into the concrete seawall near the Statue of Liberty ferry port during a dense fog? 173 were injured."

He snatched the brochure again. "Steam was used on the Staten Island ferries up until the 1980s."

"And," Winona said, reaching for the brochure. But Steve held onto it, so she leaned against him to read. "'On July 7, 1986, a mentally disturbed person named Juan Gonzalez attacked passengers on a ferry with a machete. Two people were killed and nine others were wounded.'"

"Ferries are dangerous," Steve joked. Then he started reading again. "'After the 9/11 attack on the World Trade Center, the Staten Island Ferry transported tens of thousands of people out of lower Manhattan to safety on Staten Island.'" He released a slow breath. "'The captains docked the ferries while under zero visibility as smoke and debris from the collapsed buildings filled the sky. In the following days, passengers were not allowed on the ferries.'" His voice cut off, and he handed the brochure to her.

Winona continued in a soft voice. "'The fleet was used to transport emergency personnel and equipment to and from lower Manhattan. In addition to the emergency personnel and equipment, the ferries were also being used to transport military personnel and equipment to Governors Island and lower Manhattan. Included in this were U.S. Army tanks. Since that day the Staten Island Ferry no longer carries cars.'" She blinked rapidly as the words swam before her. She couldn't read any more.

Steve slipped the brochure from her hands and folded it. Then he put his hand over hers and threaded their fingers together. The feel of his hand warmed the rest of her as they stood watching the New York skyline, not saying anything, not needing to.

NINE

Steve realized he was holding Winona's hand; he'd hardly remembered doing it. Maybe it was just his natural reaction while reading about the sobering details about 9/11. She didn't pull away though, and that made Steve's heart skip a beat.

But she's an artist.

And she's Genevieve's niece.

Two things that should make her off-limits. And she lived in California. Three strikes.

But he liked her—although that hadn't been his purpose in holding her hand. It might be why he was *still* holding her hand, though.

She'd been quiet for several moments as they looked out over the harbor. Steve stole a couple of glances at her. He was glad that she'd finally come with him. It was probably doing her a lot of good to take a break from her work, just as it was doing him a lot of good. Having Winona's company was a bonus.

On the ferry's return route, her phone rang, and she let go of his hand to pull it out of her pocket. She looked at the caller ID then sent the call to voicemail.

"Boyfriend?"

"Client. I'll call him later—he likes to go over everything on the phone instead of through email." She scrolled through what had to be texts on her phone.

"Do you have a boyfriend?" Steve asked.

"Had." Winona's voice sounded a bit uneasy.

Steve cursed himself. He'd been an idiot to bring it up.

"My aunt is a bit worried about me because I haven't dated in several months, since . . . well, since Paul dumped me."

So she was willing to talk about it. Steve took that as permission to ask another question. "He dumped you, huh? Been there."

Winona turned toward him, and he was glad he saw humor, not sorrow, in her gaze. "Which? *You* dumped, or you *were* dumped?"

"Mostly *I* get dumped." He quirked his mouth into a questioning smile. "I don't get it. I'm pretty much perfect. Maybe it's the AA meetings."

Winona laughed. "Yeah, that could be a deterrent." She turned back and looked over the water. "Or maybe it's because your girlfriend called you a two-timer."

Steve snapped his head to look at her. "I don't have a girlfriend." Then it hit him. "Oh, you mean Leisa . . . She's a disgruntled artist. Thinks she should be featured in my gallery."

Winona's expression looked relieved. Steve wasn't sure

what that meant. Unless . . . "She's not good enough?" Winona asked.

"She's good, but she's what I call *a dime a dozen* artist." He saw the confusion on Winona's face. "Not to be cruel about Leisa's talent, but it doesn't stand out. There are dozens of other artist who paint landscapes like her. When I mentioned it as gently as I could, she switched to nudes. Said that would get her some attention."

Winona was staring at him. "Did it?"

"Not yet."

"Maybe if she painted *you*?"

Steve nearly choked on his laughter. "Don't think she hasn't asked. A nude painting of me would surely ruin her career."

Winona's brow arched. "Maybe not."

He was turning red; he knew it. *Wow.* "I'd have to start drinking again."

Winona nodded, a small smile on her face. "Then you should probably avoid Leisa and her penchant for nude paintings."

Steve chuckled. "Believe me, I'm trying my best."

"It wouldn't scare me off, of course." Her smile was coy.

"What?" He teased. "A nude painting of me?"

"That, or AA meetings."

Steve felt his breath leave him, but he quickly recovered and said in a casual voice, "Good to know."

"I mean, you *are* clean now, right?"

"Yes. Six years."

"What have you done to celebrate?"

Her question surprised him. "Nothing."

"Steve," she said. A shiver traveled through him at the sound of her saying his name. "You need to celebrate."

"What do you have in mind?" Steve half-hoped that the celebration would include her.

"Have a medal made?" she suggested.

He laughed. "I could wear it to the gallery opening."

She was looking at him again, and he steeled himself against getting too caught up in her hazel eyes. Her mouth was quirked into a smile. "Maybe not. Something less loud?"

"Definitely less loud."

"Lunch? After the ferry? You choose the place, and I'll buy."

Steve couldn't move for a moment. "All right," he said, or at least he thought he did. She had turned to look over the railing, and he gazed at her profile. Did she just set up a lunch date with him? Winona Grant was becoming more interesting by the moment.

TEN

"Price isn't a concern," Winona said as she and Steve walked off the ferry. The more time she spent with Steve, the more she let down her guard, which wasn't as painful as she thought it would be. "But it has to be in New York. I'm not flying you to Paris or Rome."

Steve grinned. "It seems that price really is a concern."

She nudged him with her elbow. "Expensive is okay, but within reason."

"I think I know a place, and we can walk from here. Follow me." The crossing light turned green, and Steve touched her back as she stepped off the curb, as if he were watching over her.

It felt nice to be with a gentleman. And it was nice to tease him, as if they were good friends or even siblings. Winona stopped short at that thought as they reached the other side of the road. *Not* like siblings. There was nothing in her feelings toward Steve that resembled anything she felt for a family member.

She admitted that she was attracted to Steve—which probably wasn't much of a feat for him. He was good-looking, charming, sweet, and his smile was contagious. And he was flawed. She hadn't had too much time to analyze how she felt about this growing friendship with a recovering alcoholic. When he'd told her about his past, it hadn't bothered her. She hadn't wanted to take off or never see him again. If anything, she wanted to get to know more of the real Steve.

"This is it," he said, stopping.

Winona looked up at the sign above the restaurant windows. "The Italian place? It's just a small café."

He was watching her with a smile, as if he had been waiting for her to say that exact thing. "Yes, and you'll love it."

She moved her hands to her hips. "Why don't we go someplace fancy and memorable? Six years deserves a big celebration."

"Don't you like Italian?"

"I love it, but I thought you'd want to go to someplace where you have to know the manager to get a reservation."

Steve tugged her hand from her waist and squeezed it briefly, then let go. "What's better than eating my favorite Italian food with Genevieve's favorite niece?"

Winona could still feel his warm fingers against hers. "Are you sure?"

"It will be the perfect celebration. Besides, they know I don't drink."

Good point. Winona felt as if she'd had a tiny glimpse into the many challenges he must encounter on a regular basis. "Then it's settled."

Steve stepped forward and opened the door for her, and she walked into the quaint restaurant. Soft music played, and small lamps glowed on each table. One wall was taken up entirely by a seascape painting. The floor was made of beautiful marble tiles. Only three tables were occupied; they'd likely missed the lunch rush.

A hostess stepped around the podium and kissed Steve on each cheek. "Welcome!" She drew back, her lipsticked mouth a wide smile. "We've missed you."

She was probably in her mid-thirties, and she was stunning in the natural way Italian women were blessed with.

"Cynthia," Steve said, "this is Winona, Genevieve's niece."

The woman practically flew at Winona and proceeded to kiss both of her cheeks. "How wonderful to meet you! Genevieve is our favorite." She flashed Steve a smile. "After Steve, of course."

Winona checked Cynthia's left hand for a wedding ring. There was one. Winona let herself relax. Then she berated herself. She was *not* interested in Steve. She'd be here for the summer only, and besides, the Paul-disaster made her want to put off dating anyone else for at least a year.

But as Steve casually took her hand and led her to the table Cynthia showed them, Winona found herself swallowing back a hard lump in her throat. It had been months since she'd had a man's affectionate touch. Granted, Steve wasn't being affectionate—just courteous. Even so, she could almost let her mind wander and enjoy the way he held her hand.

It was over in moments when Steve released her hand and pulled out a chair.

"Would you like to see the wine menu?" Cynthia asked Winona.

"No, thank you," she said.

"Ah." Cynthia arched a brow at Steve. "You brought a good one."

Winona was sure that every part of her turned red. "We aren't dating," she said, only making herself blush more.

"We're celebrating," Steve jumped in, saving Winona from her awkwardness.

Cynthia tilted her head, looking back and forth between Steve and Winona, clearly not buying that this was not a date. "Oh?"

"Six years dry."

"Wonderful!" Cynthia beamed. She squeezed Winona's shoulder. "He's a good man." She bustled away before Winona could respond. "I'll bring appetizers," Cynthia called over her shoulder. "They're on the house!"

"How are you doing?" Steve asked, throwing Winona for a loop.

Was he referring to how she'd embarrassed herself? "You've missed, what, three hours of work? Is it driving you crazy yet?"

"Not really." She'd been too caught up in everything else to think much about work. The realization stunned her. "The ferry was fun."

"Your aunt will be so pleased."

"I didn't do it for her."

His eyes widened slightly at that, but then he covered his almost-confession up with taking a drink of water. She smiled. She was flirting, and he knew it. *What am I doing? I am going to so regret this.* Someone needed to pinch her, hard, to remind her about how Paul had dumped her flat on her—

"Tell me about your last boyfriend," Steve said.

He did not just ask that. But apparently he had. "Oh,

well, you know. The usual . . . boy meets girl, girl falls in love with boy, boy falls in love with another girl, boy dumps first girl, first girl falls apart and becomes a hermit."

Steve didn't laugh. "If that were the usual story, no one would ever leave their houses."

"What about your last girlfriend?" she asked.

He grimaced and took another swallow then he ended up coughing into his napkin.

"That bad?" Winona said.

He lifted his glass. "We probably would have stayed together if I were drinking this."

"Ah." She understood. He didn't need to say anything more. But did that mean he hadn't had a girlfriend since getting sober? For six years? He seemed to read the question in her eyes.

"It's true," he said. "I haven't been serious with anyone since I dried up. Ironic, I know. It seems I only attract women when I'm messed up. No one likes sober Steve."

"Leisa seems to."

"I wouldn't consider that a compliment." He smirked, his blue eyes focused on her. "She probably has a crush on you too."

"Who has a crush on someone?" Cynthia showed up carrying a platter of hors d'ouevres, which looked like a variety of melted cheese sauces and thick slices of crusty bread.

"We're talking about Leisa," Steve said.

Cynthia laughed. "Still after you, huh?"

"She's after the gallery."

Cynthia kept laughing while she nodded. "What'll the two of you have?"

Only then did Winona realize they hadn't been given menus.

"Are you okay if I order for both of us?" Steve asked.

"No problem." She leaned back in her chair. She'd never had anyone order for her, and she was impressed when Steve did so in Italian. But that also meant she had no idea what she'd be eating.

When Cynthia left, Winona said, "Are you Italian?"

"Nope. I know about three dozen words—and they're all related to food."

"Sounded good to me," Winona said. "What did you order?"

"It's a surprise." His gaze held hers. "But you'll love it."

ELEVEN

Steve leaned against the wall of the corridor, exhaling. Seconds ago, he'd seen Winona to her door. And he'd almost kissed her. Almost.

He was being an idiot. Winona was completely off-limits, and one part of him wondered if that was why he was attracted to her. But the other part of him knew that wasn't true.

It was time to put a stop to all of this temptation. He pulled out his cell phone. One thing that he'd learned in his AA group was that he always had to be completely honest. Any lie he allowed into his life would multiply faster than he could blink, and soon he'd be back to pacing in front of the liquor store. The first lie to Genevieve had been pretty white, but now he was getting in too deep. He typed out a text to her.

I have to bail on your niece. She's beautiful and sweet, and I'm attracted to her. Sorry to let you down, but I can't keep my promise of being her tour guide. Hopefully she's seen enough of the city to venture out on her own.

Steve pressed send then pocketed his phone, already feeling better. That lasted until he got on the elevator and the doors shut, then he felt lousy. He missed Winona already. The way she'd opened up to him had been charming. Beneath her reserved shell was a soft, warm woman who was the most unselfish person he knew.

Over lunch, she'd become more and more comfortable with him, and soon she'd told him things he was sure she'd rarely talked about. She'd given up a sure promotion to help her aunt this summer. When her ex-boyfriend had broken her heart by cheating, she'd felt like it was her fault. She was afraid to let anyone down, especially her boss and her clients, often revising ad campaigns to their specifications at all hours of the night. And she'd wanted to celebrate six years of sobriety with someone she barely knew.

He hadn't felt judged by her; she hadn't been repulsed by his confessions. She'd focused on his successes, not his long list of failures, which he'd told her plenty about. And she'd been nonplussed about it all. She'd even given him a tight hug at her apartment door. Thus, the almost kiss. It would have been natural, and he could have sworn that she would have welcomed it.

But he couldn't do that to Genevieve, who trusted him. Steve could never disappoint her.

As Steve stepped into his apartment, the empty rooms brought on a familiar loneliness. He locked his door and flipped on the lights—too bright for his somber mood. He turned them off again and crossed to the window to look out over the late-summer New York afternoon. Clouds had stirred up, and it looked like it might rain again.

He thought about the two hours he and Winona had spent talking at lunch. She had brought up a good point. Why had he hardly dated since he became sober? Was it because his past relationships had brought him too much emotion? Was he afraid to feel something that might tempt him to go numb again?

His phone buzzed, and Steve checked it, surprised that Genevieve had texted back already. It had to be after midnight in Europe.

I thought I could trust you. I'm sorry too.

Steve blew out a frustrated breath. He moved to his couch and sat down, composing an even longer text. *Don't worry. You can trust me. I'm staying away. It would tear me apart if I thought I hurt her. I want to be completely honest with you so you know why I'm not touring with her anymore. Winona is unexpected. And to tell you the truth, it scares me. I'm sorry.*

He leaned his head back and closed his eyes. Instead of blackness behind his eyelids, he saw Winona's expressive face as she sat across from him at the restaurant. The gold and green in her eyes as she asked about previous girlfriends. How she looked away as she talked about Paul cheating on her. Heard her laugh when he told her about his worst disaster-date ever, which had involved a taxi, an angry actress, and four hundred dollars. Then he watched Winona grow mellow talking about her mom.

And he still hadn't seen her art. But he knew, without even looking at it, that it would be multi-faceted, like her.

Someone knocked on his door, and his eyes snapped open. If it was Leisa, he hoped she'd give up soon and go away. The person knocked again, and Winona called his name.

Steve shot up off the couch and ran his hands through

his hair. What did she want? He'd just told Genevieve that he was leaving Winona alone.

Before he could talk himself out of it, he opened the door. Winona was back to wearing her lounge pants, which he found completely endearing.

"Genevieve called," she said.

Steve's heart froze. Had Genevieve told her what he'd said? He couldn't tell by Winona's expression whether she was mad or annoyed.

"She did?" he asked.

Winona stepped forward, surprising Steve, and even more surprising, she put her hand on his chest and pushed him back into his apartment. Then she shut the door. Her eyes looked dark in the shadows of the room.

"Yes, she did," Winona said in a quiet voice. "You might think I'm crazy, and I probably am, but . . ." She placed her hands on his shoulders and tugged him down toward her.

She's going to kiss me, was the last thing Steve thought before Winona pressed her mouth against his.

TWELVE

I can't believe I'm kissing Steve. Heat shot through Winona's arms, moving to her torso and throughout the rest of her body. Thinking about kissing Steve had made her warm enough, but actually kissing him made her melt.

When Genevieve had called her and confronted her about what was going on with Steve, Winona was floored. Steve had feelings for her? It seemed impossible, but Winona knew she returned the feelings.

She'd spent an hour in her apartment, pacing. Trying to talk herself out of going up to Steve's place. Trying to deny what she felt, what she thought. Maybe if she kissed him, she'd get over him and she'd realize that all guys were the same.

But now she knew—kissing Steve was *not* the same. He'd certainly been surprised, but once he got over that, he took his time exploring her lips, then her jaw, then her neck. She found herself gripping his hair and pulling him closer.

For a brief moment, she wondered if she was doing this because she was lonely, simply craving affection. But deep down, she knew she was okay with loneliness. She was okay by herself. His mouth was slow and caressing now, as if he didn't want to let her go. And that was fine with her.

His hands moved up her back, and he moved his mouth to kiss next to her earlobe. "Good talk with your aunt?" Steve whispered.

"No," Winona said, completely breathless. She drew away so she could meet his gaze. Her heart thudded at the serious look in his eyes, and something else, something she couldn't exactly name, but that she feel too. "It was an awful conversation. She said I should go home. She doesn't want me to rebound."

"What did you say?" He was equally breathless.

"That I'd think about it," she said. "But I want you to know it's *my* decision. Not my aunt's."

He straightened, his hands staying at her waist, his eyes intent on hers. "Kissing me?"

"As long as you don't mind, I think I can make this kind of decision."

"Genevieve asked me to stay away from you." He let out a small sigh. "I promised her I would, but now I'm regretting that." He leaned his forehead against hers. "How mad will Genevieve be if I go back on my promise?"

She touched his face, running her fingers over the scruff on his cheeks. "How mad will *I* be if you don't?"

"Hmmm. Only you can answer that. What's your vote?"

"Genevieve will get over it."

He grinned. "That's what I was hoping to hear." He brushed his lips against hers. "Besides, I still have to take you to see The Metropolitan."

Her lips quirked into a smile. “Maybe I should stick around one more day then.”

He leaned his forehead against hers. “What about the Empire State Building? You can’t go back to California without seeing it.”

Her hands snaked around his neck. “I saw it as a kid.”

“It’s completely different now,” he said.

She wanted to close her eyes and melt against him. “Really? Then I’d better see it again.”

“Then you can’t leave until at least Saturday.”

She laughed. “I hate traveling on weekends. Too busy.”

“And there’s nothing better than Central Park on a Sunday.” Their mouths were so close together that Winona wasn’t sure which breath was hers and which was Steve’s. “The Italian restaurant has a Monday night dinner special, and Broadway is best on Tuesdays.”

“Hmm,” she said. “What will Genevieve think?”

His lips found hers for a long kiss. Winona was now melting even faster. Even though she knew it was a bit crazy to be kissing Steve, she let her instincts guide her for once.

When he pulled away, he said, “I’ll tell her that you can make your own decisions.”

“But I’m in her apartment.”

“Then stay here.”

She let out a small gasp. “Steve!”

“I’ll sleep on the couch.”

She started to protest again, but it was lost in another kiss. His phone buzzed, and although it was nice that he was ignoring it for her, it kept buzzing. “You can get that.”

“It can wait.”

She disentangled herself from him and stepped away. “What if it’s Genevieve?”

His eyes shot to hers, panicked. “Do you think she planted a camera?”

Winona laughed. His phone started buzzing again, and he finally pulled it out of his pocket. "I *should* get this. I've been waiting for this call for three days."

THIRTEEN

"Jeanmarie," Steve said, his heart thudding, both from kissing Winona moments before and now finally speaking to the elusive artist he hoped to book.

"Steve," the woman's cool voice came through the other end. "I don't know how you expect me to be in your show with such little notice."

"I understand, and that's why I offered to lower the commission by ten percent." Thirty-five was standard; he'd offered her a good deal.

"Ten."

Steve exhaled, glancing over at Winona, who had busied herself sorting through his vinyl record collection. Normally, it would have bugged him to have someone touch his records, but he knew she would be careful. "Twenty-five is more than fair."

Jeanmarie barked out a laugh without a trace of humor in it. “Twelve percent.”

Steve exhaled. There was no easy way around this, especially since his mind was spinning circles around what just happened with Winona. “Let me run some numbers, and I’ll call you back.” He hated to disconnect, especially when she’d waited three days to call him back. But he couldn’t think straight. Not with Winona in the room. He was tempted to turn down Jeanmarie and use Leisa anyway, although that would be no better than gallery suicide.

Winona sat on the couch now, thumbing through an art album on the coffee table. She didn’t say anything when he sat by her. He watched her profile, wondering at the conflicting emotions she’d stirred inside him. He also wondered how real her feelings were for him. Her aunt had warned him that she was fragile.

But when she turned to look at him, all he saw was determination in her gaze.

“My aunt is not going to be happy about this,” she said, her smile wide.

Steve’s mind took a second to catch up. He reached for her hand and linked their fingers. “Are we going to rebel, then?”

She nodded, and he thought his heart might have skipped a beat.

Her phone rang, and he said, “You can answer that.”

She pulled it out. “My mother. I’ll call her later.” She ended the call, and Steve found himself staring at her screensaver. Something told him it was Winona’s work. “Can I see that?”

Winona looked down, and her face flushed. She made a move to pocket her phone, but Steve put his hand over it. “Please?”

Winona exhaled, then released the phone. He felt her eyes on him as he studied the piece—a regular photograph enhanced with bursts of color. The girl in the picture looked about fifteen. She sat on wet sand near the ocean, her knees pulled up, a too-big prom dress flowing around her. The girl's eyes were soulful, like her prom date hadn't gone well. Yet, the spark in her eyes told Steve that she'd be okay; she was a strong girl turning into a strong woman.

"This is gorgeous," he said when he found his voice. "Are there more on your phone?"

Winona leaned over. She swiped the screen then tapped the photo icon, then scrolled to a picture file and opened it.

Steve tapped on picture after picture. Each photograph had been digitally altered and colored, adding explosions of color and emotion. They were breathtaking.

"Have you ever sold any of these?" he asked.

"A few for book covers." Her voice sounded timid. "I took those off the market so the images aren't duplicated for covers."

"How long does one take you?"

"The actual work is only a few hours, but the decision-making process can be days or weeks." She reached for the phone. "But I'm not ready to make them public. They're sort of my way of journaling, I guess."

He was currently looking at an image of a stormy afternoon. A young man stood near a tree, his eyes hooded. Darkness swirled about him, while the clothing around his heart was brilliant orange. It made Steve think of a young man standing in the middle of turmoil with a soul was determined to fight through it.

Winona slipped the phone from his fingers. "I don't know how to explain it, but after selling a few for book covers, I felt like I was letting a part of me go. I took them off the market. They can still be seen at a digital art site, but I've turned down any inquiries."

Steve stared at her. One part of him said that she was crazy—she created beautiful, modern art and could make good money selling it—but the other part of him said that she was simply amazing. She created art for art's sake, not for profit. Artists of that caliber were rare.

Before he could say anything, her phone rang. Her mother again.

"Maybe I should take it this time," Winona said.

Judging by the one side of the conversation he heard, it was clear that Genevieve had called Winona's mother. When she hung up, Steve braced himself to hear that even though they'd only kissed once, they were done.

"Wow." Winona turned to him. "She called you *rebound guy*. I feel like I'm fifteen, being lectured on the boy who asked me on my first date."

"Was *his* name Steve?"

"Jack," she said, letting a small smile break through.

"And what did you do when you were fifteen? Did you go out with Jack?"

"I did." Her smile grew.

He laughed. "So there's a history of rebellion in you after all. With the way your mom and aunt are taking this, you'd think I'd just asked you to elope."

Winona nodded, her eyes dancing with amusement. "They *are* taking this a little too seriously."

"Not that I don't want you to take this seriously." He felt his face heating up, but he plunged on. "I mean, I don't take it lightly that you burst into my apartment and threw yourself at me."

She leaned closer, their faces only inches away. "Is that what happened?"

"It's how I remember it."

"Hmm." She eyed him. "So what *is* going on? That's what my mother asked."

"I can only speak for myself, you know. But as I told Genevieve, I like you. I haven't dated for a long time, and I wouldn't mind changing that with you."

She looked down at their hands, which Steve had intertwined together. "That doesn't sound too horrible."

"So I'm *not* rebound guy?"

"Of course you are," Winona said, looking back at him, eyes soft. "Do you mind?"

He closed the distance and kissed her gently. "Not at all." He lifted his hands and placed them on both side of her face, slowly running his fingers along her cheek then neck. "I want you to think about something. You don't have to answer right away."

"What?" she breathed.

Steve hesitated, wondering if he was about to commit career suicide. But his gut wouldn't leave him alone. He hoped that he could still trust it. "I want to debut your artwork in my gallery."

FOURTEEN

Winona couldn't sleep, and every time she tried, she couldn't get Steve out of her mind. It was four in the morning, and she was wide awake. She climbed out of bed and went into the kitchen to make some tea. It had been three days since he'd asked her to debut her digital art in his gallery. She'd told him he was crazy, that she couldn't be the downfall of his opening weekend. He'd stopped asking, but the offer was constantly in her thoughts.

And the attraction between them was stronger than ever. Maybe she shouldn't have kissed him, and maybe she shouldn't have kissed him the next day and the next. The man hadn't dated for six years. She was on the rebound. Feeling Steve's arms around her and his touch on her skin was the perfect antidote for thoughts about Paul. In fact, she could barely remember what he looked like.

Her heart no longer hurt like it used to. There was still an emptiness in her heart, but Steve was filling it up fast. A warning voice whispered that this was too good to be true. That she was wearing rose-colored glasses. She was in New York only for the summer. This couldn't last.

Tea ready, she cradled the steaming cup in her hands and went to sit on the couch. What if she did agree to be in his gallery? What if the exhibit was an epic failure, and the write-ups in the paper were cruel criticisms of the most private part of her? She didn't know if she could recover.

Worse, she didn't know if she wanted to end things with Steve—and she would certainly have to.

Winona groaned. Why did she have to go make things complicated? Or was this Steve's fault? If he hadn't been so sweet and charming, she would have been able to stay away. She took a sip of tea and closed her eyes, letting the warm liquid calm her.

Her phone chimed. Who texted at four in the morning? She set the tea down and walked to the bedroom for her phone, dreading the sight of something from her aunt, who had not been happy when Winona had informed her that she would be dating Steve for the rest of the summer. Only time would tell where it would go. After Genevieve's initial lecture and admonition to stay in her apartment after all, she'd been remarkably quiet.

Winona looked at the text.

I can't sleep. Please say yes.

Steve. By *yes*, he meant *yes* to debuting in his gallery.

She sat on the bed, reading his text again. *I can't sleep either*, she typed back.

Breakfast?

She hesitated. *Ok.*

Be over soon, sweetheart.

Winona stared at the word: *sweetheart.* Steve was so unassuming, so straightforward. He just embraced things; he didn't let fear stop him from going after what he wanted. Which was ironic, because he used to drown his fears in alcohol.

She wished she could be more like him—brave enough to put her art in a gallery, tell her boss to save the promotion for her, explain to her mother that Steve was not Paul, and not be so afraid of taking a chance.

Knowing that he was bringing her breakfast, she got dressed in lounge pants then straightened the kitchen and living room.

She was expecting him, but even so, when Steve knocked at the door, her heart thudded. She opened the door, and he came inside, smiling and carrying a couple of sacks. After setting them on the counter, he pulled Winona into a hug.

"I need to show you something," he said against her ear.

Winona was enjoying his arms around her and didn't want to separate. The moment he'd touched her, her anxieties had fled. "Are you going to bribe me to be in your gallery?"

"Yes." He pressed a kiss on the top of her head. "Let's eat first."

They sat down to muffins and coffee, Winona trying to get more information out of him. Steve remained quiet and only flashed her the occasional smile. When they finished, he rose and held out his hand. "We're going outside, so I'll give you the choice of whether to get dressed first."

Winona looked at her lounge pants. She'd grown quite fond of them, and besides, the sun wouldn't be up for another two hours. "I'm fine."

Steve grinned and tugged her toward him. "Be prepared to be amazed."

Winona let him lead her out of the apartment. Once outside at the street curb, he hailed a taxi. Winona climbed in, and when Steve settled next to her, she said, "Where are we going?"

He placed his arm around her shoulders and pulled her close. "Just wait. You'll love it."

"You say that a lot," Winona said, letting a smile fill her face. "How do you know what I love?"

He chuckled, and she nestled closer, feeling cozy as she leaned against him. About fifteen minutes later, the taxi stopped, and Steve told the driver to wait for them. Then he opened the door and climbed out.

Winona followed and looked up at the awning on the building. *Monti Gallery.* The windows were dark and the neighborhood silent.

"What are you up to? I already told you I'm not ready."

"I know." He kissed her cheek. "I want to show you something."

He unlocked the door and led her into the entryway. It was nearly impossible to see anything. They shuffled in the dark toward a set of stairs, and Winona's eyes gradually grew accustomed to the gloom.

"It's upstairs," Steve said, leading her by the hand. At the top, he said, "Wait here and keep looking forward."

A chill crept up Winona's back at his sudden absence and at the fact that she was standing alone in a dark building. Then, about ten feet ahead, a bank of lights came on. Winona stood a few feet from a balcony rail. Below was an entire room dotted with display consoles. The balcony was level with another one on the opposite side, which was lit up. In its center was a massive canvas.

Winona stared at the lit canvas—a duplicate of her screensaver, the photograph of the girl by the ocean, which

Winona had digitally enhanced. It was amazing. Beautiful. Intense.

"Wow."

Steve's hand touched her arm then slid down to capture her hand. "Exactly. *Wow* is what every person will say when they see your work."

Winona's eyes stung with emotion. The art expanded to nearly life-size, powerful and captivating. It made her heart swell to the point of pain. "I don't know, Steve. I just don't know."

He turned to look at her, and his other hand brushed her cheek. "Give it this one chance. If you hate it, I'll never ask you to do it again. But, if you love it, then you can worship me for the rest of your life."

Winona laughed, but it came out as more of a cry. She wrapped her arms about him, squeezing him as tight as she could. "I'm afraid."

He squeezed her back. "I know. But I'll be here with you."

Winona closed her eyes, taking comfort in his words. "Okay."

"Okay?" Steve moved his hands to cradle her face. "Really?"

She nodded.

He brushed his lips against hers, softly. "I can't wait."

FIFTEEN

Two weeks later

"Ready?" Steve grasped Winona's hand and guided her out of the taxi. Steve had wanted to arrive a block away then walk up to the opening, surprising those on the lookout.

Winona's heart had been thumping like mad for the past few hours. Tonight was the opening, and the media had already gathered outside Monti Gallery.

"The crowd is huge," Winona said as they approached it. Steve had told her to expect a good showing—primarily for the other two artists. "I hope I don't disappoint the others' fans."

"They're in for a treat," Steve said, leaning down and kissing her cheek.

The gesture went straight to her heart. Steve seemed so

comfortable around her, as if they'd known each other for years.

For a moment, Winona wished it could be the two of them walking into the gallery, holding hands and looking at all the art pieces. She'd felt more and more attached to Steve over the past two weeks. He'd been frank about how much he cared for her, although they hadn't discussed the end of summer.

Her stomach was a horde of butterflies as they reached the gallery entrance.

"Mr. Monti, tell us about the new exhibit," a young man called, stepping in front of them and holding out a microphone. A cameraman edged toward them, filming every word.

Steve introduced Winona to the reporter then answered a couple of questions. They spoke to two more reporters before making it inside. There, Steve introduced Winona to those milling about on the main level. A server brought a tray over to Steve and handed him a champagne glass of water.

"Thank you," Steve said, then picked up another glass with champagne in it and handed it to Winona.

"I'll have water too," she said.

The server took the glass, and a few moments later brought her a new one with water.

"You didn't have to do that," Steve said.

She simply smiled and took a sip. Soon they were surrounded by art patrons. Between introductions and conversations, she examined the artwork. The collection of traditional sculptures beside modern art was electrifying.

"Are you Winona Grant?" a woman asked. Her fitted yellow dress screamed for attention. The woman was tall, with sleek black hair, and could more than pull the look off.

"I am," Winona said.

"Rachel," Steve said to the woman, leaning over to kiss her cheek. "Wonderful to see you."

"Bringing in digital art was a brilliant move, Steve. Others have been reluctant to embrace technology. I love a forward-thinking gallery." Rachel smiled at Winona. "Ms. Grant, I love your work. I've already put in a bid on two pieces, although I expect to be outbid before I finish off this champagne."

Winona tried not to let her mouth hang open. Bids had already been entered on her pieces?

Steve grinned. "Good to hear."

Rachel was watching Winona closely. "Are you two . . .?"

"We are," Steve said, his voice confident.

Winona could tell that she was blushing.

"Splendid," Rachel said. "It's about time."

They laughed together, and Winona found herself smiling.

Rachel touched Winona's arm. "I can tell—you two are a good match."

It was just casual conversation—a lot of people would probably comment on their relationship tonight—yet she couldn't help but let Rachel's words warm her through.

No one had ever said that she and Paul were a good match—in fact, they had always commented on how opposite they were. Winona was the organized, hard-working woman, while Paul had the devil-may-care personality.

"Let's go up to see your display," Steve said.

She tuned back in, wondering what she'd missed of Steve and Rachel's conversation.

"You haven't seen it yet?" Rachel asked. "Come on." She

linked arms with Winona and walked with her toward the stairs. This was all so surreal.

Suddenly, a woman who was the exact image of Genevieve appeared at the top of the stairs. Winona refused to believe her eyes.

"Darling." She certainly looked and sounded like Genevieve. She wore a Italian silk suit and more diamonds than the British royalty. Her blonde-colored hair had a pixie cut.

"Aunt Genevieve?" She hurried up the stairs.

"I see Steve talked you into displaying your art. It's breathtaking." Genevieve swept her into an embrace, and the next thing Winona knew, her aunt had hugged Steve as well, then began talking animatedly with Rachel.

Winona stared at Genevieve. She'd hardly spoken to her aunt for the past two weeks, and Winona had thought she'd burned plenty of bridges by dating Steve. She turned to him and whispered, "What's my aunt doing here?"

Steve winked, then looked away, as if he was suddenly interested in a couple who'd come up the stairs.

"Steve?" Winona grabbed his hand.

He smiled, but before he could answer, Genevieve was back at her side, slipping an arm around Winona's waist. "When he said you were debuting your work, I couldn't not come."

"But I thought you were upset and—"

"I was. Then I got over it," Genevieve said. "I guess I was too curious. I had to see the two of you for myself." She flashed her a brilliant smile. "I must admit, you make a good match." Then Genevieve was off again, talking to an ancient-looking man who seemed pleased with the digital art display.

A good match. Winona had heard that twice tonight.

"I agree," a whisper was spoken right next to her ear.

Winona turned. Warmth shot to her toes at the way Steve was looking at her, his expression questioning, open, tender.

"Do you agree?" He said it with a smile, but his eyes were serious.

"I think I do," she said. "And I think you may have a hard time getting rid of me come August."

His fingertips brushed hers. "I wouldn't have a problem with that. There are a lot more places I need to show you. And when it starts snowing, I'll buy you a warm coat."

"You think I'm staying until it snows?"

"You can't miss Rockefeller Center during the holidays." He leaned close, and his lips brushed her ear as he said, "Besides, come June, there's no one I'd rather celebrate seven years with."

Winona wanted to kiss him right then, but they were surrounded by the public. "As long as we celebrate by you ordering in Italian for me."

Steve's fingers intertwined with hers. They stood close, and although only their hands were touching, Winona felt as if she were wrapped in his arms.

"I know the perfect place," he said. "You'll love it."

Winona let a sigh escape. She hadn't had a drop of champagne, yet she felt as if she were floating. "It's a date."

ABOUT HEATHER B. MOORE

Heather B. Moore is a *USA Today* bestselling author. She writes historical thrillers under the pen name H.B. Moore; her latest is *Finding Sheba*. Under Heather B. Moore, she writes romance and women's fiction. She's one of the coauthors of The Newport Ladies Book Club series. Other works include *Heart of the Ocean, The Fortune Café,* the Aliso Creek series, and the Amazon bestselling Timeless Romance Anthology series.

For book updates, sign up for Heather's email list: HBMoore.com/contact

Website: HBMoore.com

Blog: MyWritersLair.blogspot.com

Twitter: @HeatherBMoore

DULCE DE LECHE

Lusia Perkins

OTHER WORKS BY LUISA PERKINS

Dispirited
The Book of Jer3miah: Premonition
Done & Done

ONE

Marisol absolutely had to land this job; that meant nailing the interview. After getting on the elevator to her potential employer's penthouse apartment, she checked her resume for the hundredth time. Professional, detailed, clean, understated. She put it back into her bag and then surveyed her outfit in the dark glass of the elevator wall. Dumpy, boring, dependable. Perfect.

The nanny agency had told her that this family was a little desperate, and that if she got it, the job would start the following week. That was perfect, as far as she was concerned. The reality was that Marisol needed this job as desperately as the employer needed it filled. This was the one. It had to happen.

She rotated her neck and shoulders, trying to release the tension she felt whenever she thought about her current situation. *Current for the next eight days*, she corrected herself. She'd nannied for the Rubin family for three years, working hours and whole days of overtime without pay. She'd shared a bedroom with Tikva, the older daughter, and had basically been a full-time occupational therapist for Bayla, their special needs younger girl. Most exhausting was enduring the contempt, insecurity, and jealousy of Miriam, the girls' mother.

At first, she'd thought Rubins had paid her pretty well—until she realized that it worked out to about five dollars an hour. Regardless, she'd ignored every humiliation until Monday night.

After the girls had gone to bed, the Rubins had asked her into Bob's study—a room normally off-limits to Marisol. They'd sat her down, which never meant good news was coming. What had she done wrong this time? Had she left the kitchen light on again? Forgotten to latch the door to the dog run on the side of the townhouse?

What they'd told her had been much worse than their usual nit-picky reprimand. "We're letting you go, Marisol. We're moving to Paris in two weeks. We'll let you work right up until then, and then give you three weeks' extra pay as a bonus." Bob Rubin had sat back with a self-satisfied air, apparently impressed with his own generosity.

"Two weeks?" Marisol echoed. "That's not much notice for you to get your family ready to move all the way to Paris."

Rob's gaze slid sideways to his wife. *Aha*. They'd known about the transfer for far longer but hadn't told her on purpose. It was more convenient for them to have her unaware—and their convenience trumped everything.

Marisol glanced over at Miriam. Her expression was smug, even triumphant. Miriam had never kept her feelings about Marisol a secret. She fumed any time the girls clung to

Marisol instead of running to her—which only made their clinging worse. She constantly urged Marisol to put on a sweater, complaining that her clothes were too tight or revealing. She took every opportunity to complain about Marisol's cooking or cleaning or caring for the children—yet the Rubins had kept her on all this time.

Marisol had walked out of the study numbly, not bothering to argue or negotiate for more money. She went to the tiny room she shared with Tikva, holding back tears so she wouldn't wake the girl. Lying on the bottom bunk, she pulled up her nanny agency's website on her laptop and sent them an urgent message.

The end of May was the worst possible time of year to try to get another nanny job. Was it even worth the bother of applying? But she was so close to graduating. For years, she'd taken night classes at City College several blocks downtown, paying as she went.

Just two more semesters of night classes, and she'd be done. She had to find a way to push through. She was already twenty-seven, far older than the traditional graduate. But if she could get another nanny job, she'd finish college without any student loan debt. That meant she'd have a prayer of being able to afford to live and work in Manhattan after graduation. She'd finally realize her dream of being permanently independent of her family, and she'd be free to explore the endless wonders of the greatest city in the world.

Now, as she gazed at the dial that showed the elevator's laborious progress, Marisol took a series of deep breaths. This new job opportunity wasn't perfect—it was only for the summer—but it *would* be the ideal bridge to September, which was prime nannying season. It would get her through the crisis the Rubins had thoughtlessly put her into.

Finally, the elevator reached the penthouse level. Marisol relaxed her shoulders and smoothed her long, shapeless skirt. She'd consciously copied the dress of the Orthodox Jewish women who lived around her in Washington Heights, not wanting to draw attention to her body. Her potential employer was a single dad, and Marisol didn't want any favors or even any extra attention. She'd seen the way Bob Rubin's eyes had lingered on her chest and hips lately when she played Legos on the living room carpet with Bayla and Tikva. As much as she'd resented Miriam's urgings of uber-modesty, she could now see the wisdom in it too.

After she exited the elevator, Marisol lifted the heavy brass knocker on the polished mahogany door and knocked. A moment later, the door opened. Marisol looked up—way up. She was short and used to looking up into people's faces, but this guy made her neck hurt. He looked a bit like Will Smith, only younger—and much taller.

"May I help you?"

"I . . ." Marisol was confused. Had she gotten off the elevator on the wrong floor? Downstairs, a woman's voice had answered when the doorman had announced her over the intercom; single dad or no, she hadn't been expecting a man to answer the door.

The man raised an eyebrow at her. His height, his beautiful amber eyes, and his eyebrow all intimidated Marisol. But she had to nail this.

"I'm Marisol Flores. Team Nanny sent me. I'm here to interview for the job. Is this the right apartment? I'm looking for Dr. Jackson."

Now the man frowned, looking her up and down. "There must be some mistake."

"Oh . . ." So this was the wrong floor after all. Marisol turned to the elevator, and then looked back. "This isn't the penthouse, then?"

"Yes, it is. What I meant was that the agency made a mistake. You're not at all what I asked for."

Oh. "Dr. Jackson?"

"Yes. I'm sorry. You won't work out. Not your fault. I'll call to let the agency know." He took a step backward and turned away.

"Wait!" On a wild impulse, Marisol lunged forward and stuck her hand out, keeping Dr. Jackson from closing the door all the way.

He looked at her, impatience furrowing his brow. "What is it?"

"The subway ride here took forever. Could you at least look at my resume? And maybe . . . may I use your restroom?"

The doctor looked at Marisol for a long moment, and then relented. "Sure. Come on in. The bathroom is on your left. Give me your resume. Come down the hall to the living room when you're done. I can't give you more than a minute, though. I need to get the agency on the phone to see if they can send over someone else before I have to get to work."

TWO

Darius watched the young woman go into his bathroom, her ugly black skirt sagging in the back. Walking into his living room, he scanned the paper in his hand. She'd been a nanny for three years, and before that had worked at a special needs daycare in Inwood. She hadn't included any education details, other than a CPR and lifesaving course she'd taken the summer before.

Darius flopped onto his long, leather couch and fumed. What had the agency been thinking? He'd specifically requested someone older. Well, he couldn't say that straight out because of anti-discrimination laws, but he'd asked for a college degree and a minimum of fifteen years' nannying experience. He couldn't stand a repeat of last summer's disaster.

Ever since he and Phoebe had split up and she'd moved to Las Vegas, they'd shared custody of Reese and Seth. And when Reese had started school, Darius had consented to the boys spending the school year in Vegas as long as he had them all summer. It was a less-than-ideal arrangement, but Phoebe had been dead-set on accepting the prestigious position as Head of Bariatric Surgery at UMC.

Darius was ambitious too, and, especially in this day and age, he'd be the worst kind of hypocrite to demand that his ex-wife not further her own career. He ached for the boys all fall and winter—and then during the summer months, worked as little as possible so that he could spend every free minute with them.

But that still meant he needed a full-time nanny during the summer. Anesthesiologists couldn't just take three whole months off. "Working as little as possible" meant keeping his schedule to thirty-five or forty hours per week plus on-call time, instead of the sixty or seventy he was used to.

Last summer, he'd settled for a college student. It had made sense at the outset; she wanted work only for as long as he needed her. But he hadn't counted on the constant flirting and overt bids for his attention. Chelsea had been so over-the-top with her low-cut blouses and push-up bras that even his boys had noticed—and they'd only been six and four at the time.

This year, he was adamant. He wanted a matronly grandmother type. No one who was going to see his ringless left hand and start scheming. He was willing to pay a full year's salary for the next three months if it meant getting someone who would focus on his boys and not him.

The woman—Ms. Flores—had come out of the bathroom and into his living room. She looked at him with solemn, dark eyes. He thought about her long commute via subway to his apartment and felt a twinge of guilt.

"Please, sit down for a moment, Ms. Flores. Can I have

my housekeeper get you a drink of some kind? Tea, water, juice?"

"No, thank you." Her voice had a slight lilt to it. South American, maybe? Her accent wasn't Mexican or Dominican.

"Well, I'll insist on paying for a taxi back to wherever you live—or over to Team Nanny's office, if you prefer. I'm sorry that they've wasted both of our time. The fact is, I'm looking for someone more experienced. And with more education."

The woman's face fell, and she rooted through her briefcase. "But I have excellent references. My current employer—"

"I'm sure your references are fine."

"Then why won't you give me a chance?" she blurted. A second later, she looked mortified, as if she regretted her outburst.

"It's complicated." Darius exhaled and rubbed his forehead. "I only have my boys for three months of the year. Last summer, I hired a college student to watch them while I was at work. It seemed ideal, but it . . . wasn't."

No need to share the sordid details with a stranger. Chelsea walking around in her lingerie after the boys were in bed . . . Chelsea "forgetting" to close her bedroom door when she undressed . . . Darius cleared his throat and continued. "For one thing, my older son has Asperger's, so I need someone with a high degree of patience, and someone with competence in dealing with special needs children. For another . . ." Darius looked into the woman's deep brown eyes and lost his nerve.

She rushed to fill the momentary silence. "One of the girls I take care of now has Sensory Processing Disorder. I know it's not the same, but if you read my references, you'll see that I come highly recommended for special needs kids. I've worked really closely with Tikva's occupational therapists for the past three years, and I've picked up a lot of techniques. If you would just give me a chance . . ."

Her bottom lip trembled the slightest bit, and she looked like she might be close to tears. Darius felt bad for her, but he had to do what was right for his boys. He steeled himself. "I'm sorry." He stood and fished his wallet out of his pocket. Handing her a twenty-dollar bill, he said, "This should cover your cab. Thanks for your time. And good luck."

She took the money without a word, ducked her head, and headed for the door. After she got on the elevator, he phoned the agency.

Team Nanny's owner took the call herself and cut him off mid-complaint. "Dr. Jackson, hiring a caregiver isn't like ordering a pizza. Marisol Flores is the only available candidate we have that has any special needs experience at all. The rest of my roster this time of year is pretty thin. You may want to double check with another agency, but I've already made some calls to colleagues, and trust me: Marisol fits your profile best."

Standing in his entryway, Dr. Jackson swore under his breath, then punched the intercom button. For once, he thanked heaven for his pre-war building's ancient, snail-paced elevator. "Eddie? Has my guest left yet?"

"She just walked out, sir. Hank is hailing her a cab."

"Can you do me a solid and run out and grab her? Tell her I've changed my mind."

"Yes, sir!"

Five minutes later, the elevator clanked its way up to the penthouse again. Darius opened his door before Ms. Flores could knock. Her dark, cautious gaze met his.

"I was too hasty, Ms. Flores. Please forgive me. The job is yours if you still want it."

Her face lit up with relief and hope. "Thank you, Dr. Jackson. You won't regret this."

I hope you're right, he thought, swinging the door open all the way. "Come on in," he said. "I'll show you around."

THREE

"Mami, *por favor.*" Marisol groaned into her cell phone as she glanced over at Reese. He was still contentedly arranging his collection of plastic spoons while Seth watched a cartoon.

"What?" her mother asked. Pots and pans clattered; Carolina Flores was surely getting an early start on *onces*—Chile's version of afternoon tea. Her mother could afford a cook but preferred to reign supreme in the kitchen. For good reason—her cooking was legendary. "You can't blame me for dreaming, *gordita*. He's a doctor, he's single, and he lives in a penthouse. And that photo you sent me of him and his boys. *Es bien encachado*. It actually worries me that you don't find him attractive."

Marisol lowered her voice so that the boys couldn't hear. She and her mother were conversing in Spanish, but she couldn't be too careful. She'd already learned that Reese was sharper than a tack and had picked up all kinds of random information purely by listening when others spoke too freely. "Of course he's attractive. But he's my boss. And I'm a professional." She looked at the clock. After this show was over, Seth would run out of screen time for the day, and Marisol would have to help him make the transition to other summer activities. Maybe they'd go to the park.

"Professional," her mother scoffed. "Taking care of someone else's children is not professional. It's being a servant."

Marisol rolled her eyes. They'd had this conversation a million times. Her parents employed several servants and hated the idea of their *preciosa* lowering herself to such a thing. They also couldn't understand her fixation with finishing college—and doing it all her way, without accepting help from anyone. She knew what was coming next: the plea to return home.

Right on cue, her mother begged, "Come back to Chile, Marisol. Your Tia Gabriela has a new tenant who's just a little older than you. He's a builder, but he owns his own business, and he's saving up to buy his own ranch. I want you to meet him."

"Mami, I'm not interested in any more blind dates, and I'm not coming back to Chile. You know I love you and Papi and the rest of the family. But New York is my home now. As soon as I finish my degree and have a real job and my own place, then I'll think about dating. Not before. Please don't ask me again."

A heavy sigh traveled the five thousand miles between them. "I pray for you three times a day, Mari."

"*Sì*, Mami. I know." Marisol glanced at the television. "But I've got to go now. It's time for us to go to the park."

At the Bleecker Playground, Marisol shadowed Reese. Despite her brave speech to her mother, she felt a tidal wave of homesickness wash over her. Life in New York was exhilarating, but it wasn't easy. If her parents had any idea how many times she'd been tempted to forget about college, pack up, and move home to Santiago . . . well, they'd probably push a lot harder for her to come home.

The past two weeks had been great, though. Reese and Seth were high-energy, but lovable. Marisol had her own room in Dr. Jackson's penthouse apartment—something she'd never had before. And the pay was phenomenal; Marisol had been calculating whether she could actually go back to sharing a studio and paying rent in the fall instead of having to find another nannying job. If she could swing that, she could go to school full-time and graduate in December instead of June. She'd be that much closer to her goal—if she was very, very careful.

When two of the playground swings freed up, Marisol stopped doing mental math and coaxed Reese and Seth away from the sandbox. Both boys loved to swing, and it was great therapy for Reese in particular. She could push them both for a while, and then she'd tempt them away from the park with a trip to the Magnolia Bakery across the street. She'd quickly learned that with Reese, transitions between activities were a lot easier with some sort of carrot—in this case, a carrot cupcake with mounds of cream cheese frosting.

FOUR

As Darius pushed open the double doors of the employee exit of St. Vincent's Hospital, the familiar wave of summer humidity hit him and chased away the artificial chill of the air conditioners. He breathed in deeply, letting the tension of a particularly difficult shift roll off his shoulders. He texted Marisol to let her know he was on his way but immediately got a reply that they were at the playground.

I'll meet you there, he texted back.

Marisol was pushing the boys on the swings. She moved over so that she was behind Seth and let Darius take over with Reese.

"I told them we were almost done," Marisol said, a little out of breath.

"How long have they been swinging?"

Marisol glanced at her watch. “About forty minutes.”

Darius laughed. “Wow, that’s quite the workout for you.”

“I don’t mind. They both love it, and I promised them we’d go to the bakery on the way home.”

“Daddy! We’re getting cupcakes!” Seth crowed.

Darius looked away. Overall, Marisol had done a great job with his sons over the past two weeks, but clearly, they were starting to get into some bad habits.

“Let’s buy the cupcakes and have them after dinner,” he said.

“No. Mari said now!” Reese said, turning around so far in his swing that it got off balance.

Darius stopped it and started it up again. He frowned at Marisol. “I guess there’s no negotiating. Cupcakes it is . . . this time. But they’ll ruin their appetites for a proper dinner.”

“I’m sorry,” she said with a beguiling smile. “It’s just that it’s almost five o’clock. I’m used to *onces*—tea time in my country—with a small supper later in the evening. *Onces* is every Chilean’s favorite meal, and we do usually eat a lot of sweets. A cupcake from Magnolia is exactly what my body wants this time of day.”

Darius looked down at Marisol’s body, which was swathed in layers despite the heat. “Well, I don’t know where you put it all. Clearly, you have genetics on your side. But African-Americans are particularly prone to type II diabetes. My mother died of complications from it last year, so I’m trying to instill healthy eating habits in my boys.”

Marisol turned back toward Seth. “Again, I apologize. It won’t happen again.”

Once they got to the bakery, Reese got the very last carrot cupcake of the day, averting crisis yet again. Darius knew that his son liked what he liked and had difficulty with change of any kind. During Marisol's first week of work, Reese had asked over and over again where Chelsea was. Marisol had eventually won him over, but it had taken days.

For the moment, though, Reese seemed content, methodically licking the cream cheese frosting off his treat. Seth happily buried his face in his vanilla buttercream, while Marisol took a huge bite of a caramel cupcake. She rolled her eyes in obvious pleasure.

"Almost as good as an *alfajor,*" she murmured. "Are you sure you don't want one?"

Darius shook his head. He hadn't ordered anything in an effort to make a point, but now he secretly regretted it. All of the baked goods looked amazing, and he hadn't eaten since an early lunch many hours before. "I'm not hungry right now," he lied—and immediately his stomach growled, loudly betraying him.

The boys burst out laughing, and a moment later, Marisol joined them. Darius looked at them sternly, his pride stung. *Idiot,* he said to himself. He got up from their table and walked to the counter.

"Is Daddy mad?" he heard Seth whisper. Darius glanced back. Marisol looked up at him, then shook her head at the boy with a smile.

"I changed my mind," Darius announced to the cashier. "I'll have a banana pudding."

He sat down with his snack and tried to act casual. But after his first bite, he had to keep himself from moaning. Fresh bananas layered with homemade pudding and delicate vanilla wafers . . . heaven.

Marisol smiled at him knowingly, her gorgeous eyes crinkling up at the corners. "See? How can something so delicious be bad for you? Savor the moment with your boys."

Spooning more of the velvety pudding into his mouth, Darius decided he'd do just that. This time.

FIVE

Darius knocked on Marisol's door then opened it without waiting to be invited in. She looked up at him in panic, shoving papers underneath her pillow. What did she have to hide? Darius wondered, but didn't have time to speculate.

"I've been called in to work," he announced. "Emergency surgery for a traumatic brain injury. Can you take over?"

"Of course. I'll be right there."

Darius closed the door again and went to the living room to say goodbye to the boys.

"What about our movie?" Seth whined in protest.

Reese just sat and glowered, shuffling his plastic spoons back and forth. "Not good, not good, not good," he muttered.

Darius groaned inwardly. Being on call was the worst part about handling life with Reese, who depended on routine and consistency to cope. Darius tried to hug his older boy but got a stiff-armed rejection. He looked up at Marisol, who had just come in.

She sat next to him and put her hand on the boy's shoulder. "Hey, Reese, I know you're disappointed, but remember? When you can be flexible, I can give you extra flex points."

Flex points? Darius raised his eyebrows at Marisol, and she made a circular, *Just go with it* movement with her arm.

"Not good," answered Reese.

"I know, Reese. It's not good that your dad has to go, but someone at the hospital needs his help. Since it's an emergency, this is definitely worth a *lot* of flex points. Like, maybe fifty."

Reese looked at her sideways and paused his shuffling. Then he glared at Darius. "Can I use flex points for more screen time?"

Darius glanced at Marisol. Her eyes were big, and she nodded very slightly.

"Absolutely," he said, improvising, and hoping he was doing it right. "Flex points can definitely be traded for screen time."

"So your dad needs to go now, but I'll watch the movie with you," Marisol said. "But before that, guess what. Something special, on top of the flex points . . ." she teased. "Tomorrow is Father's Day. I thought we'd make a surprise for your dad. Can you both help me? It's a three-person job. I especially need someone who's good at math."

"Reese is good at math!" his younger brother cried—and Reese favored Marisol with his full regard.

"That's perfect, Seth," she said. "We have a lot of math to do for this surprise. Can you handle it, Reese?"

Reese nodded. He gathered up his spoons, put them into their zipper-lock bag, and hopped off the couch.

Darius exhaled with relief. Glad to have the boys distracted from their disappointment, he backed out of the room and headed for the door. He'd have to get the details on "flex points" later. Marisol had a great way with both boys, especially Reese. They were only three weeks into it, but this summer had already been far less of a rollercoaster than last year. Part of it was that Reese was a year older and had benefited from an extra year of occupational therapy, but Darius knew that the rest of it was due to Marisol's intuition and patient strategizing.

Of course, he suspected that Marisol's special surprise had something to do with a sugar-laden treat, but hey. It was Father's Day tomorrow, and it would be nice to be celebrated for once.

SIX

Marisol looked around at the mess in the kitchen. Dribbles of thick golden *dulce de leche* dripped off the edges of counters and down the fronts of cabinets. Powdered sugar and cornstarch coated every horizontal surface, including the tile floor. A large platter of misshapen but delicious *alfajores* was the fruit of their afternoon-long labor. Reese and Seth had "helped" Marisol make the South American delicacy for hours: rolling out, cutting, and baking the shortbread cookies; sandwiching them with the homemade caramel; and finally dusting them heavily with powdered sugar.

All the while, Reese had marked up Marisol's mother's recipe as he enthusiastically calculated conversions from the metric system to US measurements. Marisol had double-checked his math, and he'd been right every time.

The sticky boys had happily taken their baths, sure that their daddy would be impressed with his delicious surprise. They'd also eaten several samples, all in the name of scientific testing. Now they were asleep, Marisol having managed to coax them each to eat an organic hot dog during their movie so that she could honestly report they'd had a "proper" dinner. After their culinary exploits, she was worn out.

But no way could she leave the mess for the housekeeper. Edna wasn't due back to the apartment until Monday, and Dr. Jackson liked to cook on Sundays. Usually something involving kale and quinoa and egg whites. Marisol shuddered at the memory. All the more reason to conceal the evidence of just how much sugar had been involved in today's adventure.

Marisol set to work scrubbing and sweeping, managing to finish just as Dr. Jackson walked in the door. She hurriedly laid a clean dishtowel over the platter as he walked into the kitchen.

"You're still up?" he said, setting down his keys and walking over to the platter.

"No peeking," she warned. "It's not Father's Day yet."

Dr. Jackson looked at the clock, which read a few minutes shy of midnight.

"Please?" he said, with a wide smile. "Whatever it is, it smells great, and I'm starving."

"No way. Reese counted how many were left. He'll know if you eat even one. I can make you a protein shake, if you like."

"Not to worry. I'll do it myself. You should have been off the clock hours ago."

Marisol moved toward the kitchen door but stopped when Dr. Jackson caught her hand in his. He dropped it almost immediately, the skin of his neck flushing a bit darker. He looked down at the floor, and then met her eyes.

"Stay for a few minutes? I'm always wired after emergency surgeries, and I could use a bit of company."

Marisol hesitated before shrugging. "Sure. '*Comer solos es muy amargo*,'" she murmured.

"I beg your pardon?"

"It's from a poem by Pablo Neruda, the great Chilean poet . . . 'Eating alone is very bitter.'"

"Ah. True." Dr. Jackson grinned. "I do know who Neruda was, by the way. It wasn't all chemistry and biology in college."

"Sorry." Marisol sat down at the breakfast nook and idly thumbed through a medical journal while Dr. Jackson made himself a smoothie. He put the inevitable kale in his fancy blender, followed by cucumbers, celery, and some hemp protein powder. Marisol suppressed a shudder, even though Dr. Jackson had his back to her.

"I'm sorry I'm so late, but it was a complicated surgery," he said over his shoulder.

"Successful, I hope."

"Should be. The patient was in good shape when I left." Dr. Jackson poured his green *abominación* into a tall glass and sat across from her. He took a swallow, his nostrils flaring ever so slightly.

SEVEN

"How is it?" Marisol nodded at the glass, her eyes dubious.

Darius did his best to keep a poker face as he gulped down another mouthful. The emulsion of this particular smoothie recipe was short-lived; he knew that from experience. He had to get the whole thing down before it separated and became undrinkable. "Healthful. Refreshing."

Marisol let out a giggle at that—and Darius couldn't keep from staring in appreciation. She was always pretty, but when she smiled? She looked like a movie star. She had Sofia Loren's exotic, tilted eyes and Liv Tyler's generous lips. And her creamy, satiny skin . . . Darius downed the rest of his shake, the internal equivalent of a cold shower.

"Wow. That was bitter even with you here. I can't

imagine how it would have tasted if I'd been alone," Darius joked, and was rewarded with an outright laugh this time.

"*Pobrecito,*" Marisol said, still chuckling. "Here. I'll take pity on you and give you something to take that taste out of your mouth. I'll tell Reese I had to test one more for science's sake."

She went to the covered platter and brought him back something covered in powdered sugar. After handing it to him, she unconsciously licked her fingers. Darius felt his face go hot at the sight, and hurriedly took a bite of the cookie. Then he forgot everything else.

Buttery, crumbly shortbread melted on his tongue, followed by the most voluptuous caramel sauce he'd ever tasted. He chewed slowly, savoring every morsel. "Happy Father's Day to *me*," he murmured.

"You like it?"

"It's amazing. Did you make the caramel?"

"Yes. It's called '*dulce de leche.*'"

"It's perfect. Not too sweet, but so rich. There's amazing depth to the flavor. Wow." Darius swallowed the last bit with real regret. "I never thought I'd say this, but that was better than anything Magnolia makes. You should open your own shop. Where did you learn to make those . . . whatever they are?"

"They're called *alfajores*. It's my mother's recipe, and she would probably die of shame if I opened up a shop."

"But she's okay with you being a nanny." It was out before he could stop it. Marisol's face fell, and Darius mentally kicked himself. "I'm sorry," he said, reaching across the table to touch her forearm. "That was a stupid thing to say. I always turn into a tactless idiot when I'm sleep-deprived."

"It's fine." But she avoided his gaze. "No, actually, she's

not okay with me being a *servant*, as she calls it. But that's my problem, and I have my reasons for doing what I'm doing. And I take pride in my work, even if it's menial."

"It's really important work, and you're really good at it," Darius said, but it was clear that the damage was done.

Marisol stood up. "It's late. I should get to sleep. The boys will be up early." She finally glanced his way. "Promise you'll act surprised when the boys bring you some *alfajores* with your coffee tomorrow morning."

"Cross my heart," Darius said, hoping for another smile from her. He was disappointed. As she crossed the threshold into the hallway, he called her. "Hey."

She turned, her lovely face in the shadows. "Yes?"

"I really am sorry."

She nodded once, formally. "I know. Good night."

EIGHT

Marisol didn't mind Dr. Jackson's erratic schedule. It meant that she worked some weekends, but as a tradeoff, she had some weekdays off in the city, which always felt like a treat. It meant that she could take care of errands when things were less busy—like today, when she'd had to register for her fall classes. On the way home from the university, she'd opted to get off the train a few stops early and walk the rest of the way downtown. It was hot, but it felt good to be out and moving.

She walked through the thick August air on the shady side of Seventh Avenue, not caring that the humidity had frizzed her hair into a halo around her face. Her last semester approached; she could hardly believe it. After years of work, it was difficult to imagine not having homework to turn in and tests to study for.

She was almost all set for September. Her class schedule was chosen and paid for. She'd found a studio to share with another student only blocks from campus in Harlem. With the help of Dr. Jackson's lavish salary and the bit of money she'd saved while working for the Rubins, she would make it until graduation, and even a few weeks beyond. In the meantime, she'd be applying for jobs, hoping to start work in January. She knew she could go to her father for a bridge loan, but she wanted to avoid that at all costs.

But as excited as she was to be a full-time student, she'd definitely miss the Jacksons. She and Reese and Seth had developed an easy rhythm to their days. Marisol had come up with a winning formula: an unvarying routine of plenty of exercise and occupational therapy, lots of messy fun, flex points, and a fair amount of secret treats to balance out all the vegetables their father made them eat. Just that morning, Seth had thrown his arms around her legs and told her that he didn't want to go home to Las Vegas when school started.

It had given Marisol a bit of PTSD. She didn't ever want to incur the wrath of a jealous mother again, even if that mother was two thousand miles away. Seth was just exuberant in his affections. Yet she doubted he'd have much trouble making the transition back to life with his mom.

Reese was another matter. He'd gotten fiercely attached to her, wanting to hold her hand when they watched movies, wanting her input on his complex plastic spoon arrangements, and demanding ever longer bedtime stories featuring the three of them whenever Marisol had to put the boys to bed.

She wondered whether she should bring Reese up with Dr. Jackson. He'd gotten called in nearly every time he'd been on call, meaning that he'd worked far more than he would have liked to with his boys home. Marisol had done her best to make up for his absence. She didn't want to seem boastful, but Reese really had connected with her in a way that had surprised his father. He'd have to agree that Reese would probably have a hard time when it was time to go back to Las Vegas. Marisol didn't know what could be done about the situation, though. Maybe she should keep it to herself.

As for Dr. Jackson . . . Marisol would never admit it to her mother, but she'd probably gotten overly attached to him, as well. It was one of the reasons she insisted on calling him "Dr. Jackson" instead of "Darius," even though he consistently begged her to call him by his first name. She had to maintain a professional distance from her employer.

He never dated; that would take time away from his children. But Marisol saw how women eyed him when the four of them were out at the park or in a restaurant. With good reason. His stunning good looks and firm but affectionate manner with his boys would make any woman look twice.

Since Father's Day, Dr. Jackson had asked Marisol more than once to make *alfajores*, and she'd happily done so. She'd also had the boys "help" her make empanadas and *sopaipillas*, all of which everyone ate with gusto—always following some sort of giant salad.

As an employer, Darius Jackson was everything the Rubins had not been: generous, considerate, and respectful. True, once in a while he was the tiniest bit condescending, but Marisol hadn't ever known a doctor—her brother included—who wasn't somewhat arrogant. She could make allowances for that. Besides, he'd never, ever called her into his study for some imagined infraction. All in all, Marisol had felt as though this summer had been a healing respite after the trauma of her previous job. Was that strange? She hoped not.

A few blocks from Bleecker Street, her phone buzzed. She looked at the caller ID. *Hablando del rey de Roma . . .*

"Hello, Dr. Jackson. How are you?"

"Darius. Please, Marisol. And I'm fine, thanks."

"What can I do for you, Dr. Jackson?"

"I'm sorry to bother you on your day off, but I was hoping we could talk. Do you have time now?"

Marisol felt a twinge of dread in the pit of her stomach. What could this possibly be about? "Sure," she said, forcing a smile into her voice. "What's up?"

"Are you nearby? I'd rather speak to you in person, if that's all right."

Marisol sighed. Had she jinxed herself by celebrating her reprimand-free summer? Had the boys ratted her out about the Mexican hot chocolate she'd made them yesterday? "Of course. I was on my way home, anyway. I'll be there in a few minutes."

Dr. Jackson met her at the door and silently ushered her into his den. Marisol gritted her teeth against the memory of the way her last job had ended and sat on an overstuffed leather chair. Dr. Jackson didn't go around the desk, but instead sat next to her. Grabbing a sheaf of papers off the corner of the desk, he said, "Why didn't you tell me?"

Tell him what? "I'm sorry about the hot chocolate—" she started.

"What? Never mind that. I'm talking about your schooling. Why didn't you tell me that you were in college?"

Oh. Marisol thought for a minute and then shrugged. "It never came up. I'm a private person, Dr. Jackson. My education has no bearing on my job here . . . and I remembered that you had a bad experience with a college student last summer, so I thought . . . How did you find out?"

"The registrar at City College called a little while ago.

Apparently they overcharged you by several hundred dollars when you registered for next semester, and she wanted to let you know that they'd be sending you a refund. They faxed me a statement, along with the transcript you requested." He held out the papers.

Marisol took them. "Oh, wow. That's good news. Thanks. I appreciate it." She stood up to go. Why had Dr. Jackson felt the need for her to rush home so that they could discuss this in person? "Was that it, then?"

He looked up at her, his eyes hurt. "I . . . I suppose. I was just surprised. I thought we were friends, and that you would have mentioned your plans for the future at some point."

Marisol was puzzled. "But you never asked," she said gently.

Dr. Jackson looked at his hands and pressed his lips together. He nodded once. "You're right. I'm sorry."

She turned to leave.

"Wait, Marisol. Can't we talk about this? I'd really like to know what you're doing in the fall. It's clear that I've made certain assumptions about you. I'd love to hear the real story."

Marisol huffed a short laugh. "Assumptions?" Dr. Jackson was kind, but his ignorance of who she really was felt like the last straw. All of the prejudice she'd encountered since she'd come to the United States flooded through her mind. "As in, your assuming that I'm a pretty, uneducated Latina with an accent, possibly not legal in this country, nannying because it's the only honest work I can get? No ambitions other than to take care of someone else's children and live in a corner of someone else's house for the rest of my life?"

She sat back down, her cheeks burning. She angrily brushed her out-of-control hair away from her face. "My father is a legislator in the Chilean Congress. He has a Ph.D. in Economics from Yale. He arranged my visa, by the way, so, yes. I *am* here legally. My parents live in Lo Barnachea, a chic suburb of Santiago. My older brothers are both married. One is a lawyer; the other one is a pediatrician. I'm the baby of the family, and after I finished high school, everyone expected me to marry some professional man just like my father and brothers had, then settle down and have kids.

"But I wanted something else, something more. I do want a family of my own someday, but all my life, my family has defined me. I came to New York seven years ago to find out who I really am, independent of them. And I've done it all on my own, without any help from my parents, because their gifts always come with strings attached. It's taken me all of this time to finish college, but I've done it myself. And I've learned a lot about who I am along the way."

Marisol sat back. "There. How about those assumptions now, Dr. Jackson?"

She stared at him, her furious eyes welling with tears, her loose, wavy hair making her look like a medieval madonna. Darius had never felt so ashamed.

"I'm sorry," he repeated. "You're right. Please forgive me." He tried to smile. "But admit it: you had assumptions of your own about me on the first day we met. I saw how surprised you were when I answered the door. You couldn't believe you were at the right apartment. You hadn't ever met a black doctor before, had you?"

Marisol stared at him. "It wasn't that. I was surprised because I heard Edna's voice on the intercom downstairs. And you looked so . . . young," she finished lamely.

Darius briefly wondered why she was blushing, then sighed. "Aha. So I'm the only racist in the room. All right; I own it. Some enlightened, twenty-first century feminist I am. My mother, God rest her soul, would've had a fit if she'd witnessed this scene."

Marisol crossed herself. "Maybe she's looking down on you from Heaven right now, shaking her finger at you." Her lips twitched until she pressed them together.

Darius seized his opening, barely daring to hope that she might be able to forget his bigoted idiocy. "I want us to be friends. Let me make it up to you. I'll cook you dinner tonight after I've put the boys to bed, and you can tell me everything. Your plans, your hopes, how far you've come. I'll ask lots of questions. Please? Can we be friends?"

Her smile made his heart rate increase by at least ten percent. "On one condition, Dr. Jackson."

"Anything."

"No kale."

Darius guffawed. "Done."

NINE

Darius's BMW sat in weekend traffic on the Long Island Expressway. The drive out to the Hamptons was long under the best of circumstances, but the Friday before a long holiday weekend was the worst possible time to make the trip.

Fortunately, the boys were happily engaged with a game on Darius's iPad. He hoped that would last, because they were still at least an hour away from his boss's weekend house in Sag Harbor.

"Sorry," he said to Marisol. "I know this is probably not the way you wanted to spend your Labor Day weekend."

Reese had thrown a fit when Darius had told him about Steve Bradshaw's invitation. He'd thought both boys would be thrilled about spending three days at the beach before heading back to the endless desert of Las Vegas. But Reese had shocked him with his vehement refusal. "We're leaving on Tuesday, and I'll never see Marisol again in my whole life!" he'd shouted. "I'm not going."

Fortunately, Marisol had taken pity on all of them and agreed to come along. "Classes don't start until next week. I'll have plenty of time to get settled. I've never been to the Hamptons. It'll be fun."

Now she shrugged and smiled. "You're paying me, and I'm glad for some extra time with . . . the boys." She turned her head sharply and looked out the window.

Darius stared back out at the endless line of cars ahead. "Me, too."

Ninety minutes later, he buzzed the intercom box outside the gates of the Bradshaws' estate. "We're here, finally."

"Wonderful! We'll meet you on the porch. Come on up."

The massive wrought-iron gates swung open, and Darius drove up the winding drive. He'd been here once before, but the opulence still stunned him. He'd made a very comfortable life for himself, but this was another reality entirely. Steve's wife, Jane, was a Van Doren, and this house had been in her family for decades; no modern doctor, however prosperous, could afford a place like this.

Three figures stood on the wide, columned porch. After he parked on the circular gravel drive, Darius looked into the back seat and eyed Reese and Seth's sweet, sleeping faces apprehensively. The boys didn't move a muscle once the engine stopped. Darius mentally crossed his fingers. Reese would do so much better if he could sleep through this transition and wake up in the morning fresh.

He glanced at Marisol. "I'll introduce you to Steve and Jane, and then if you can help me get Reese and Seth to their room without too much drama, I'd be grateful."

"Of course."

They slid out of the car, shut the doors as quietly as possible, and went up the steps. "Steve, Jane, this is our nanny, Marisol. Marisol, this is my boss, Dr. Stephen Bradshaw and his wife, Jane."

Marisol extended her hand graciously to each of them and inclined her head. "I'm very pleased to meet you. Thank you for including me in your invitation."

Steve shook her hand a little too enthusiastically. "Our pleasure. Whatever makes life easier for Darius is great by us." He winked at her and turned to Darius. "We have someone we want you to meet too." He beckoned the third figure forward out of the shadow of a fluted column. "This is Beth Thomas. She's a partner at Weiss Scarpa, and she acts as outside counsel for St. Vincent's."

Beth smiled at Darius, and he nodded back. "Nice to meet you." He glanced back at the car and saw Reese stirring. "Can we talk in just a bit? Everything will go better if we can get these boys into bed while they're still unconscious."

Steve chuckled. "You're the anesthesiologist; you know best. I'll lead the way if you want to grab your rug rats and follow me."

"You get Seth, I'll get Reese," Darius said to Marisol as they walked back to the car.

She shook her head. "I'll get Reese," she offered. "That way, if he wakes up, I can whisper one of my stories to him to help keep him under." She glanced up at the huge house, her eyes nervous. "That is, if the bedroom isn't too far away."

From what Darius remembered of his last visit, that wasn't likely. Reese was almost as big as the petite Marisol, but she did have an excellent point. "Deal," he said, mentally making a note to give her an even bigger bonus as combat pay.

True to his suspicions, the boys' assigned bedroom was in a remote wing of the mansion. They got them into bed without incident, stopping only to pull off their shoes before tucking them in. He'd come a long way as a dad this summer, giving in to abundant sugar, adopting Marisol's genius flex-point method of negotiation, letting them sleep in their clothes. What was next for his boys? he wondered wryly.

He watched as Marisol tenderly tucked Reese's ubiquitous bag of spoons in next to him and kissed his forehead. Reese responded by smiling in his sleep, burrowing into his covers, and turning over with a sigh. Marisol was a miracle worker.

In the hallway, Steve gestured to the room next door. "We've put you in there, Maria," he said.

Darius opened his mouth to correct Steve, but then thought better of it. He'd find a more tactful time to remind his boss of Marisol's name.

Steve continued, apparently unaware of his mistake. "José will be round with your bag in a minute or two. Please ring for the housekeeper if you need anything at all, from extra towels to a midnight snack."

He smiled and turned to Darius. "How about you, my good sir? Jane's sent a nosh platter and drinks into the billiards room. Are you up for a game? It'll help you unwind after that hellish drive. Beth keeps claiming she breaks a mean rack, and I believe her." He walked away, obviously expecting Darius to follow.

Darius looked at Marisol helplessly. They'd been living in a bit of a bubble for the past few weeks, the four of them. Now, being with her around other people, he suddenly realized that he'd stopped thinking of Marisol as just an employee quite some time ago. But in the context of the rest of society . . . their relationship was definitely unique. He hadn't counted on how complicated his feelings for his nanny had gotten.

Marisol smiled tightly and patted his arm. "I've been dismissed," she whispered with false cheer. "Don't worry about me. Schmooze with your boss. That's one of the reasons why we're here, isn't it? The kids are asleep, and I'll be here if they have any trouble. That's why you paid me to come, remember. I'll do my job. You go do yours."

"I'm sorry," he murmured, covering her hand with his own for just a moment. So warm and soft. He dropped his arm to his side and sighed. "Thanks again. I'll see you tomorrow." It seemed like all he'd done lately was apologize. He turned away abruptly and followed his boss down the labyrinthine hall.

TEN

Marisol watched him go, still stinging from Dr. Bradshaw's blithely getting her name wrong and treating her like a second-class citizen. Then again, why wouldn't he? She was just the nanny, and Marisol had witnessed nannies treated this way for years. She should be used to it, able to let it roll off her back by now.

She went to her doorway and flipped on her bedroom light. As spacious and comfortable as Dr. Jackson's apartment was, his living room would probably fit in this room with square meters to spare. She went to the window and peered out the sheers. A huge expanse of lawn ran down to the ocean, where wave after gentle wave broke on the wide, smooth beach. The water glittered under the light of a full moon.

Snobby hosts or not, this place was heavenly. She hadn't

been to the beach in years; she needed to put her petty hurt feelings aside and make the most of this weekend. Because after that . . .

Tears filled her eyes, and she turned away from the window as a knock came at the door. "Miss?" A man peeked around the door. "I have your bag." His English was heavily accented.

Marisol crossed the room. "Thank you!" She smiled at the short man and took her suitcase from him. "*Muchas gracias,*" she added.

He bowed his head in a courtly gesture. "*De nada, señorita.*" He continued in Spanish. "I'm José. If you need anything, the intercom is next to the light switch. Do you want any food or drink?"

"No, thank you. You're very kind." She made a guess as to his accent. "Are you from Ecuador?"

He nodded, clearly delighted. "Yes, very good. I'm from Quito. And you, miss?"

"Santiago de Chile."

"Ah. It's beautiful there. Well, good night, miss."

"Good night. Thanks again." Marisol closed her door.

She got ready for bed in the luxurious en suite bathroom, forcing herself to count her blessings all the while. She'd spent a lovely summer with nice people and fulfilling, lucrative work. She had enough money saved to get her through the fall and winter. She would be a full-time student with plenty of free hours to study and prepare for classes. She had her health and no debt and a bright future.

Then why, she asked herself as she lay in bed, gazing at the moonbeams filtering through the curtains, *why* was she so miserable? As soon as she asked the question, she knew the answer.

She'd known the Jackson family for three short months,

but already they felt like family to her. *This is the flip side of having a kind employer*, she thought sourly, impatiently brushing away the tears that threatened to trickle down the sides of her temples and into her ears. She'd gotten too attached the boys . . . and, if she was honest, to their father.

Since their kale-free make-up dinner a few weeks ago, they really had become friends: debating everything from politics to music, joking, even cooking together. He'd relaxed his vegetable regimen; she'd experimented with making *sopaipillas* with whole wheat flour. And as they'd talked and eaten and laughed and taken care of the boys, she'd even dared to dream about him asking her to stay once the summer was over.

But if anything could impress upon her the impossibility of a future with Darius Jackson, tonight's events had. No matter how egalitarian American society considered itself to be, the class system was still going strong. She was the help, and nothing more. Never mind that at home in Santiago, she'd gone to the most exclusive all-girls' private school, and that her parents moved in the highest social circles. In the United States, she was a Hispanic woman with an accent, and that would always be held against her.

She lay awake, thinking about her employer and injustice and irony and bad timing, until the incessant waves outside lulled her into a troubled sleep.

ELEVEN

Darius sat under a beach cabana with his boss, sipping homemade lemonade and watching Marisol and the boys dig in the sand at the water's edge. Marisol wore a black, one-piece bathing suit—modest, but perfectly highlighting her gorgeous, lithe figure. After months of seeing her dressed in baggy shirts and jeans, the sight of her now was breathtaking.

Steve echoed his thoughts, after a fashion. Eyeing Marisol appreciatively, he said, "I have to hand it to you, Darius. You sure know how to pick 'em. She is quite the specimen."

That rankled. "I had no idea, Steve," he said, a little too sharply. "You should see how she dresses most of the time; you'd think she was Amish. And I hired her because she had experience with special needs kids. You can see how amazing she is with the boys."

"I can certainly see how amazing she is," Steve answered absently, fortunately not noticing Darius's cranky tone. But then, looking beyond Darius up the beach, he sat up a little straighter and cleared his throat. Darius turned and followed his gaze. Jane and that lawyer, Beth, were walking toward them from the estate's tennis court. Beth was tall and blonde and lean, her pleated tennis skirt setting off her tanned, muscular legs.

Despite her classic American good looks, Beth had a hungry look about her; in fact, last night, as they'd played pool, she had reminded Darius a bit of his ex-wife, Phoebe. Their coloring was completely different, true. But there was something underneath, something almost predatory. He'd found Phoebe's aggressive nature appealing when they'd been in medical school together, but it had turned out to be . . . difficult to live with. He shuddered slightly at the memory. Steve and Jane might have invited Beth out this weekend with the idea of setting him up with her, but if so, they'd gotten his taste—at least, his current taste—exactly wrong.

Jane and Beth sat down in the empty beach chairs under the cabana and helped themselves to lemonade.

"Good match?" Steve asked.

"Great match," Beth answered. "Jane beat me in straight sets. It's good for me to play someone better than I am. Do you play tennis, Darius?"

Looking into her avid, blue eyes, Darius decided to play to stereotype. "I'm afraid not," he drawled. "Basketball's always been my game."

That actually was true; he'd grown up playing on the ragged asphalt courts of the Hamilton Heights housing projects just north of Harlem. His street skills had landed him a spot on the team at Horace Mann, one of Manhattan's most prestigious private high schools; from there, he'd gone on to Duke, and then to Harvard Medical School.

But Jane noticed his coy retreat and wouldn't let him get away with it. "Beth went to law school at Harvard," she said. "You might even have been there at the same time."

Darius opened his mouth, automatically about to start the inevitable Harvard "do you know" game. He'd played it for years at cocktail parties and conferences and other gatherings; the world of Manhattan professionals who also attended Ivy League graduate schools turned out to be boringly tiny. That wasn't what he wanted anymore, he realized. What he wanted was right in front of him, down by the water. He shut his mouth again and grinned. "Harvard, yeah? Seems like ages ago, right?" Without waiting for an answer, he got up to go join his boys and Marisol.

"Daddy!"

Marisol looked up at Seth's happy shout. Dr. Jackson stood smiling down at them just a few feet away.

"Hey, boys. How's it going?"

"Great! Come help us build the *palacio*, Daddy!"

Dr. Jackson obeyed his son, sitting cross-legged in the sand next to them. He was careful not to disturb the plastic spoon forest Reese was constructing with geometric precision.

"A *palacio*, huh?" Dr. Jackson smiled at Marisol. "Why not a regular old sand castle?"

Seth kept working in the damp sand, sculpting and smoothing a corner tower. "Mari lived in a *palacio* when she was my age. She can't take us to visit it, but she said we could build it."

Seth handed Dr. Jackson a tiny plastic shovel. "You work on the courtyard," he directed. "I'm going to get more shells for the roof." He got up and marched down the beach a few steps, scanning the shoreline as he went.

Marisol turned to Reese. It had taken a lot of work to get the poor kid up, fed, and out of doors this morning. Pulled out of his routine, waking up in a strange place, knowing that he'd be leaving for Las Vegas in a couple of days . . . Reese had done remarkably well so far today, considering all the triggers he was dealing with. The sensory input of a long, barefoot walk the three of them had taken along the beach had helped soothe him, and Marisol could tell that his intricate spoon work was also a key part of his coping strategy.

She touched his arm gently but firmly, and waited until she sensed that his attention had shifted to her. "Reese, are you okay?"

He just nodded, which was enough for now. Marisol looked up to see Dr. Jackson looking at them, a half smile on his face.

"What is it? What's on your mind?" she asked, smiling back.

"I was just thinking. You come from a faraway *palacio*, and now, at least for two more days, you're a nanny. The best nanny in the history of nannies, by the way. I came from the uptown projects, and now I'm a doctor who lives downtown. We've turned our worlds upside down. Neither of us is who or where other people expect us to be, are we?"

"I guess not." Marisol looked out at the horizon, a lump in her throat. She wished her boss would go back up to the cabana with his friends and that skinny lawyer and leave her alone—not sit down next to her and make her want to cry for no reason at all.

"Which gives me pause," he went on after a moment. "I wonder . . . do you think maybe there's a chance that, precisely because we're both so different . . . maybe we belong together?"

Marisol whipped her head back toward him, her mouth open in shock. Had he just really voiced the midnight aching of her heart from hours before?

He swallowed, then smiled his devastating smile at her again. It didn't quite reach his eyes, though. Marisol sensed anxiety there.

He went on. "So, you asked what was on my mind. That's what was on my mind. Also . . . I was thinking about asking you if you'd be willing to kiss me . . ." He trailed off, staring intently at her.

Warmth rushed through Marisol's core, and she brushed impatiently at her traitorous eyes. "So then ask me, Dr. Jackson," she said simply, trying to remain dignified.

Again, that blinding smile. "Ask me, *Darius*," he corrected.

"Ask me, Darius," she repeated, unable to stop grinning. "Ask me to kiss you."

Darius glanced at Reese. He sat frozen, listening intently, a spoon held in mid-air and a small smile playing around his lips. Then Darius moved closer to Marisol, reaching out to her across the sand walls and towers of the *palacio*. "Will you kiss me, Marisol Flores?"

"*Sí*, Darius Jackson, I will."

ABOUT LUISA PERKINS

Luisa Perkins is the author of the dark fantasy novel *Dispirited*, the conspiracy thriller *Premonition*, and the cookbook *Comfortably Yum*. She has had short stories and essays published in numerous print and online anthologies. She and her husband, Patrick, have six children, and they live in a small town in Southern California. Luisa blogs (infrequently) at: kashkawan.squarespace.com.

Follow Luisa on Twitter: @LuisaPerkins

TAKE A CHANCE

Sarah M. Eden

OTHER WORKS BY SARAH M. EDEN

Seeking Persephone
Courting Miss Lancaster
The Kiss of a Stranger
Friends and Foes
An Unlikely Match
Drops of Gold
Glimmer of Hope
As You Are
For Elise
Longing for Home
Hope Springs
The Sheriffs of Savage Wells

ONE

Miguel Santos boasted a long list of cities he'd visited by means of airport layovers. His experience with Phoenix was limited to Sky Harbor. His time in Chicago was spent exclusively at O'Hare. It seemed LaGuardia was to be his only glimpse of New York City.

He'd heard enough about the Big Apple to know he was getting a raw deal. His one-time girlfriend Jane loved New York; she'd told him so dozens of times. She'd also said she loved *him,* so he figured she was probably only interested in New York as a friend, since that's what "I love you" turned out to mean.

"This isn't what I want. It isn't what I ever wanted." Her words were tattooed on his mind. He'd been expecting a simple "Yes, I'd love to marry you." At least the jeweler had given him a full refund on the ring and a coupon for 5% off a future purchase of $1000 or more. Yup. That made it all better.

"Ladies and gentlemen," a voice came over the speakers in the airport terminal, "for those of you flying with us to Denver, we have an important announcement."

Miguel, along with the rest of Gate 5, turned to face the airline agent at the counter. Their flight was due to depart in only five minutes, and the plane they were supposed to board hadn't even arrived.

"The National Weather Service has issued severe weather alerts for most of the Midwest, in effect until seven p.m. local time."

The announcement was met with groans from many of the other passengers. Miguel had endured more than his share of weather delays. Getting upset hadn't helped with any of them.

"The weather has delayed your aircraft, along with many others," the agent continued. "Please know that we are doing all we can to get you to your final destination and will update you as more information is known. Thank you."

Miguel silently counted, watching the counter. He knew what came next. *3 . . . 2 . . . 1 . . .*

Right on cue, floods of angry passengers stormed the counter. Though he couldn't hear their demands, he knew what they were. Someone would be insisting the airline get them to Denver on time because of something important. Someone else would be yelling about how unacceptable the delay was and threatening to talk to the media or their lawyer or the FAA. Almost everyone would demand an exact timeframe for departure despite having been told already that there wasn't one.

Travel didn't generally bring out the best in people.

Miguel pulled out his phone and checked the weather

for himself. Sure enough, the radar map was lit up from Canada to Texas, Nebraska to Tennessee. *We're not going anywhere anytime soon.*

A burly man in a business suit sat on the stool next to Miguel's and slammed his forearms down onto the table. LaGuardia, at least the terminal Miguel had seen, was filled with stools at long tables and short booths with charging stations. If they were stuck here all night, there'd probably be a battle to the death for the few old-fashioned row seats scattered around the terminal. There'd be nowhere else to lie down other than the floor.

"Ridiculous," the businessman muttered. "They say the flight may be cancelled."

Miguel clicked through to the current weather warnings. "With weather like this, flights will be cancelled all over."

"The airline should do something about it."

"About the weather? I think you're confusing airlines with God."

That earned him a muttered observation about Mexicans and idiot Catholics. *The guy demands that the airline magically wave away a storm system, and* I *am the idiot?*

"I'm going to do something about the delay," Miguel said, pocketing his phone.

The man eyed him doubtfully. "What could *you* do about it?"

"Buy myself a magazine and get comfortable."

His fellow passenger repeated his earlier observation, though more clearly stated this time. So Manuel responded in Spanish with one of his *abuela's* favorite observations about enduring the company of ignorant people.

"Don't even have the decency to speak English," the man muttered.

Why was it that hearing Spanish made so many people in America bristle so much? It wasn't as if Miguel hadn't just had a detailed conversation with the guy in perfect English. The fact that he could speak a second language would have been a point in his favor anywhere else.

Miguel left the grumbler behind and headed toward the nearest newsstand. He'd done more reading in airports than almost anywhere else. He thumbed through the racks. Which did he want this time? Sports? News? Anything but celebrity gossip, really.

"Attention, please. Passenger J. Schoonenburg, please see an airline representative at Gate D5. Passenger J. Schoonenburg."

Miguel spun around. *Schoonenburg*. Jane's last name was Schoonenburg. How many J. Schoonenburgs could there be flying from New York, Jane's favorite city, to Denver, her hometown? He rushed from the newsstand empty-handed, back to the gate. He kept a safe distance from the counter, watching for "Passenger J. Schoonenburg." The place was chaotic. TVs blared the news with word of widespread weather alerts sliding across the bottom of the screen. Agents were attempting to calm frustrated passengers. Miguel eyed them all, searching.

Out of nowhere, there she was. Jane. Dressed like she'd just stepped out of a fashion magazine. Cool. Collected. Beautiful.

He hadn't seen her since she'd told him she didn't want to marry him. Three months that had felt like years. Now here she was, on the same flight he was taking home, stuck in the same terminal at the same airport.

The only question was, should he go talk to her—and risk the possible humiliation—or do his best to stay out of her sight?

"I'm Jane Schoonenburg. I was paged."

The agent nodded and reached under the counter. "Your boarding card was found and turned in."

Jane thumbed through the outer pocket of her carryon, where she always kept her boarding cards. "I didn't even know I'd lost it." Sure enough, it was missing.

"I'll need to see your ID," the agent said.

"Of course." Jane pulled her driver's license from her wallet and handed it to the agent. After a quick moment, she received it and her boarding pass back. "Thank you."

"You're welcome."

Weather information flashed across a nearby TV screen. "Any word on when or if we might be in the air?"

"We have no new information, but we will be certain to pass it on once we do."

Jane offered an empathetic half-smile. "I am probably the hundredth person to ask."

That brought a bit of humor to the agent's face. "Two hundredth, at least."

"And how many have demanded that you fix the weather?"

"Most." The agent laughed the word. "If airlines could control the weather, believe me, we would."

"Well, for everyone's sake, I hope the weather clears quickly." She checked one more time to make certain her boarding card was safely stowed in her bag, then stepped away from the counter so the next irate passenger could demand answers.

Jane visited New York several times a year on business, though she always made time for enjoying the city. She'd never made a single trip here that didn't have its share of chaos. She'd learned to simply roll with the punches, both in travel and in life.

She sat at one of the booths near the gate. Life had certainly dealt her its share of punches. Not a day went by that she didn't think of Miguel and wonder what might have happened if he hadn't ruined everything between them.

Coming to New York was supposed to clear her head of all that. Her head and her heart. It hadn't worked at all. At least this trip had given her a little time away from home and all of the things there that reminded her of him. If she could just get him out of her thoughts, she could move on.

That's what you've got to do. Get him out of your thoughts.

It was simple enough.

"Hey," someone said.

She looked up, directly into the chocolate-brown eyes of Miguel Santos.

TWO

Miguel was already second-guessing his decision. "I heard them call your name." *Is that really the first thing I said to her?*

"What are you doing here?" Hers was not a tone of pleasant surprise.

Awkward.

"My latest Layover Vacation." He tried to play it cool, but knew he was failing miserably. "Now I can say I've been to New York."

"LaGuardia doesn't count as New York. JFK, *maybe.* But definitely not LaGuardia."

Making small talk about airports was almost as bad as chatting about the weather. They'd once been able to talk about anything. "How long were you in New York this time?"

"Four days," she said.

Miguel nodded. The nod didn't mean anything, he just couldn't think of anything else to do. He stood there looking at her, while she fidgeted in her seat. "Did you see a show?"

"*Newsies.*"

He nodded some more. All the times he'd thought about running into her again, he'd never pictured himself acting so stupid. But this was Jane, the woman he still loved. The woman he would probably always love. Acting stupid seemed unavoidable.

"How are your parents?" he asked.

"They hate each other and demand that their children do the same. So, same as always." She shrugged as if her family being completely dysfunctional didn't bother her, but he knew better. Her parents had divorced when she was a teenager and had been going for each other's jugulars ever since. "What about your family?"

"Still loud and nosey. And still bribing the police with tamales to look the other way when their backyard parties get a little out of hand." He could still remember the horror on Jane's face the first time she'd attended one of their extended-family parties. The music was loud. The people were louder. The neighbors often complained—those who hadn't accepted the invitation to join in. But she'd adjusted quickly and soon fit right in. "Mamá asks about you. They all do. They—*we* miss you."

"Don't, Miguel." She stood and pushed past him. "Just don't."

Well, that *didn't work.* He watched her take long, determined strides to the other side of the gate area and drop into a different booth. It was impossible to misinterpret that.

The Santoses had always been superstitious. His grandfather had gone to bed with socks on because *his* father had died barefooted. Miguel's mother always ate nuts in even numbers so she'd never accidentally eat thirteen. For some reason, she felt that nuts were the unluckiest food. His brother couldn't see a black cat without spitting. If fate, chance, divine intervention, or whatever it was, had brought Jane back into Miguel's life by stranding them both at the same airport, he wasn't going to turn his back on the chance to try winning her over again.

Big words, considering she isn't even talking to you.

"Attention, passengers. We have updated information regarding flight 884 to Denver. We are looking at a delay of at least two hours. We ask for your continued patience. The weather has delayed flights throughout the country."

The response was immediate. Some were angry, others clearly worried. Jane's gaze darted to Miguel. For a moment, she looked wary, vulnerable. But just as quickly, the look was replaced with defiance. In an instant, she had her phone out and her attention diverted.

A man could come up with a lot of plans in two hours. He'd try every single one of them if he needed to. Jane had once said she loved him. Even as she'd turned down his proposal, she'd said she loved him. That she didn't want to marry him, but she loved him.

They'd dated for a year. He'd known she was the one in the first month. That she didn't run away screaming the first time she'd been introduced to his crazy extended family only made him more certain. But she *had* run screaming from the prospect of wearing his ring. She wouldn't even give him a reason beyond, "This isn't what I want."

The three months since she'd ended things had been miserable. Living without her had convinced him that if marriage wasn't what she wanted, he needed to find out what she *did* want. If there was any way he could find to make her wants meet his somewhere in the middle, he'd do it. In a heartbeat.

But how are you going to find that out if she's putting the length of a terminal gate between you? He sat in the booth she'd been in. He knew her better than anyone else. If he gave it some thought, he could come up with something that would pierce her armor just enough to get her to talk to him. But what did he have to work with?

New York was her favorite city. But apparently LaGuardia didn't count.

She liked musicals. But he didn't have a Broadway cast on hand to stage a musical number right there in the airport. He also couldn't sing. Or dance. Or act.

She was a big Robert Downy, Jr. fan. But, honestly, if he'd had Robert Downy, Jr. on speed dial, Miguel would have had *him* handle the proposal in the first place, and he wouldn't be in this mess.

Jane loved Mamá's tamales—who didn't? But Miguel didn't have any handy.

What do *you have handy?* He set his carryon bag on the table and dug through it. A protein bar. A dog-eared paperback of *Variant.* His wallet, though offering Jane the seventeen dollars in there wouldn't do any good. A half-empty bag of trail mix. The bottle of water he bought after his was confiscated at security. Last, and definitely least, his ratty old sweatshirt. A pathetic collection of potential offerings.

Dude, you're such a loser.

His bag of tricks had failed him. Time for more desperate measures: buying overpriced goods at an airport newsstand and offering them up as a bribe. He had seventeen dollars, after all. And a credit card.

He passed the magazines—giving her reading material

would defeat his purpose—and went straight for the snack section. He knew Jane's junk food habits well. Funyuns. Oreos, Double Stuf. Washed down with Dr. Pepper. And for dessert, gummy peach rings. He grabbed them all, plus a few things for himself. If he was going to stage a dead-relationship intervention, he needed the strength that came from a full-size bag of Cool Ranch Doritos and Sunkist.

He walked back to the gate with his arms full of loot. With an empty calorie count like he was lugging around, Jane wouldn't be able to resist talking to him. At least she wouldn't have been able to resist it if she had still been sitting where he'd last seen her.

Where'd she go? He didn't see her anywhere. Maybe she'd sensed the approach of irresistible cuisine and took off. He dropped his armful onto the booth table where she had been sitting and sat on the bench. The gate had calmed. Plenty of passengers still glared and fumed, but they were doing it sitting down rather than gathered around the counter.

Jane had disappeared. Maybe she'd decided to wait out the delay somewhere else in the terminal, banking on hearing the announcement over the loudspeakers. That took a level of desperation even Double Stuf Oreos wasn't likely to overcome. But the newsstand and the vending machines didn't carry cheesecake, her go-to in a crisis. He was more of a *dulce de leche* man, himself.

He eyed the Funyuns. *Traitor.* He pushed the bag aside. He needed a new strategy. If only he'd run into her in the TSA security line. They'd have had endless hours in each other's company, and she would have had no escape.

That's a really nice thing to wish on the woman you'd hoped to marry.

"You stole my seat."

"Jane." How long had she been standing there? "I came over, but you were gone."

She motioned to the table. "Have you taken up snack hoarding?"

He picked up the Funyuns bag. "You know how much I love these."

"You *hate* them." Her gaze scanned the rest of the loot. "Double Stuf Oreos. Dr. Pepper. Wait a minute." She skewered him with a suspiciously glare. "Is this a bribe?"

"That depends. Is it working?"

"Maybe," she said hesitantly. "What is it you're hoping I'll do for all of this?"

"Just talk." He could see her defenses going up immediately. "Nothing too personal. Just a chat between friends."

Come on, Jane. Don't leave me hanging here.

"I *do* like Funyuns." But she still looked uncertain.

"I might even share my Doritos with you."

Her nose wrinkled up. "But they're Cool Ranch."

He shook his head and sighed dramatically. "You never were a connoisseur."

She laughed, her lips pulling upward in the dazzling smile he'd missed so much over the past three months. They'd been happy together. They honestly had been. There had to be a way of getting that back again.

THREE

The fact that Miguel knew her favorite junk food was not reason enough to stay and talk to him. Yet Jane sat across from him in the booth without further argument. He'd said they wouldn't touch on difficult topics, and she would hold him to that.

She pulled her share of the goodies over to her side of the table. "How is your grandma Alena?" she asked as she opened the Funyuns. "Is she still fighting to keep living on her own?"

He opened his Doritos. "She moved in with my aunt Rita last month."

"Rita. That's the daughter she—"

"—claims to have adopted at a pet shelter." Miguel's dark eyes danced. He'd always been the most naturally happy person she'd ever known. "Mamá made them both go in and talk to the priest; that way, when they kill each other, it won't be on her conscience."

She loved Miguel's family. They were funny and quirky and a breath of fresh air.

He paused with a chip partway to his mouth. "How's work? Did they ever merge those two branches?"

Of course he remembered that. She'd dated a few guys who probably couldn't have come up with the name of the company she worked for, let alone what was going on with her job. Miguel had never been like that.

"They did. And I got promoted to account executive."

He quickly swallowed a mouthful of soda. "That's awesome. Did they give you a raise, too?"

She nodded. "And a bigger cubicle. I'm not corner-office material yet, but I'm working on it."

"As hard as you work, you'll have that corner office in no time."

She dug into her Funyuns. "Tell that to my family. They all either think I'm in a dead-end career or I'm working too many hours. It's the only thing they debate as often as which parent everyone dislikes the most."

"Do either of your folks claim to have picked you up at a pet shelter? 'Cause that'd make the choice a little easier."

She didn't often laugh about the mess that was her family, but she did then. And she had many times over the year she and Miguel had been together. Somehow he managed to joke about it without making light of it all.

"I'll have to ask whichever one of my parents I have to spend Fourth of July with," she said between sips. "Dad planned this big elaborate barbeque. Then Mom found out and announced she was hosting a dinner party at the exact same time. It's like the Hunger Games, except everyone is begging to get killed off."

Miguel pointed a Dorito at her. "What you need is to get yourself invited to something else that day so you don't have to go to either one."

"Next time I'm on Craigslist, I'll be sure to search for 'Parties for People Avoiding Their Feuding Families.' That ought to do it."

His warm, genuine chuckle rumbled through him. "That's a good way to get yourself murdered. It'd be a lot safer to come to my family's Fourth of July party. You remember it from last year. A ton of people and a ton of food."

"We're not—we were dating last year, so it was okay for me to go then."

He was shaking his head before she finished her protest. "No one'll care if we're not there as a couple. I mean, they'll *care* because they're all still in mourning over our breakup. Mamá lights a candle for the two of us every time she goes to mass."

If not for the laughter in his tone, she might have been worried. Either he was indifferent, or he thought that seeking the help of the divine for an ended relationship was taking things a little far.

"Fresh salsa again this year?" She was honestly considering it a little. A very little.

"And live music." He wiggled his eyebrows as if offering a temptation she couldn't possibly resist. "And, as if that weren't enough, at least half of the people there will speak entirely in Spanish. You won't understand a word."

She finished off her Dr. Pepper. "I wonder what it would take to get my family to talk only in languages I don't understand."

"Things sound even worse with your family than they were before." He set aside his snacks and gave her his full attention. "Are you all right?"

She slumped a little on the bench. "It's really not any different than before. I guess I just notice it more than I used to." Knowing Miguel's family and watching how they interacted with one another had changed the way she saw her own family.

"Then maybe it's a good thing you've been away from them the past few days."

It was, and yet . . .

"What is it?" he asked.

The confession that came next surprised her. "This trip was a little lonely. I always come here alone, but I really felt it this time."

He reached across the table and set his hand on hers. She ought to have pulled away, but found she didn't have the heart. His touch was as gentle and tender as she remembered, and she'd missed it. She adjusted her hand enough to thread her fingers through his.

"Where did we go wrong, Jane?" he asked quietly. "We were always so good together."

Regret trickled over her. "We just wanted different things, I guess."

His brow pulled downward. His gaze grew more intense. "You didn't want to spend the rest of your life with me."

That wasn't it exactly. "I didn't *not* want it."

He blinked a few times in rapid succession. "But you turned me down. You said no."

She realized quite suddenly how personal their discussion had become. This was exactly the topic she'd wanted to avoid. Thinking about their breakup made her emotional, and she wasn't about to start crying in a crowded airport.

She pulled her hand back. "Thanks for the snack break."

"Jane, I—"

"Ladies and gentlemen, we have updated flight information for our Denver passengers."

Jane turned her gaze to the gate counter.

"Due to ongoing weather problems throughout much of the Midwest, delays and cancellations are widespread throughout the country. The delay of this evening's Denver flight has been extended. We do not, at this time, have an estimate for when the flight will depart."

Not even an estimate? That is not a good omen.

"Passengers wishing to rebook for a future day may speak with any of the gate agents who have now arrived for that purpose. For those choosing to wait, we appreciate your continued patience, and we will keep you updated. Thank you."

A few passengers jumped up immediately; others seemed to be debating. An indefinite delay most likely meant an eventual cancellation. But there was still a chance. And rebooking wouldn't necessarily make a difference. If flights were being delayed and cancelled across the country, travel would be chaotic for days.

She met Miguel's eyes once more. What did he mean to do about his flight? If they both intended to stay and wait out the delay, that'd likely mean more awkward conversations, more confronting her own regrets and confusion. She wasn't sure she was ready for that.

But airlines didn't provide hotel accommodations when weather was to blame for flight problems. And this trip hadn't been business. She'd come to clear her head and try to get herself back on track. She'd paid for the entire thing herself. She didn't have the budget for another night at a hotel.

"What are you planning to do?" she asked. "Wait it out or reschedule?"

His smile was slow and soft. "I have all the time in the world, Jane. I'm willing to wait."

She shouldn't have liked the sound of that, but she did. She very much did.

FOUR

I *didn't not want it.*

Miguel wasn't sure what she'd meant by that, but he liked what it hinted at. He figured she'd turned down his proposal because she didn't want to be with him. But that, apparently, wasn't entirely true. He had to figure out what *was* true.

He sat in their booth, finishing off his chips, trying to decide what came next. It had been almost thirty minutes since she'd taken up her bag and offered him a "talk to you later." He was determined to hold her to that. Of course, there was a fine line between being determined and being a stalker.

He slouched low on the bench. "Love is a pain," he muttered.

"Tell me about it," someone answered behind him.

Miguel looked back. A guy in the skinny-jeans-and-tee-shirt look only a person who was both young and crazy in-shape could pull off sat there alone, but with several mismatched carryon bags.

The guy nodded. "I'm Tim," he said.

"Miguel." He turned a little on the bench, stretching his legs out the length of it, sitting full profile to the guy, who sat the same way.

"How long do you think we'll be stuck here?" Tim asked.

Miguel motioned with his chin toward the TV. "With that kind of weather, I'd guess all night. If the flight doesn't end up cancelled altogether."

Tim pushed out a huff of breath. "Just my luck. My first week off in eighteen months, and I'm going to spend it here in the airport."

"Is New York home or Denver?"

"New York is, Denver *was.*" Tim crossed his Converse at the ankles. "Some friends and I were going to spend some time enjoying nature. LaGuardia's not exactly what we had in mind."

Miguel could appreciate that. "This airport is all I've seen of New York. It's not exactly Broadway, but I guess it has its own charm."

Another guy, dressed in slacks and a tucked-in button down shirt, joined Tim at his booth. Their styles were different, yet something about the two of them was very similar.

"This is Darren," Tim said. "Darren, this is Miguel, who just attempted to compare the charms of LaGuardia to Broadway."

Darren eyed Miguel disapprovingly, though with enough drama to make the look hilarious. "We burn people at the stake for that kind of heresy."

Miguel silently chuckled. "My girlfriend would probably be the one to light the torch; she's crazy about Broadway. Well, my *ex*-girlfriend. But I'm working on that."

Tim's brow shot upward. "Ah. Now we've stumbled on the reason for your earlier declaration about love." He turned to Darren. "That's how I met Miguel. He was emoting about the pains of love."

"'Emoting'?" Miguel laughed. "I only said four words."

Darren shook his head. "You can emote without any words if you try hard enough. But back to the 'I'm working on that' part. You're trying to win your ex back?"

Miguel gave the two a very quick, very vague version of his current predicament, minus the personal reasons for their breakup. He found in them a very sympathetic audience.

"And she's *here*?" Tim's eyes darted about, looking for her, though he couldn't have known what she looked like. "That is fate. You can't ignore fate."

"Fate seems to be ignoring me," Miguel said. "We talked for a while over junk food, but as soon as I brought up anything even kind of personal, she took off."

Darren scratched at his chin. "Took off in a huff, or just took off?"

Miguel didn't think she'd been in a huff. But he wasn't really sure.

Darren waved over three more guys. Anyone looking would have pegged the five of them as a group. Same commitment to style, same mannerisms. "Miguel here is trying to make his ex-girlfriend his ex-ex-girlfriend. And he is failing miserably."

"Thanks," Miguel muttered.

Darren waved it off. "He hasn't seen her since she broke up with him, and then, boom, here she is waiting for the same flight."

One of the newcomers turned wide eyes on Miguel. "This is meant to be. You have to do something."

Miguel held his hands up in a gesture of helplessness.

"Chocolates?" Wide Eyes suggested.

"She's more of a salty junk food kind of person. But I tried that already and didn't get very far."

"Flowers," Tim said. "Oh, but where would you get them here?"

"Maybe he knows origami," one of the others suggested.

Miguel just shook his head.

Two of the hipsters sat at his booth and furrowed their brows in thought. "What are some of her favorite things?" one asked. "Besides all the junk food you already bought."

"Food and New York City, especially Broadway."

"Plays or musicals?" Darren pressed.

"Musicals." Miguel knew that for a fact. "But as you've already explained, LaGuardia is about as different from Broadway as you can get."

"How did you ask her forgiveness when you were still together?" Tim asked.

"Homemade tamales. A foot rub. Begging forgiveness in my best Ricky Ricardo accent."

His five newest best friends pondered his list. Authentic, homemade tamales, they acknowledged, couldn't be had in an airport terminal. Not one of them recommended a public foot rub. But they seemed in favor of his Ricky Ricardo impression. Darren, especially.

"It's like an inside joke for the two of you," Darren said. "Go with that. It'll remind her of happy times."

He had a point. "She might laugh, anyway. But what if she won't talk to me? I just want a chance, even if it doesn't work out."

Darren and Tim exchanged glances then caught the eyes of their three other friends.

"We may have a plan," Tim said. "Will you be around here for a while?"

Where did they think he was going? "I'm here until the plane takes off."

Darren was on his feet in a flash. "Give us like thirty minutes."

The five guys hurriedly stepped over into a far corner of the gate area. Miguel didn't know what they were up to, but he was definitely intrigued. And if their plan helped convince Jane to talk to him, then he approved completely.

Jane was stepping out of the women's restroom and walking back toward the gate. Should he go talk to her as soon as she came near enough, or would he do better to wait a while? If he did the first, he would probably come across as desperate. He was desperate, but he wasn't big on advertising that. If he waited, he might not get another opportunity.

I can always tell her I'm not trying to be a stalker. Which is pretty much the surest way to make sure I seem like one.

She sat a few booths over and pulled out her phone—the universal signal saying, *Do not disturb.*

What now? There had to be a way to let her know he was around and wanted to talk without making it seem like he didn't respect her decision to avoid him. *Maybe I'm overthinking this.*

She was on her phone. Had she changed her number since they broke up? If she hadn't, he had an idea.

Miguel pulled out his phone and typed out a text. *I'm going to the newsstand. You need anything?* He sat with his thumb hovering over send. Chances were good he'd almost passed from kind of annoying to definitely annoying. But a text was less annoying than marching up to her and begging her to talk to him.

He sent the text, then held his breath. He forced himself

not to look at her or his phone. Just because he was pathetic, he didn't have to act pathetic. But man, if her number was different now and he'd just texted some random person . . .

His phone beeped. Miguel forced himself to pull it out slowly, casually. He held his breath and opened the text.

Are you bribing me with more junk food?

Miguel gave a mental fist pump. Not only did he have her number, but she'd responded with something other than, "Leave me alone, creep."

He quickly typed back. *Or a U-shaped travel pillow. Everyone needs a good travel pillow.*

Tim, Darren, and crew were across the gate deep in conversation. Miguel hoped whatever they were planning worked. He wasn't failing completely, but he could use all the help he could get.

A new text came through. *What about a keychain with my name on it? Or I <3 NY?*

Jane hated the cheesy touristy souvenirs. *A tacky keychain? I don't know who you are anymore.* This was working even better than he'd hoped. She must not have completely hated him if she was joking around.

He watched her out of the corner of his eye. She laughed as she read the text. Miguel couldn't help grinning. She might not have wanted to marry him and was hesitant to even talk to him, but she was laughing and willingly texting with him.

You. Me. Newsstand. Person who finds the cheesiest souvenir buys the other one a drink.

It was exactly the sort of thing Jane would have suggested while they were dating. *You're on, Schoonenburg.*

He didn't wait to watch her get the text. She was likely watching him already. He jumped up and rushed to the newsstand. Jane arrived behind him.

"No cheating," he said, pretending to block her view of the rows and rows of souvenirs.

"Just know, if you're reaching for the Statue of Liberty rubber duck, I can top it with at least a dozen different things."

He gave her a suspicious look. "Lucy, you have some 'splainin to do," he said in his Ricky Ricardo voice.

She laughed.

Thank you, Darren!

"You've done this souvenir hunt before," he said.

Her bright eyes sparkled with mischief. "It's a good way to pass the time in an airport."

Miguel shook his head. "You're such a cheater."

"Maybe, but this cheater's gonna win." She folded her arms across her chest and tossed him a look of challenge. "Do your best, Ricardo."

He looked over the souvenirs then let his hand hover over a neon-green Statue of Liberty bottle opener.

"I could top that with the box of taxi-shaped butter cookies," Jane said smugly.

He took another look at the selection. "What about that puzzle of the Empire State Building?"

"That's the *Chrysler* Building." She shook her head in disappointment. "I'm going to have to dock you points for getting that wrong."

"Did I mention I haven't even left the airport?"

She set her hands on her hips. "No excuses, Santos. Make your choice."

"Okay, but you have to make your pick without seeing mine."

They'd always enjoyed goofy games like this. She stepped away, and Miguel got to work. *Think cheesy.*

Postcards, pencils, mugs. None of those things would

cut it. But then he saw exactly what he was looking for: a snow globe with King Kong inside climbing the Empire State Building, overlooking bumper-to-bumper taxis and the Statue of Liberty glued to the top of the clear plastic dome. Around the bottom was the *I Love NY* logo with the heart symbol replaced with an apple. Oh, yes. This was a winner. He grabbed the globe, and, keeping it carefully out of Jane's sight, wandered over to the other side of the newsstand.

He sent her another text. *I got this in the bag, Schoonenburg.*

A minute passed. Jane sauntered up, her hands held behind her back. "Ready to be humiliated?"

"I'm *always* ready to be humiliated." With a flourish, he presented his snow globe.

Her brows shot up and her eyes pulled wide. "Wow. That is . . . horrible."

Miguel grinned. "I know."

Jane sighed. "A good try." She held up a Statue of Liberty bobble head.

"That's it?" He tsked. "A little lame, but not lame enough."

She held up her right index finger and very slowly pressed a button at the base of the statue. An ear-grating rendition of "New York, New York" echoed out of Lady Liberty. Jane flicked the statue's crown, and the head bobbled to the beat of the music.

Miguel set his pathetic snow globe on a nearby shelf and stepped closer to Jane. "At least I didn't go down without a fight." He tapped the bobble head, setting it wobbling faster.

She grooved a little to the ongoing music.

Miguel laughed; he couldn't help himself. "I believe I owe you a drink. What's your poison?"

She jerked her head in the direction of the newsstand

refrigerator. "Apple juice?" Her mom was an alcoholic. To Jane, "having a drink" always meant soda or juice. Mamá had always made sure to have Dr. Pepper for Jane at every family gathering.

"Apple juice it is."

He grabbed a bottle, and they walked together to the cash register. Jane moved to set the Statue of Liberty bobble head back on a shelf.

"Wait," he said. "That, too."

She was surprised, but didn't argue. She set it on the counter beside the juice bottle. "I didn't realize you liked this so much," she said with a smile.

"It's a souvenir of my first trip to New York." He paid then handed the juice to Jane. "I'll put it on my coffee table and tell everyone who comes over that you picked it out."

She bumped him with her shoulder. "Don't you dare."

"Sorry, Jane. It's already decided. Nothing you can do about it."

They ambled back toward the gate, weaving around people. More and more flights were being delayed, and the airport was getting crowded. "Looks like you might need that U-shaped travel pillow after all," Miguel said. "We could be camping out here tonight."

She smiled at him. He'd always loved her smile. Seeing it again gave him hope that there might still be something between them. Friendship, at least.

"It's good to see you again," he said. He held his breath, waiting for her to turn on him.

She hesitated only a moment. "You too, Miguel."

FIVE

Being with Miguel had once been as easy as breathing. She'd almost forgotten how nice that was. The past twenty minutes, laughing with him at the newsstand and now sitting in a quieter corner of the gate area, just chatting, had reminded her with great force how much she enjoyed his company.

"After all the Funyuns and Oreos, I really shouldn't still be hungry." Jane made the declaration as she took another handful of Miguel's trail mix. "My only excuse is that I missed dinner."

"Works for me." He tossed back a handful as well. "Besides, we met over a bag of trail mix, so this isn't new territory for us."

"Trail mix and flag football." She settled more comfortably into the corner between the wall and the booth bench. "It doesn't get more romantic than that, does it?"

"At least I knew right off how competitive you were. The first thing you said to me was, 'Well, this should be an easy win.'"

She rolled her eyes. "I wasn't talking about your team versus mine, and you know it."

He pretended to really ponder it. "Are you sure? 'Cause that's not how I remember it."

She pointed at him with her apple juice bottle. "Then I hope you remember how things went down when my team finally did play yours. That was a bloodbath, my friend."

He shrugged and took up his water bottle. "It's hard to be embarrassed by a flag football game after covering yourself in cheese and marinara sauce on a first date."

Jane laughed at the memory, and at Miguel's mishap with a very large, very full piece of ravioli.

He swallowed a mouthful of water. "I sat there waiting for you to leave me in the restaurant and never look back."

"I actually liked you more after the ravioli incident. If you could laugh at something like that, then I figured you were the kind of guy I wanted to know better."

Why was she admitting all of this now? She knew the answer, even if she wasn't ready to admit it to anyone else. Her feelings for Miguel had never changed. She'd wanted him in her life, needed him there. If not for his very different view of where their relationship ought to have been, they might have even still been together.

"I told my mom about the ravioli," Miguel said. "She said, 'Don't worry, *m'ijo*. You bring her here for tamales, and she will forget that you don't know how to eat food like a real person.'"

Jane loved Miguel's mom. Had from the very first time they'd met. "That is a far better reception than my mom gave you. 'You didn't tell me he was Mexican.'" Jane cringed at the memory. Her mom had made the observation as if Miguel had been a rabid bat or something.

He reached across the table and took her hand in his. "She wasn't the first person to say something like that to me, *querida.* And she won't be the last."

Jane held fast to his hand, relishing the familiarity of it. "I know, but I still wish she hadn't said it. Said it *or* felt it."

"You can't change who your parents are. And they shouldn't be held against you." He raised her hand to his lips and kissed her knuckles.

Jane closed her eyes and let the warmth of that gesture trickle over her. He'd always had a way of melting her, and she wasn't one whose head was easily turned.

"I have a question, Jane."

Her heart dropped. She'd sensed this coming. He'd want to talk about what had pulled them apart. She took a breath and opened her eyes once more. Even with the nervousness of broaching this difficult subject, she found tiny sparks of anticipation bursting within her. Whispers of hopefulness tiptoed over her skin. Though she couldn't imagine how, talking about the chasm between them might help them find a solution. Maybe it was time they tried.

"What's your question?" She barely managed to speak louder than a whisper. Her pulse strummed in her neck. The thought of talking about what had happened between them scared her, but at the same time she truly hoped he would bring it up.

"If I had come to New York with you like we talked about, where would you have taken me?"

That was it? He wanted to talk about the city? She didn't know whether to be relieved or disappointed. Both emotions tugged at her equally. Maybe he wasn't as interested in trying again as she was.

"Well . . ." She forced her heart and her head to focus once more. Falling apart wouldn't help anything. "For starters, I'd take you to the Chrysler Building, since you clearly don't know what that is."

He chuckled. She smiled a bit at the sound.

"And Broadway," she said. "I would definitely take you to a musical on Broadway."

"Still trying to convert me?" He popped another handful of trail mix into his mouth with his free hand.

She kept her fingers entwined with his. "Absolutely."

His gaze held hers for a long, drawn-out moment. A question hung there, unspoken, but understood. *What is happening between us?* She wished she knew exactly.

"Ladies and gentlemen."

Jane cursed and blessed the gate agent all at the same time.

"As we are certain you have realized from watching the news on the terminal televisions, weather continues to be an issue throughout the country. We apologize for the ongoing wait. However, for those of you at Gate 5 here in the Delta terminal, we have a special treat for you."

That sounded intriguing. She shot Miguel a questioning look. He just shrugged and shook his head.

"We have five cast members from the Broadway cast of *Mamma Mia!* on our flight today, and they have offered to help pass the time by performing for us."

The gate erupted in applause. Jane squeezed Miguel's hand. "I love that show," she whispered to him. "Who do you think the actors are?"

She looked all over the gate, hoping to figure it out. She didn't have to wait long. A tall guy in skinny jeans and a knit beanie belted out above the crowd, "If you change your mind, I'm the first in line . . ."

Two other guys joined in with the backup parts, and then another two. Man, they were good. Perfect harmony and perfectly in sync without a single instrument to back them up. The singers moved around, engaging the crowd. In no time, the waiting passengers were clapping along. After a moment, many started singing, something the performers encouraged.

Jane leaned across the table toward Miguel. "This is the best flight delay ever!"

He was grinning in a way that immediately made her wonder what was going on in his head.

"What?" she asked.

"I met those guys earlier, but I had no idea they were Broadway singers."

One of the performers reached their booth. He held out a hand of invitation to her as he kept singing.

"Go for it," Miguel encouraged, loudly.

She didn't need any more of a push. She took the guy's hand and let him pull her to her feet, where she joined many other passengers dancing and singing along. An instant later, Miguel was up as well, and all five of the performers gathered around him.

Above the ongoing sing-along, the lead called out, "Take it, Miguel."

Jane started to laugh, trying to imagine him belting out ABBA. For one thing, he likely didn't know the words. For another, he was not a singer. But her chuckle died in the instant Miguel jumped in as impromptu lead singer.

Though he didn't get every word right, and he got every note at least a little bit wrong, his version of the chorus was contagiously enthusiastic. He took her hands in his and danced with her. As much as he wasn't a singer, he was even less a dancer. He threw himself into the moment with a grin.

It was ravioli all over again.

She'd always loved that about him. He could take an embarrassing moment and turn it into a barrel of laughs.

The actual singers took over again. Miguel wrapped his arms around her and spun her about, still dancing in his ridiculously ungraceful way. His laughter was contagious; Jane couldn't keep singing, she was laughing so hard.

Jane leaned into his embrace, still laughing at his antics as the song ended.

The lead singer stepped up close to the two of them and whispered, "Take a chance on the guy."

Quick as that, he rejoined the other performers and they launched into "Dancing Queen." Passengers began arriving from nearby gates for the concert. Jane, however, settled her attention on Miguel.

"Did you put them up to this?" She hadn't decided what she hoped his answer would be.

He held her tighter. "I didn't, but I'm not complaining."

Jane set her arms around his middle. "This doesn't fix things, you know."

"I know. But we're here, together, and you're smiling at me again. This is the best day I've had in three months."

Me, too.

SIX

First chance he got, Miguel would thank Tim and Darren and crew. Serenading Jane with a Broadway musical number had been genius. And, if her willingness to walk the concourse hand-in-hand with him were any indication, it had worked at least a little.

"If Mamá were here, she'd swear this was fate. You and me, at the same airport, on the same flight, with Broadway actors, and a nationwide thunderstorm trapping us here."

She smiled up at him. "And your mom would bite our heads off if we didn't take advantage of it."

He rallied his courage. "Then I'm just going to jump right in and ask my question. What happened between us? How did we fall apart?"

She swung their arms between them. "We didn't want the same things."

"You said that before, but it doesn't explain anything. I don't know what you want that I don't."

She stopped walking. Something like pain pulled at her expression. "*You* wanted what *I* didn't."

Too many people stood nearby. Miguel motioned her to a quieter corner of the concourse. "What I wanted was to spend the rest of our lives together. You didn't want that?"

She shook her head, but the pain and confusion hadn't left her eyes. "I didn't *not* want that."

"Jane." He sighed in frustration. "That doesn't make any more sense now than it did then."

She paced away. "You were so sure about marriage. We were going along fine, getting closer and stronger. You were so sure about marriage being the next step." She rubbed at her neck as she turned away from him. "You were ready to take that huge leap. I'm not a 'huge leap' kind of person, Miguel."

So it was marriage that had scared her off. "We'd been dating for a whole year, and, like you said, we were happy together. Things were great."

She gave him an exasperated look. "'A whole year' you say, as if that's an eternity. It took my parents ten years to figure out that they hated each other."

"And you think that'll happen to us?"

"No. Maybe." She held her hands up in helplessness. "My parents regretted marrying each other. My sister hates her ex. None of my grandparents stayed married. Only one aunt is still married, but she and her husband are just as unhappy as all the others were."

Things were starting to make more sense. "My family doesn't have a perfect track record," he said. "But there are a lot of happy marriages there."

She turned away again. "Rub it in," she muttered.

"No, that's not what I meant." He stepped around and faced her. "I just didn't think of it that way. Marriage didn't feel like a huge leap to me, so I didn't realize it was for you. All you said was you didn't want that—you didn't want to marry me. You never said why."

"What was I supposed to say?" She looked away. "That while you think marriage is this wonderful, happy thing, it scares me half to death? That while I want to believe we would beat the odds, when I look around at my family, I can't help wondering if those odds are even beatable?"

"Yes. That's exactly what I needed you to say." He gently tipped her head back so he could meet her eyes. "If I had realized all of this, I would have happily stepped back and taken things slower. I just didn't know."

She didn't look surprised, thankfully. But she did look embarrassed. "I guess I couldn't admit that my family and my childhood were this messed up, especially when you were so sure."

Miguel set his hands on her arms. "What I am sure of is *us.* All I need from you is to stick it out with me. I'm not asking for huge leaps, just a hop now and then."

Her brow pulled in tight. "But you shouldn't have to give up what you want."

He shook his head at her misunderstanding. "*You* are what I want, Jane. Us. Together. What can I do to help you believe that?"

She set her hands on either side of his face. "Time," she said. "And baby steps."

For a second, the enormity of what she'd said didn't hit him. Time. She was saying she would give them time. She was coming back. He was getting another chance.

"I'll give you all the time in the world," he promised.

Her hands slid to his chest, her eyes remaining locked with his. "I've missed you," she whispered.

He answered, not with words, but with a kiss. A kiss filled with months of missing her and loving her alone, filled with the relief that came from having her back. She wrapped her arms around his neck as the world around them disappeared.

SEVEN

"Ladies and gentlemen, we will begin boarding our Denver flight in about thirty minutes."

Jane wasn't quite awake enough to make sense of the announcement at first. She shifted, her back loudly protesting the night she'd spent on the airport floor. She forced one eye open, and then the other. Miguel didn't look any more awake than she did, and he looked far more uncomfortable.

"I told you not to sleep sitting up," she said groggily.

"The way they designed this terminal, I don't know that there were many other options except the floor." He turned his head from side to side, as if working out a kink. "Booths as far as the eye can see."

Jane sat up. Miguel's sweatshirt slid off her shoulders. He'd insisted she use it as a blanket. "We're boarding in half an hour."

Miguel stood up and held his hand out to help her to her feet. She stood and stretched.

"I'll go grab us something to eat." He gave her a quick kiss on the cheek and took off.

She watched him go, smiling to herself. She'd missed him the past three months. How did she ever get lucky enough to find a guy like Miguel, let alone get a second chance with him? She pulled their carryons over to an empty booth. Thankfully, she always kept a brush and gum in her bag.

She'd barely made herself presentable when one of the guys from last night's *Mamma Mia!* tribute approached the booth.

"It's Jane, right?"

She nodded. "Great job last night. You guys were amazing."

"Thanks. It was fun." He motioned toward the opposite bench. "Do you mind?"

"No. Go ahead."

"I'm Tim," he said, taking a seat. "Is Miguel around?"

"He went to grab us some breakfast."

"'Us?'" Tim's eyes pulled wide with excitement. "Are the two of you together again?"

She nodded. "He said he met you last night. Apparently you talked about a lot."

Tim glanced back over at his fellow performers, who were watching from a distance. "We can be a little nosy," he admitted. "But Miguel looked so broken up about it all."

Jane could appreciate that. "We split up three months ago, and I think we've both been miserable ever since."

"I'm no expert in love—I haven't ever managed a long-term relationship—but both of you being miserable without the other seems like a sign to me." Tim's look was one hundred percent empathetic. "Miguel's a great guy, from what we learned of him in the thirty minutes we talked last night. And you seem pretty wonderful as well."

"Well, I am."

At first Tim didn't seem to catch her joking tone. But then his smile blossomed, and his laugh followed shortly after.

"Thank you, again," she said, "for the song last night. The not-so-subtle message hit its mark."

"You're going to take a chance on him?" Tim pressed.

Jane nodded. "Happily. And hope for the best."

He turned a bit on the bench to fully face his friends and gave them two thumbs up. The group exchanged high fives. Jane couldn't help but laugh. These strangers were nearly as happy about her and Miguel reconciling as she was.

"Oh, hey, Tim." Miguel stepped up to the table and set a yogurt and an orange in front of Jane.

She scooted over to make room for him on the small bench. "Tim was checking to see if their serenade last night had the desired effect."

Miguel set his arm around her shoulder. "I'd say it was a success."

The others joined them, sitting in nearby booths. The next few minutes flew by as they chatted about the theater, Denver, love, second chances. Through it all, Miguel kept his arm around her. Jane couldn't say for certain that everything would work out between them, but having him with her again felt so very right.

The official boarding calls began. Changing flights had allowed for the changing of seats as well. Jane and Miguel now sat beside each other. Once they were settled in, he took her hand.

"Thank you," he said.

"For holding your hand?"

He shook his head. "For giving me another chance. I know things aren't perfect between us, and I know that commitment is a hard thing for you. So, thank you for trusting me enough to try again." He raised her hand to his lips and pressed a kiss there. "I love you, you know."

"I know. That's why I'm willing to try. Well, that and the fact that I haven't had a decent tamale in three months."

He laughed long and deep. From across the aisle, Tim gave them both an enthusiastic thumbs up.

Jane set her head on Miguel's shoulder. The path ahead of them wouldn't be all sunshine and roses, but being with him again, knowing he hadn't given up on her, gave her a hope she'd seldom known in her life.

And hope made all the difference in the world.

ABOUT SARAH M. EDEN

Sarah M. Eden is the author of multiple historical romances, including *Longing for Home*, winner of *Foreword* magazine's IndieFab Gold Award and the AML's 2013 Novel of the Year, as well as Whitney Award finalists *Seeking Persephone* and *Courting Miss Lancaster*.

Combining her obsession with history and affinity for tender love stories, Sarah loves crafting witty characters and heartfelt romances. She has twice served as the Master of Ceremonies for the LDStorymakers Writers Conference and acted as the Writer in Residence at the Northwest Writers Retreat. Sarah is represented by Pam van Hylckama Vlieg at Foreword Literary Agency.

Find her online at: SarahMEden.com
Follow Sarah on Twitter: @SarahMEden

FIRSTS AND LASTS

Annette Lyon

OTHER WORKS BY ANNETTE LYON

Band of Sisters
Coming Home
The Newport Ladies Book Club series
A Portrait for Toni
At the Water's Edge
Lost Without You
Done & Done
There, Their, They're: A No-Tears Guide to Grammar from the Word Nerd

ONE

Dani stood on the sidewalk, looking up the grand staircase outside the Metropolitan Museum of Art. Although she'd seen the building several times during her six months in Manhattan, she'd never really stopped to *look* at it, and she'd never been inside.

People rushed past her as they went their different ways up and down Fifth Avenue. She could easily identify the residents over the tourists. Real New Yorkers moved with a quick, no-nonsense stride. Businesswomen in dress pants and jackets often walked in sneakers. Dani had learned that they kept high heels in their purses or at the office to switch into after they got to work. She could hear the whoosh and honks of traffic behind her.

Several strollers passed, making Dani step out of the way. Some were pushed by mothers, others by nannies. Dani glanced at a pair of women pushing strollers with toddlers about the same age. They chatted and laughed—and looked completely at home.

I want that—to feel at home here. But she didn't, not after six months, not after experiencing a New York winter turned to spring, and not now that this was the official first day of summer, either. By some miracle, the humidity was low, but the air was hot, alleviated slightly by a cool breeze blowing down the corridors of the streets as if through a canyon. Standing so close to Central Park, she could feel the coolness there like an oasis beckoning her to come in and escape the heat.

She still related better to the other people walking the streets, the ones who were obviously tourists. They had that starry-eyed gaze as they consulted maps—whether on paper or on their cell phones—and argued about whether to see the Statue of Liberty or go to the top of the Empire State Building. They were the ones whose chins often tilted back as their eyes searched for the tops of the skyscrapers.

Dani had done that too when she'd first arrived. So maybe she wasn't exactly a tourist anymore, not in the typical sense. She could get around without a map. She knew which trains to take to get from point A to point B.

But so much was still foreign, even the sounds. She hadn't quite gotten used to having the constant energy and buzz of a city that never slept. The busiest street back home in Pekin, Illinois, paled in comparison to the sea of yellow taxis and buses passing her now.

She'd come here to pursue her dreams of performing on Broadway, yet here she was a step away from leaving it all.

Her mind and heart warred against each other, and had for weeks. Her mind—which tended to echo her mother's sentiments—insisted that she'd given it her best shot and needed to go back home. She should settle down into "real" life. But her heart cried out that six months wasn't enough, that she needed more time to give this dream thing a shot. That she was *good* and just needed to get in front of the right directors and producers at the right time, with the right project, to get her big break. Her mother wanted her to return home, find a man, have a litter of babies, and spend the rest of her life doing nothing more remarkable than canning peaches.

But the bitter reality of having run out of money was the weight that had finally tipped the scales in the direction of the logical mind winning out over her heart. The jobs she'd found as a waitress, dishwasher, and cashier at a souvenir shop had paid her bills—barely—but they also required her to work intense hours, leaving her almost no time for auditions or callbacks. She was here, so close to her dream, but unable to grab the brass ring.

She'd been through these thoughts and arguments over and over again. Time to stop thinking about it all and just enjoy today for what it was, to fully embrace all of the sights she would see for the first—and likely last—time.

Again she raised her eyes to the top of the wide staircase, which had students, tourists, and others walking up and down, some sitting in various spots. Her eyes stopped at the grand white building that was the Metropolitan Museum of Art—what she still called "the Met," even though she'd recently learned that New Yorkers typically thought of "the Met" as the Metropolitan Opera, and the museum as the MMA. Further evidence that she hadn't managed to fit in. She wasn't really a New Yorker.

Last month, some of the biggest celebrities in the world had gathered here for the annual fashion show. Dani wished she'd slowed her life down enough to notice it at the time, to have come up here from her apartment to watch the stars walk the red carpet in their magnificent gowns instead of merely seeing it all reported on during the morning news shows like the rest of the country.

As vast as the museum was, it seemed to be almost nestled within the greenery that was Central Park, safe and secure. From where she stood, she could feel the cooler temperature wafting off the park, a respite in the middle of an ocean of concrete and asphalt. Dani had half a mind to go to Central Park now and wander the miles and miles of paths until she got lost, just so she could say she'd seen everything there was to see inside it—every statue, bridge, path, and street performer. The zoo. The restaurants. The open-air theater. She could see herself spending hours at the Conservatory Garden alone.

Maybe tomorrow. Today, she'd give her time to the Met. *The MMA*, she corrected herself. She'd heard that a person could spend a week or more in there and still not see everything, but she'd do her best to see as much as she could today. She had too many other things on her first-and-last list to be able to give more than one day to it.

"Gorgeous, isn't it?" a deep voice said beside her. "Going to the museum today?"

Dani startled and turned to her right to see a man somewhere in his upper twenties grinning at her.

"Do I—know you?" she stammered. Maybe she'd met this guy somewhere and didn't remember. They could have crossed paths at an audition or something. He couldn't be from one of the awful cattle calls she'd been in; she'd remember every face she'd ever seen during those.

One thing she'd learned during her time here was that the people were far friendlier than the New Yorker stereotype suggested. But that didn't mean they struck up conversations with total strangers on busy sidewalks.

"No, I don't believe we've met," he said, holding out a hand. "Mark Potter. No relation to Harry."

Dani's eyebrows went up, and she almost laughed. He was funny, and he didn't seem like the Ted Bundy type. Before she could speak, he went on.

"And yes, I actually have been asked that—more than once." He looked at his hand, still held out to shake hers.

She eyed it. Maybe she looked like a gullible tourist, and this guy was going to try to rip her off with some trick. He seemed a little too nice, a little too sure of himself. But she found herself reaching out to shake his hand anyway. There couldn't be any harm in that, surely.

"Nice to meet you . . . Mark."

Now it was his turn to raise his eyebrows, as if he'd caught how she'd deliberately not said *her* name. As they shook hands, his was warm and his grip firm but not hard.

I could get used to holding that hand, she thought, then immediately snapped herself out of the fantasy and slipped her hand away.

Mark pointed up the stairs at the Met. "You going inside?"

Should she tell the truth and risk having a potential creeper following her around, or should she hedge and lose him? Maybe she could grab a taxi and have it drive around for a while until he was gone.

Except his warm eyes kept drawing her gaze, and he seemed to be sincerely interested in her response. And, if she was being entirely honest with herself, she wouldn't mind having company for this first-and-last stop.

She found herself nodding. "Yeah," she said. "I've never been inside, which is crazy."

"Me, neither. Crazy, especially considering that I've lived here for five years. I guess it's easy to put off seeing the sights when you're right among them."

"It really is," she said, still hedging, not saying how long she'd been here.

He was right, though; she'd grown up not far from Chicago, and while she'd visited the city a few times, she'd never seen the Frank Lloyd Wright home or Wrigley Field. She'd seen the Trump Tower in Manhattan, but not the one a few hours from home. She'd done the same thing in college; she'd attended Arizona State but had never managed to visit the O.K. Corral to the south or the Grand Canyon to the north. So odd how that worked.

She glanced over at Mark, deciding what to say. She wasn't a tourist, but she wasn't a local, either. Not really. But today of all days, she didn't want to be seen as an outsider.

"So what are you doing here?" she finally asked. "Visiting the Met for the first time too?"

"I am now, if you don't mind the company." He grinned, something that made her stomach flip deliciously. He cocked his head as if awaiting her answer, and a cowlicked piece of hair fell onto his forehead.

She sensed something else behind his smile—another emotion she couldn't pin down. It intrigued her. Maybe a couple of hours with this guy would tell her what that was all about. Besides, the Met had to be one of the safest places in the City, with all the security that had to be in there. She could ditch him later if she needed to. And she could definitely find worse things to do with her day than spend it with a hot guy.

"Sure," she finally said. "But I'm hoping to see the American Wing first, if that's all right with you."

"Sounds good to me." He turned toward the stairs, and she started up them at his side as he went on. "I looked at the directory once and had no idea how I'd pick where to start. Figured I'd get here one day."

"And it only took you five years," she said, half teasing.

"Sort of," he said, jogging up the steps beside her. "I was raised in the Hudson Highlands, an hour's drive or so, depending on traffic. I came into the city a few times growing up—family outings, school trips, that kind of thing. But the one year our class had a field trip to the museum, I had my tonsils out. My parents were always attending symphonies and fancy restaurants, but very few touristy areas. Dad hates those. So he always said we'd visit the MMA on a Sunday, when the crowds weren't so big." He shrugged. "That Sunday never did arrive. I could list off some of the best places to eat in the city, but not a single painting from inside there. Let's rectify that."

When they'd reached the top of the stairs, Mark held one of the glass doors open, and Dani went inside. Two steps in, she could already *feel* the history, as if it had soaked into the stone floor below her feet. In spite of herself, her head tilted back, just like a tourist, so she could take in the tall walls that rose to meet arches. The lobby alone looked like a cathedral, only with gargantuan flower arrangements that were works of art themselves. It all gave her half a mind to shush the people milling about. She could have stayed there all day, enjoying the vast foyer.

When they reached the ticket counter, Mark paid for two and handed Dani hers before she could object. She took it from him, their fingers grazing. A zip of electricity went up her arm.

"Thanks." She should have said so much more—how she was running low on funds, which was why she was leaving, so she appreciated the gesture even more. But the single word was all she could manage.

"No problem," Mark said as he unfolded the pamphlet he'd been given and found the museum map, which he examined. "I hear the restaurant somewhere over . . . *here* is excellent." He tapped a spot that looked to be past a long gallery of sculptures. "But I have a better idea for lunch—the best hot dog stand *ever*. It's not too far from here."

"Sounds good to me," Dani said. You can't live in the city long without expecting to walk blocks and blocks every day. A short trip to a food stand sounded good.

And after seeing how much Mark had paid for the two of them to get in, she was more than happy to have a cheap lunch—assuming that she still wanted to hang out with this guy in a few hours. One thing she'd learned during her time here was that street vendors' unhealthy food was far cheaper than groceries and far easier to get home than schlepping bags of food for blocks and blocks to cook in the tiny apartment kitchen.

"This guy's food is good," Mark promised. He rolled his eyes like a puppy in ecstasy. "Heaven on a bun, I promise."

"Let's do it," Dani said. "After we go through the . . . the American Wing, at least. We can come back to go through more of the museum after that."

"Perfect," Mark said. "Lead on."

They meandered through hallways and climbed stairs that looked old; Dani wished she could put her hand against the walls and *feel* the history inside them. She would have loved to know what these walls had seen and heard over the years. They reached the American Wing, where, to her surprise, the walls weren't white, but an almost pinky salmon.

"Huh. Not what I was expecting," she said, looking about. But soon her attention was diverted from the color of the walls to the paintings hanging on them.

She'd seen many in textbooks and elsewhere over the years, but these were the originals. Many were downright huge compared to the inches-wide images she'd become accustomed to—some were taller than she was and two or more yards across. Others would have taken up a whole wall of her bedroom back home.

They wandered through the maze of the gallery, somehow staying side by side the entire time, their arms almost brushing each time they moved from one painting to another. Dani was used to friends and family laughing at her insistence on stopping at every display at a museum to really appreciate it and even read the signs. Her older sister insisted that going to a museum with Dani was seventy-five percent an exercise in waiting for her. But even though Mark didn't stop to read as much as she did, he seemed happy to move at her pace. They gazed at each painting, and only after spending enough time to truly appreciate the work did they make a move to continue to the next. Dani found the relaxed pace oddly refreshing—no pressure to hurry up and move. She'd thought she was the only person in the world who took so long in museums.

Eventually they reached an area that must have belonged to a different wing, because she immediately recognized European works, especially several paintings in one room. Only one painter she knew of used those contrasting browns and whites and worked that way with light and shadow, along with those big ruffed collars on his subjects.

"Rembrandt," she said in awe.

"Wow," Mark said, following her.

Standing several feet back, Dani studied one painting, amazed at how lifelike the ruff looked—she couldn't make out individual brushstrokes. Hands behind her back so she wouldn't accidentally touch anything, she stepped closer. But she still wasn't close enough to see the small details. She took another step closer still. Another.

And that's when Mark tapped her arm. "Uh, Dani?"

"Yeah?" she said absently, glad to finally be close enough to see the brushstrokes—twelve inches away, perhaps.

Instead of Mark replying, a different, somewhat nasal voice did. "Miss?"

Dani turned to see who was addressing her. A security guard stood there, rocking back and forth from heel to toe. "The cameras just took a picture of you." He looked both serious and amused. But his meaning didn't register.

She took a step toward him. "Excuse me?"

He nodded at the Rembrandt. "You were too close. The security cameras took a picture of you in case you damaged the painting. You'd better stay back."

"Oh." Dani deliberately took two long strides backward, putting several feet between her and any painting. Any chance of seeing Rembrandt's individual strokes was gone. "Better?"

The security guard didn't even answer. He just walked off.

"Didn't expect that," Mark whispered with a chuckle. "Had I known I was inviting myself to come along with someone who is practically a felon . . ." He shook his head.

"Oh, please." Dani slapped his arm playfully and laughed as she headed to the next painting, another Rembrandt. "Really, how do they expect anyone to appreciate the work if we don't get to actually *look* at it? Three feet away is too far; that painting looked just as it did in my humanities textbook in college. But up close—that was seriously cool."

Mark put his hands in his pockets and stopped by her, admiring the next piece. "I dare you to do it again."

She looked over and raised her eyebrows. "Yeah, no,"

she said, unable to hide a smile. "I have no desire to have my face sent to security or for me to be escorted out for endangering a priceless work of art." Dani looked away, because eying him was quickly becoming a dangerous act. She could have sworn he got better-looking with each glance. She studied the painting in front of her, even though her mind was now elsewhere.

You can't let yourself get hung up on some guy you don't even know, she reminded herself. *Not when you're about to move a thousand miles away.*

"But I have no regrets about getting that close—once—if that's what you're asking," she added, holding up her index finger to emphasize her point.

Mark didn't so much as look at her when he spoke next, but he did lean close and whisper in her ear, giving her a hint of his musky cologne. "I *double-dog* dare you."

At his nearness, Dani's knees threatened to give way, but she wouldn't let him see that. Wanting to smell him again, she leaned in—slowly, to prolong the moment—and whispered her reply in his ear. "Not. On. Your. Life."

Their eyes caught, and they both grinned. She sauntered off, and she couldn't help feeling a bit of a thrill when he grinned and followed behind. After a few more rooms, they reached a corridor that marked the end of this particular wing.

They headed down a staircase, with Mark ahead of her. At the bottom of the wooden steps, he paused and looked back. "Time for hot dogs?" he asked. "Or do you want to go see some Egyptian mummies or maybe the Ancient Near Eastern Art? African? The Costume Institute?"

"I thought you didn't know much about the museum," Dani said, raising one eyebrow. Under normal circumstances, she would have preferred to stay in the museum all day, but she found herself saying yes to lunch—and meaning it. "A hot dog sounds perfect about now," she said, even though she'd already had half a dozen in the last week.

TWO

They walked down Fifth Avenue, chatting about the museum and how they really should have gone before, although truth be told, Mark was rather glad that his first introduction to the MMA was with Dani.

Approaching a good-looking, unknown woman had never been part of Mark's MO. For that matter, he'd *never* done it until today. But today, he'd needed a break from everything. As of this morning, he'd had another flop of an audition, racked up with all the others he'd thought had gone so well but had still yielded rejections.

So he'd tucked his oboe case into his backpack then headed to the park. His original intention was to get *away* from the City, and the park was about the best he could do without actually leaving the island. He missed his family's house back in Cold Spring, with its aging shade trees, green bushes, and flowers in a thousand varieties and colors. They'd be in their prime about now, mid-June: after budding and blooming but before the weather got too hot.

Dani talked about her home in Illinois, a town much different from one he'd ever lived in, surely. He couldn't quite imagine what living in the Midwest would be like, with its rolling plains and cornfields.

"I'm glad I came to New York," she said. "But I do miss home."

Mark found himself nodding. "I totally get that."

He missed home too, in a lot of ways. He didn't want to go back, though, not until he had something to show for his efforts. This morning, he'd failed again. He'd come to the park—and then to the museum—to shake off the voice of his father, which always set up shop and lived in his head, whispering about how he'd failed again and always would be a loser.

Oboe performance? Really, son? That's ridiculous. Don't go studying music and then, when you can't support yourself, come limping home, expecting to stay in your old room.

His father had a point in some ways, Mark supposed. Had he picked one of the STEM majors, he could have been making money at some big technology company or something by now instead of serving tables, eking out a living, barely able to pay rent, always hoping that the next audition was the one. He managed to make ends meet by playing freelance gigs like weddings and corporate parties, sometimes on the piccolo or bassoon—instruments he could play that weren't as common.

He'd walked past several groups of children at various statues, and as they'd played tag around the figures in the Alice in Wonderland statue, he'd noticed the magic in their eyes that always seemed accompany children's play.

Just as Mark's doubts had come to a crescendo, he'd left the park and reached the sidewalk. Instead of hailing a cab as intended, he'd spotted Dani at the base of the stairs. She'd stood there, looking up at the museum as if it held some last scrap of hope for her. That expression was exactly how he felt.

And it was also why he suddenly found himself walking up to her and acting so entirely out of his comfort zone. If she brushed him off, so be it; he'd go inside and visit the museum alone. If he got to meet that beautiful woman on top of it all, so much the better.

The worst that could happen was being rejected, right? And that had already happened today. So he'd gone over and found himself talking to a perfect stranger—and connecting with her so completely in almost no time at all. The beautiful woman had turned out to be intelligent and witty and fun and so much more.

Now, as they walked down the street, he couldn't believe that two hours before, they'd never laid eyes on each other.

He glanced down, where her arms swayed with each step. Their hands were so close that they might as well be touching. He could slip his hand around hers without much trouble . . . but how would she react?

And why did he suddenly care so much about that?

"We really should go back there someday," he said, breaking the silence that had consumed them both for the last moment or two.

She nodded but then shrugged. "I doubt I ever will." Her voice held a tinge of melancholy.

Never go back to the museum now that they'd discovered it? That made no sense. He stopped at the corner to wait for the light to change. "I thought you liked it."

"Oh, I did. A lot. And I'd love to see every last piece of

art in there. If E. L. Konigsburg's book is accurate, there's a whole section with antique furniture." She smiled dreamily. "I'd like to see it and imagine sleeping in one of those beds like the kids in her book. Did you ever read it?"

"Have I read about Mrs. Basil E. Frankweiler and her mixed-up files? Of course. In fourth grade, that was my favorite book. I did an oral book report about it," Mark said. "I heard that the gift shop sells copies of the book. Maybe we'll make it that far another time." He left the idea hanging in the air, hoping she'd pick up on it and give him the chance to see her again. Maybe let him buy her a souvenir on their second date to remind her of their sort-of first date. And maybe they'd arrange more dates. Together, they could see the whole museum—and then experience other parts of the city neither had seen yet.

But then the signal changed, and Dani headed across the street without answering. Mark followed, but he wasn't about to be swayed by her attempt to dodge the topic.

"So, Dani . . . why won't you go back?" he asked, catching up to her through the push of the lunch crowd.

They walked down the street again, but she stopped and looked at a store. Mark had been paying so much attention to her and his thoughts that he hadn't noticed where they were until she'd stopped: FAO Schwarz, the legendary toy store.

She pointed at the glass doors, where a man wearing a toy soldier's uniform "guarded" the entrance. "Ever been in there?" Her voice wasn't as strong as before. Something was bothering her, and Mark was determined to find out what.

"A few times, but not recently," he said. "Let's go in and walk around. It's pretty cool."

"Nah. I'm good, thanks." She shook her head and kept walking, heading away from the park, toward Madison Avenue.

Maybe she was tired of his company or thought he was a "creeper," as his roommate Brian's girlfriend called guys who made her skin crawl. Should he let her walk off alone? Say good-bye?

Not without getting her number. With determination, Mark strode along in step with her. "Let's get some lunch at that hot dog place I told you about. It's just a few blocks away," he said with a southeastward nod. "On me."

At last Dani slowed from her quick steps to a stroll and then stopped altogether, seeming to consider his offer. "Of course. Sorry. I *am* starving."

Mark led the way, and while he was enjoying himself, walking along with a pretty, smart girl, he could sense that her mood had continued to shift. And he was quite sure that it wasn't only because she needed lunch.

THREE

Dani asked for her hot dog to be plain except for a little ketchup. Judging by the vendor's reaction, one would have thought she'd requested the world to be made flat. He gave Mark an approving nod after he ordered his with the works. Mustard and relish and who knew what else smothering the poor hot dog. Another way she differed from a native.

Lunches in hand, they strolled along the street. Somehow they ended up at the south end of Central Park again. Mark must have planned their path; she hadn't paid really attention to where they were going. But when she noted a free bench under a shady tree, she was glad they'd backtracked.

She sat down, and Mark joined her on the other side of the bench. She sort of wished he were sitting closer, but as soon as the thought crossed her mind, she mentally laughed at herself. She hardly knew this guy. But she'd already taken him out of the Ted Bundy category; since leaving the museum, he'd had plenty of opportunities to pull something and had been nothing other than a gentleman. A gentleman she could relate to and laugh with, and who really did know about the best hot dog stand ever. Her dog was so good, she couldn't help roll her eyes with pleasure, even if it did have only ketchup on it.

They sat and ate in silence for a few minutes, and during that time, she made a point of not looking at him too closely, because that would make her want to get to know him better. Just because she'd taken him out of the stalker-killer category didn't mean that she would be around long enough for him to be a real prospect. She was leaving New York. In ten days, she would fly back to the Midwest, where she'd do her best to be happy.

She took another bite of her hot dog, studiously keeping her gaze on a squirrel—and *away* from admiring how well Mark's chest and shoulders filled out his shirt.

Finished with his food, Mark crunched up his hot dog wrapper in one hand then draped the other arm across the back of the bench. "So why won't you be going back to the museum with me?"

Dani glanced at him, imagining herself scooting over and sitting in the crook of his arm, which was now so available. Instead, she made a deliberate show of chewing to finish the bite in her mouth as she tried to come up with a way to answer his question that wouldn't make her look like a silly farm girl, even though she hadn't grown up on a farm—just near some.

She'd have to tell him about why she'd come in the first place, something she didn't exactly relish the idea of doing.

She swallowed and then grabbed a napkin and wiped some ketchup from the corner of her mouth. When she couldn't stall any longer, she finally said, "You'll laugh."

"No way." Mark gave a firm shake of his head. "Come on. Tell me."

For a moment, she bit her lip and actually let herself eye him—but he was smiling back, so she couldn't take in every inch without being obvious about it. His smile was enough, though—warm and inviting . . . supportive.

"I'm a walking cliché," she warned him.

"Hey, I like clichés." He grinned, showing his teeth, and she couldn't help but laugh. "As they say, time will tell if the grass is always greener. And it seems that the cat's got your tongue."

"What, no 'there's no time like the present' or I'm 'scared out of my wits'?"

"How about 'opposites attract'?" He let that cliché sink in for a second before adding a caveat, "Of course, we aren't exactly opposites, so that cliché stinks."

She tried to let the implication slip away, to not react to the very real attraction she felt for him and the implied attraction he felt for her, cliché or not.

He leaned forward. "Come on. Tell me."

Dani crossed her legs to stall then finally said, "Okay, fine." She took a breath and dove in. "I came here after Christmas and gave myself six months to make it into a Broadway show."

Yep, total cliché. Cat's out of the bag and all that. She hurried on to rescue what positive opinion he might have created of her.

"I don't expect to get a leading role or anything, especially just starting out. But I've studied voice and dance for most of my life, and I'm a decent actress, too. I'd be happy with a chorus role and the chance to work up to bigger parts over the years. But here we are, six months later, with nothing to show for it but three jobs I've been fired from because I couldn't get a replacement while I was auditioning. So I'm heading home. My flight is in ten days. And there you go. That's why I'm not going back to the museum." She paused, waiting for the expected rolling of the eyes.

But Mark didn't do any such thing. Instead, he looked genuinely interested. "And?"

Dani couldn't help but tilt her head in surprise, and a smile threatened to curl the corners of her mouth. "*And* . . . isn't the rest obvious? I never got a part, and I'm out of money."

She'd known all of that for weeks now, but saying it aloud, hearing herself say the words, made the whole thing real and painful. And pathetic. She looked away, searching for the squirrel, but it must have run off. She shrugged. "Funny how time can go slow and so fast at the same time. When I got here in the winter, six months sounded like an eternity, and some days felt like they'd never end."

"Especially when you're working dead-end jobs," Mark said. He spoke as if he *knew*.

"What do you mean?" Dani asked, hoping against hope that maybe he didn't think she was a loser for coming to New York like some backwards hick, with nothing to call her own but stars in her eyes, a girl who knew more about milking cows than the theater.

I'm not that girl.

"Well," Mark said. "Let me guess what your last six months have been like."

Dani folded her arms in challenge. "Go for it."

"You've worked any job you could get to pay rent and to

eat. You probably share a small apartment with several other women to cut costs. Auditions and callbacks rarely fit with your work schedule, so you try to get time off, but after doing that a couple of times, your bosses have had to 'reluctantly' let you go. So you're suddenly free for auditions, but broke. And so the cycle continues."

"*Exactly*!" Dani said with wonder in her voice. "I've been fired three times. I've relied on temp work mostly. How did you know? Are you an actor too?" She hadn't seen him at any auditions, but that didn't necessarily mean anything; the city had a huge number of theaters, and she hadn't shown up at that many auditions, thanks to her efforts to not starve or end up homeless.

He seemed to want to hedge, his head tilting back and forth, before he answered. "I'm a musician. I play the oboe. I know all about trying to get the gigs, including auditioning to play for Broadway. Kinda sucks, doesn't it?" And he took a big bite of hot dog, almost as if he were biting the head off some casting director.

Dani couldn't help but laugh; she had felt that way more times than she could count. "Then you understand why I'm going home. The six months are over, and it's past the end of chasing a dream. Time to return to reality." She brushed her palms together to rid them of crumbs from her bun.

Mark started shaking his head rapidly, but he held up a finger to tell her to wait as he chewed and swallowed. "Six months isn't enough to test a dream. Obviously I haven't heard you sing or seen you dance or any of that. But I can recognize the fire when I see it. You've had it for a long time, haven't you?" He said it as if he could tell that she'd dreamed of making it here since she wore pigtails. "You really aren't past the end of your dream, are you?"

He probably knew her type all too well. Over the years,

he'd surely seen a parade of wannabe actors and singers and dancers.

She didn't trust herself to speak at first. Then she cleared her throat and managed, "Of course the fire doesn't go out this fast. Making it has been a dream since I was five."

"And you're going to let six measly months and how many auditions—what, twelve or so?—change all that? No way."

Nine, she thought, mentally correcting him. He'd think she was a bigger loser if he knew that number, or that she'd been called back *twice*. This was an awfully big pond, and no one here cared that back home, she'd been an awfully big fish in a tiny pond. Out here, she might as well forget thinking of it as a pond; this was an ocean, and she was drowning. *Small or big doesn't matter; I'm not even a real fish.*

She couldn't answer his question, because yes, she was going home. Yes, she was giving up on a dream she'd held for most of her life. When he didn't say anything either, a thick silence slowly descended between them. But something was held suspended in that silence, something she couldn't identify or name. A connection.

Suddenly, she didn't feel so lonely in this vast city of millions. She was going home in a matter of days—she could count it in hours, if she wanted to—and she didn't want to leave Mark behind.

How? I just met him. Why should I care about him? He surely doesn't care about me.

Her stomach went heavy and flat; she had no more appetite, even though this was, as Mark had promised, the best hot dog she'd ever tasted. She searched for something to say to end the silence; it was growing uncomfortable, and she couldn't bear to think that what she felt as a connection with Mark was nothing more than a strand of pity, even if he had hinted at attraction with his list of clichés.

After forcing a smile onto her face, Dani tucked her hair behind one ear and leaned her head against her hand, with one elbow propped onto the back of the bench. "Okay, so if six months isn't enough, enlighten me. How long did it take *you* to make it?"

FOUR

"Touché," Mark said. He studiously looked for a trashcan for his wrapper and napkin.

Dani scooted toward him—not entirely closing the distance, but shrinking it considerably. *I could get used to this*, she thought. *But I can't.*

"Seriously," she said. "How long did it take you?"

He stood and tossed his trash into a nearby can as if it were a basketball hoop. "Three points," he muttered under his breath. He didn't say anything else for a moment, but he stood there with his back to Dani, as if deep in thought.

That's when she noticed a rectangular bulge in his backpack and instinctively knew what it was—his oboe. Suddenly, everything clicked into place: Why a guy like Mark was free on a random weekday instead of working. Why he encouraged her dreams as if he understood them. How he knew about lost jobs and auditions.

"You're *still* trying to make it . . . aren't you?" she said quietly.

"Yeah." He nodded without turning around and shoved his hands into his pockets. "I make ends meet by doing a lot of freelance gigs." He turned around and shrugged. "Helps that I can play pretty much any woodwind. But my heart isn't with the clarinet."

"Isn't the clarinet the wimpy man's oboe?" It was her attempt at a joke, but she knew there was a kernel of truth to it. The reed and breath control required of an oboe far surpassed that of a clarinet.

The softening of his mouth hinted that she'd landed on something. Yet she recognized weariness in his voice; she'd felt the same thing every minute of every day over the last six months. Looking back at her time in the city, she had to wonder how much better off she'd have been if she'd thought to work weddings and other events like Mark had. Maybe she could have saved enough to buy herself another month.

But that was all in the past—what might have been. Right now, she wanted to see and hear the enthusiasm she'd first seen in Mark—to have the spark in his eyes return, which her words had extinguished as if she'd blown out a candle with a single breath. What could she say to fix it? *Sorry* wouldn't do it. Of course he knew she was sorry that they were both failures.

No. We're not both failures. He's not one. I know *he's not. He just waiting to find his big break.*

"Play for me?" she asked quietly. She stood and reached out to touch his arm. To her relief, he didn't flinch or pull back.

He just turned his head slightly and tilted it, eyebrows raised. "Why?"

"Because I want to hear your music the way only you can play it." She hadn't planned on saying any of that, but as the words tumbled out, she meant every word. "Please?"

Mark seemed to think about it for a few seconds, but then he nodded. He sat on the bench again and unzipped his backpack, revealing the black instrument case she'd known was inside. He pulled it out it oh-so-gently, as if the instrument inside were a priceless antique. He placed the backpack on the ground near his feet, and the case on his lap. He unlatched it and opened the lid, revealing the gorgeous black-and-silver instrument that lay inside, nestled in red velvet.

One by one, he pulled out the pieces and assembled his oboe, then set the case on top of the backpack. It fell open, unheeded, as Mark put the oboe to his lips. He placed his fingers just so on the keys, moistened the reed, breathed in, and began to play.

From the first note, it was as if he'd entered a new dimension where only he and his music existed; both his body and face took on a different look—focused concentration combined with peace and a sense of increasing joy. His shoulders and face relaxed as he swayed side to side. She knew that look; she'd *felt* it on the dance floor more times than she could count.

The haunting notes of Ennio Mariconne's "Gabriel's Oboe" from *The Mission* floated around her—the very piece that had first made her love the oboe. Chills broke over Dani's arms and raced down her back. What were the chances that she would meet a man who played her favorite instrument so masterfully? Every note was infused with intense emotion: melancholy and loss, with a thread of hope and joy tying it all together. More than anything else, an overarching beauty encompassed him as he moved back and forth, music flowing from his fingertips.

The moment felt holy, as if he was baring his emotions in a vulnerable, sacred way. And hers, too.

Still standing, Dani found herself moving side to side as the rhythm and notes moved through her. She closed her eyes, unable to *not* move. She was a dancer; she couldn't feel such powerful music moving through her bones and expect to stand still.

Her sway turned to a broad, sweeping arm movement, then her core contracting and releasing. Her feet soon followed, and before she knew it, she was improvising full-out with legs, footwork, arms, her torso, even quadruple pirouettes. Her movements built from small at first to grander as the music swelled. She leapt past him, vaguely aware that Mark's focus remained entirely on his instrument; she could have been beamed to Mars, and he mightn't have noticed. She grinned, knowing exactly what that felt like: the rush of creativity and performance, even if it was for an audience of one. She danced bigger, with turns and leaps and extensions, letting her emotions from the past six months come out in a rush, the same melancholy, loss, and hope that flowed from his oboe—the sounds that connected Dani and Mark in a way she would never be able to put to words.

From the corner of her eye, she noticed people passing by on their way to the pond as they stopped, perhaps to watch, but she paid them no mind. Let them think what they would. She'd stopped caring what people who weren't casting directors—or her mother, at least—thought of her.

Mark's fingers stopped moving as he held a long note, then released the reed. The music stopped, and even the air seemed suddenly still. Dani's movements stopped too. She was breathing hard, wiping beads of sweat from her forehead with the back of her wrist, when a rousing applause and cheers erupted from the small gathering around them.

The noise broke the remaining spell, and she looked about. Some twenty people had stopped to watch. Many smiled as they continued on their way. Several walked over and tossed coins—and, in some cases, bills—into the instrument case as they passed. She bowed as she would on stage, and Mark nodded deeply to acknowledge them.

After the crowd had dispersed, her heart still pounding from her sudden exertion, Dani sat close to Mark. "That was fun." She pointed at his oboe. "And that was the most beautiful thing I've ever heard. Thanks for playing for me."

Mark wore a half-smile and pointed at the instrument case. "Look. There's got to be ten or fifteen dollars in there. Not too shabby for about five minutes of work."

Dani reached down and pulled out the bills to count them—a five and four ones. "Nine bucks. And that's not counting the coins." She peered into the case with its red velvet interior, where quite a few quarters and some other change lay. "Probably a few more dollars there. Good guess."

Mark shrugged, as if his guess was no big deal. And perhaps it wasn't. But his face had suddenly darkened, and his shoulders had fallen. Dani had no idea why, but the overall effect was such a drastic change from the way he'd looked moments before while playing, that the shift made her sad—and worried.

"Did I . . . say something wrong?" she asked, scooting a couple of inches away in case she'd gotten too close.

He shook his head and licked his lips. Then he pointed at his case and shrugged. "Truth is, I've done a lot more busking than I'd care to admit. It's how I've made ends meet when I didn't have a regular job and no freelance work came my way." He leaned forward, resting his forearms on his thighs, and began rubbing his right thumb against the back of his left hand—a nervous action if ever there was one.

"I'm so sorry," Dani said. "You're so talented—and I mean that. It's crazy to think that you aren't first chair in some world-renowned symphony."

He cracked a smile at that then shook his head and laughed sardonically. "You're too kind."

"I'm dead serious," Dani insisted. "I—"

"Here." Mark picked up his case and held it toward her. Dani put her hands together, palms up, and he dumped the coins into them. He took his oboe apart and went on as he put the pieces back into the case. "My father would have a field day if he ever found out that I busk pretty regularly. It's not exactly how I pictured myself making a living with my music, either, but sometimes you have to do what you have to do, and I'm not ready to give up."

He'd placed each instrument piece carefully into its spot, treating it with care. He closed the lid and latched it carefully. That oboe was his most prized possession; Dani knew it without asking.

"If you enjoy what you do, who cares?" she said. "Your dad doesn't need to ever know."

"He'll find out eventually. Somehow." Mark said it without looking at her. He slipped his oboe back into the backpack and zipped it shut.

A strained silence tried to come between them, but Dani pushed it away. "Can you live on what you make by busking?"

His pained expression softened as his mouth rounded in a smile. "Not like a king, but I can survive. Barely. Assuming I get freelance gigs too. And have several roommates to split rent and utilities with."

She could almost hear the words he wasn't saying: that his father expected him to have a "real" job, whether that meant in a restaurant cleaning tables or a place in that world-class symphony.

"Then do more of it," she said. "I can tell you love busking. You make your own hours, and it would give you the flexibility to go to more and more auditions, and eventually, you *will* make it big, whether you're in the pit playing for *Wicked* or playing for the Metropolitan Opera or the New York Symphony Orchestra or whatever. Someday, you'll have your own concerts with an entire symphony accompanying you, like Yoyo Ma, except on the oboe. And—"

Mark laughed and held up his hands in surrender. "Fine. I'll do more busking and freelance work. Happy?"

"I suppose." She nudged him with her elbow. "Come on. I'm thirsty. Let's get something to drink. My turn to show you something—my favorite smoothie place."

"Game on," Mark said, standing. His previously somber mood seemed to have fallen from his shoulders.

"This way," she said, walking down a path that led out of the park. "I've got a handful of quarters burning a hole in my purse."

FIVE

Dani treated Mark to the best smoothie he'd ever had—a raspberry something or other, with several additional flavors he couldn't pin down except perhaps lime. As they sipped on their straws, talking and meandering through the hot city streets, he wished they were back at the much cooler park.

Aside from escaping the heat, he would also have been quite glad to settle down to busking again with Dani dancing to his music. Maybe she could sing along at times instead of dancing. They could come up with quite a gig, the two of them, especially if he brought a piccolo and flute to change things up.

He knew all the best spots for busking—not so much the playgrounds, where young kids scrambled about under the watchful eyes of their caregivers—but where adults and, preferably, tourists, tended to congregate.

With their final slurps, the smoothies were gone, so they found a trashcan then headed for the nearest corner, where traffic had picked up considerably with the later hour. Rush hour would be upon them soon.

As they waited to cross, Mark pulled out his cell phone and checked the time. "It's already five?" How had the day gone so fast?

"No way," Dani said, checking the time on her pale pink wristwatch. "Time flies."

"Speaking of clichés," Mark said, and laughed. "I promised we'd get back to the museum, but I have to clock in at my latest temp job in half an hour." He tried to hide his disappointment by adding, "I'm a glamorous dishwasher."

"Don't worry about it. I totally understand," Dani said.

After spending so much of their day together, he knew that she really did understand, and from firsthand experience. She turned and, walking backward, faced him as she talked. "How about you walk me to my place? It's not far." Her eyes narrowed with worry. "Unless that would make you late." She didn't have to add that doing so could cost him another not-so-glamorous job.

"I think I can manage a few blocks and still get there on time."

"Great." She jerked her head to the left, indicating which way to go, and he followed.

He mentally did the math, wondering if he really did have time to walk her back to her apartment. Probably not. His boss, Andre, had promised a quick kick to Mark's butt if he arrived more than five minutes late again.

Worth the risk. This way I can see where she lives and get her number. And like she said, I can always do more busking and freelance work.

Besides, he had every intention of making good on his promise to experience the rest of the museum with her . . .

and of getting to know her well beyond that. They'd spent most of the day together, and while they still didn't know each other particularly well, his gut told him without question that this was a woman worth getting to know. It was as if he and Dani were supposed to meet today, because what were the chances of two random strangers, with so many common interests, running into each other the way they had—and in a city of some eight million people? It was almost enough to make him believe in fate.

Which meant he had to take action, because the chances of him happening to see her again if he didn't get her number were so slim he refused to consider the idea.

"Here I am." Dani stopped at a gray, nondescript apartment building. It had the typical fire escapes and locked front door. He could have passed this very building a thousand times and never noticed it, but now he paid close attention to the cross streets and made a mental note of every detail, including the coffee shop on the corner. She held out a hand as if to shake his, the way he'd done when he'd first introduced himself. "It was great meeting you today."

He just looked at her hand. "A handshake? After Rembrandt, hot dogs, busking, and the world's best smoothies?" He smiled so she'd know he was kidding. Mostly.

"A hug?" she suggested.

He opened his arms, and she stepped into them. The embrace wasn't long, but for the few seconds it lasted, Mark had never felt more content and peaceful. He didn't want to let her go. That would mean seeing her walk away. It would mean going to work and dealing with Andre. Facing the rest of his life, which was as drab and colorless as this building. The only thing that gave life color was his music.

And now, Dani.

She gave his cheek a quick peck and pulled back. "Thanks for a great day. It's been a rough spell, and I needed it."

"Likewise." He could still feel the heat of her lips on his cheek; he wanted to reach out and take her hand to draw her back into his arms. She began digging in her purse for her key—Mark's cue to speak up or miss out on ever seeing her again. "So, could I—have your number?"

Dani's head popped up from her search, and a sadness around her eyes belied her smile. She clutched a keychain in her palm and seemed to struggle for words. Mark held his breath, not wanting to be rejected. *Please just give me your number.*

"Sure," she finally said. "Except that it might not be of much use to you."

Mark tried not to let his disappointment register on his face. "Even though you're leaving, I'll still like to have it." He held his breath, hoping she wouldn't just dump him right there on the street, but somehow a pit began to grow in his stomach anyway.

She shrugged and played with her keys, avoiding his eyes. "Ten days . . ."

"Don't go," he said. "Or at least, let's spend your last days seeing cool stuff in the city."

She raised her eyes to his and nodded. "I'd like that. Truth is, I'll be spending the next week or so finishing off my list of firsts and lasts—all the things I've missed out on seeing here. All of the stuff I want to be sure to experience before . . ." She looked down and again fingered her keys.

"Yeah," Mark said, wishing he could change the future.

"Are you sure you want my number? Ten days isn't much."

The pit in his stomach turned to a bitter taste in his

mouth. "You can't really leave," he insisted. Part of that was because of her insane dancing ability, but there was also the connection between them. Surely she'd felt it. But he went for what he guessed would be the stronger argument: what had first brought her here.

"You have so much talent." He stepped closer. She shook her head, which made him put a hand out and cup her cheek to stop her denial. She didn't pull away. Their eyes caught, and they gazed at each other for several seconds before he found his voice. "What about everything you told me about sticking with it, that someday it'll work out?"

"That wasn't about me. It was about you." Dani reached for his hand and lowered it, now holding it in both of hers, as if bringing his idea back down to reality. "I'm out of money. I'm out of time. I—" Her voice cut off as if she wasn't sure what to say.

He knew the feeling. He took a step closer to her; she didn't move away. "Can I still have your number?" It was almost a whisper.

She didn't answer for a second; her eyes were shiny from unshed tears. She sniffed and then nodded, pulling her phone from her purse. "What's yours? I'll text you so you'll have mine."

Relieved at the small success, Mark rattled off his number, and she punched it into her phone. A moment later, his phone trilled in his pocket, and when he checked it, her text was there with a kissy-face emoticon. He wished he dared take her up on the suggestion, but she was probably joking.

He tucked it back into his pocket and rocked on his heels. "Are you free tomorrow? I'd like to take you out to lunch at this awesome place in Grand Central Station."

"I'd like that," she said with a nod. "Text me in the

morning."

"I will," he said, then took two steps back, letting her know that he wouldn't keep her longer.

She put her key in the door, smiled over her shoulder, and went inside.

Mark swiped the screen of his phone and typed his first text to Dani. It consisted entirely of one thing: the same emoticon of a kissing smiley face.

He wasn't kidding.

He hurried to work, walking with fast strides down the increasingly crowded sidewalk to reach the subway in time to catch the right train. Not once did he think about dealing with Andre; all of his thoughts were focused on Dani and how he could possibly convince her to stay in the city long enough to give both her career and him a real chance.

SIX

Over the next week, Dani saw Mark every day for at least an hour or two—and often for a lot longer than that. One day they went to the Statue of Liberty and then to the 9/11 Memorial. On another, they got up really early and managed to be part of the crowd outside the *Today* show at Rockefeller Center. Dani got to shake Al Roker's hand. Then they wandered around Rock Center, taking it all in. Mark bought her a *Seinfeld* poster of Kramer that completely cracked her up.

As the days wore on, she crossed more and more things off her first-and-last list: browsing in Tiffany's, even though she could never afford anything in there. Being in the studio audience of a *Tonight Show* taping. Mark took her to a few places she'd never even heard of. In addition to the place he'd already promised in Grand Central—where he'd insisted she try some oyster dish—he brought her to The View, a restaurant at the top of a skyscraper, so high that on the way up in the glass elevator, her ears popped. Inside, the tables were on a carpeted ring that slowly rotated—one full circle every hour. Between trips to the buffet, patrons could look out and spot various landmarks, like the Chrysler building.

Every day, they laughed and talked. Some days, they busked—Dani enjoyed it more now, even after becoming aware of the audience. She'd taken to singing as well as dancing, and sometimes Mark sang along, harmonizing with her. They used the proceeds to pay for dinner, a meal they shared almost every night now that Mark had been fired from yet another job. He swore he'd get another one soon, but he didn't want to miss out on their little remaining time together.

At times, she considered staying in Manhattan after all; if she could be this happy all the time, why wouldn't she? Except for the fact that the only reason Mark was being so nice was because their relationship, such as it was, had an expiration date. If she were to stay, her life wouldn't be a constant stream of experiencing new things with Mark at her side. Eventually, they would both return to reality. He'd return to temp jobs and auditions. He wouldn't have time to hang out with her. And she'd be right where she'd been the day they met: alone penniless, rejected, and eventually, heading home to Pekin. What was the point of delaying the inevitable?

As great as the last week-and-a-half had been, and as happy as Dani felt to be crossing items off her list, she couldn't help but notice with regret how close her departure date was drawing. Every night, she took her wall calendar off its nail and wrote down that day's activities. Then she counted the boxes left until she headed home. They were vanishing awfully fast.

Worse, Mark seemed determined to bring up the fact that technically, she didn't have to leave. And he did so every time they said good night.

"It's only the cost of a flight," he said more than once.

Other times it was along the lines of, "You haven't sold your lease. You still have a place to live."

Or, "Come on. Give your career another shot."

Dani always brushed off whichever version he'd used. Her mother's daily emails and calls had beaten her down enough. She'd already started imagining her life back at home, maybe using her degree to teach high-school theater or something.

At her apartment door, she always gave him a long hug—their hugs were growing longer every night. She *wanted* to give him more than a hug, but that would be asking for trouble. Getting her emotions mixed up in something temporary—more than they already were—would be a mess.

On Monday, her last night in Manhattan, they walked back to her place extra slowly. They'd gotten into the habit of having Mark walk with her up to the apartment door, where they'd chat until he insisted she needed her sleep and then, of course, make another argument for why she should stay. Often as they leaned their backs against the wall, they'd end up sliding to the floor and sitting there talking for far longer than they should have.

As much as Dani loved sharing her first-and-last list with Mark, she'd come to enjoy their talks even more, except for how they always ended. That night, as they walked up the last flight of stairs, she dreaded having a final debate with him on what she wanted to be a magical conclusion to this part of her life. She still held her keys after using them on the front door. She hadn't put them back into her purse, because she didn't know if he'd want to talk about art and books when they both knew this was their last evening together.

Just as she'd feared, when they reached her door, he didn't strike up a conversation about music or movies or anything else they normally talked about. Instead, he grew quiet, as if he'd run out of things to say even about the Broadway show they'd just come from. She gripped her keys in one hand. A metal edge dug into her palm. The pain provided a distraction from the ache in her heart.

He didn't have to say why neither of them was talking; they both knew. They'd had a final day of adventures, and this was their last goodnight. She'd already packed her two suitcases, and all that remained to pack was her carryon. Last week, she'd shipped home a few boxes filled with things she'd collected in the last six months that hadn't fit into her bags.

As she stood at her door, she could picture the suitcases her mother had bought her for Christmas, which were bright red so they'd be easy to spot on the luggage carousel. They represented her failure here in the city and a dull, lifeless future.

Mom should have bought gray.

Mark stepped closer, and then closer again. She could feel the heat of his body, and her heart staccatoed.

The image of those blasted suitcases forced themselves into her mind again. They marked the end of what could have been a wonderful thing with Mark.

No, not what could have been. What *had been* wonderful.

Eyes burning and insides tightening, she ordered herself to hold back her emotions. *Don't cry. You can still text Mark from four states and one time zone away. You can still email and call.*

But what were the chances a long-distance relationship would survive, when their time in person had existed for a matter of days? When both of them had purposely kept a slight, if deliberate, distance between them? It was as if they'd both instinctively known what *could* have been.

Now, with her head lowered, she watched as he took both of her hands in his. The keys tumbled from her grip back into her purse. He'd moved so close that she could feel his breath on her cheek. She knew without any doubt that if she looked up at him, their lips would meet. A kiss would be inevitable.

And oh, how she wanted that very thing. But two weeks from now, would she regret having kissed him, when she was home, driving past corn fields instead of exploring Times Square?

"You're trembling," Mark said, his voice soft, tender. He released one hand and cupped her face as he'd done before, but this time his thumb stroked her cheek. It was almost too much to bear. It felt so good it hurt.

"Why did I have to meet you at the *end*?" she said quietly, still looking down. Seeing his face would break her. "Why not in January, when things could have been different?"

He didn't answer, as if he was waiting for her to act or speak. After several seconds of silence, she finally lifted her face to his, if only to wait for him to speak. In spite of her efforts, a tear escaped and trickled down her cheek. "And please don't say that I could still—"

He stopped her words by pressing his lips to hers, cradling her head between his hands with a sense of urgency.

A rush of heat went through Dani. In spite of herself,

she reached up and held his face in return, kissing him back as much as she'd wanted to every day they'd been together. She poured all of her wishes and dreams into that kiss, and he returned every bit of it.

At last they broke apart, and Dani rested her cheek against his shoulder, catching her breath. Half of her wondered what kind of awful thing she'd done. The other half wanted to explode with happiness because even though she was leaving, at least she'd had that kiss.

She could feel Mark's heart pounding in his chest and knew that if she didn't get through her apartment door soon, she'd want to kiss him again and again and—

"I—I have to go," she murmured, gently pushing away. She didn't want to release her hands from his chest to let him go, but she forced herself to and somehow got the key into the lock.

She opened the door, went inside, and looked back at Mark. He had his hands in his pockets, and his expression looked as forlorn and lost as she felt.

"Thank you for everything," she whispered, and closed the door.

SEVEN

That night, Dani hardly slept; she stared at the ceiling. At her now-empty dresser. At her ugly red suitcases. At the window, where she gazed and imagined Mark sleeping in his apartment in the distance. She managed a couple of hours of unsettled sleep and woke an hour before her alarm.

She got up, ate a granola bar, and took a shower. She didn't have the heart to work on her appearance. What did it matter now? She pulled her hair into a ponytail and applied only the barest amount of makeup—a little concealer under her eyes so her parents wouldn't worry about her health, and some mascara, for the same reason; she tended to look extra tired without it.

Trying not to think of the kiss from last night—but reliving it every few minutes anyway—she finished packing up her carryon. She strapped the two suitcases together, the smaller atop the larger, and shouldered her carryon and purse. On the way to the door, she left her key on the counter next to the fridge, looked back at her three sleeping roommates—women she hardly knew even after six months—and walked out, rolling her luggage behind her.

The apartment door clanged shut and echoed against the apartment corridor as Dani made her way past the very spot where Mark had kissed her. Where she'd kissed him back.

At the elevator, she pushed the button, then, as she waited for it to arrive, she couldn't help but turn and look back at where she'd last seen Mark. All of his arguments seemed to clamor in her mind, yelling at her all at once. Accusing her of abandoning her dreams. Of giving in to her mother's cynicism and insistence on a traditional role.

Of not giving us a real chance.

If they'd met even two months ago—one month ago?—things might have been different. If they'd met before she'd given her all and failed. Before she'd lost the spark that her childhood dreams had once given her. The spark wasn't dead, but it had dimmed an awful lot in six months.

The elevator dinged, and the door opened. She pulled her luggage inside, punched the button for the lobby, and leaned against the wall, closing her eyes and wishing she could rewind time enough to relive the last week and a half she'd spent with Mark. Better yet, to go back further and try to find him earlier. To do . . . *something* that would change the inevitable outcome of two strangers meeting, only to find a spark that had no hope of lasting.

Before stepping off the elevator, she instinctively reached for her pocket to check for her phone, and with the habitual act came a rush of memories—of her first text to Mark, and his reciprocal kissy face in return.

Of their actual kiss last night.

She pulled her phone out and stared at it, trying to decide whether to send him one last text before she caught a taxi and headed for the airport. But the memory of Mark's devastated face, his desperate kiss filled with emotion, made her slip the phone back into her pocket. Mark was probably asleep—and sleeping well. She'd treated him poorly. Of course he'd be angry. He'd spent a lot of time with her. He'd spent what money he had on her. And now she was walking away. He had every right to be angry, even though she'd told him on their very first day that she wouldn't be here long.

The wheels of her luggage clicked on the seams of the lobby's tile but then stopped as her step slowed before the doors. She didn't *want* to leave. The last ten days had made New York feel like home in a way it never had in the previous weeks and months.

She'd miss everything about it, from the steam rising from the subway vents in the colder months to the heat radiating off the asphalt in the summer. The sheer energy everyone and everything exuded. The knowledge that people had walked this ground for centuries before her—many in the early years of the last century as they looked for a new life as they passed through Ellis Island.

She'd come here looking for a better life too—or at least, a different one. The day she'd headed for the Met, she'd been certain that after a few weeks back home, she'd be perfectly content to stay in the Midwest with her family. Perhaps she'd do community theater productions at times, just to scratch the itch. That would be enough. Or so she'd thought.

Go, or you'll miss your flight, she ordered herself.

Somehow that thought got her feet moving again, but as she reached for the door, her phone vibrated in her pocket. She paused and stepped back, pulling it out.

It was from Mark. A kissy face, with the words, *Have a good flight.*

Dani looked at the emoticon for what felt like a long time, until it got blurry from unshed tears, and she finally slipped her phone back into her pocket. He might as well have said, *Have a good life.* They both knew it was over.

Not trusting herself to keep her tears at bay, she wiped at her eyes to dry them completely then headed for the doors again. This time she pushed the automatic button, and the door slowly swung open on its own. She walked outside into the dim morning of Manhattan. Everything seemed gray, and though it was probably just the early morning light filtering through the buildings, it seemed like a reflection of her inner state—gray and dreary. But, unlike the city, her state wouldn't change as the minutes ticked by with the dawn, bringing the sun with it.

Dani went to the curb and raised her arm to call a taxi. But a deep voice called out to her.

"Going to the museum today?"

She whirled around to see Mark standing outside her building. She'd walked right past him. Her mind refused to work. "How long have you—what are you doing—why—" Her voice cut off as he stepped closer. He had rings under his eyes; her brow furrowed. "Have you been here all night?"

He shook his head, and she realized he wasn't wearing the same clothes as before. Silly of her to think he'd be out here waiting all night long. Her mom was right; her head was stuffed with cotton.

"I went back to my place, but I couldn't sleep. I've been here since about four—didn't want to miss saying goodbye . . . for real."

Her eyes stung at that—their goodbye, their last words last night, weren't a good way to part. But that kiss . . .

She looked at her watch; it was time to go if she was going to make her flight. "Mark, I have to—"

"No." He shook his head once and stepped closer. "Don't." Like last night, only slower, softer, he took her face between both of his hands. She tilted her head back and gazed into his eyes, lost in the moment and forgetting about JFK and her flight entirely, at least for a moment.

He looked into her eyes and raised his brows as if asking for permission. When her eyes lowered to his lips, he took that as an answer—which it was—and closed the distance. He kissed her slowly at first, and then deeper.

When he pulled back—too soon—he rested his forehead against hers. Dani's breath was uneven, and her legs trembled. She couldn't have held a solid relevé if her life depended on it. But slowly the world stopped spinning, and reality settled again.

"We've been through this," she began.

"But you haven't ever listened," Mark countered. She opened her mouth to protest, but he shook his head. "You once asked me why I keep chasing this crazy dream when I'm no closer to it now than I was six years ago."

Dani cocked her head. This wasn't the direction she'd expected the conversation to go.

Mark's face was intent. "I wasn't sure how to answer you then, but I spent all night thinking about it, and here's the truth: Dreams aren't worth chasing just for fame and fortune—and I know you said that you didn't come here hoping to get rich or famous. But you forgot what about dance brings you joy. It's the *journey* that matters as much as anything. I love music. You love dance. Artists—that's simply who we are. It's in our bones. And no, it's not practical. And yes, it's full of rejection and hard times and poverty too. But without those lows, we'd never get to soar in the amazing highs, either."

A dawning of understanding came over Dani. "Like when we first busked in the park." She'd found the joy of dance again in those few moments. Pure, unadulterated joy that had had nothing to do with what a casting director was looking for.

"We're two of a kind, Dani. You understand me. I understand you. Don't say it's not true, because it is. And in more ways than other artists understand each other. We have something special—something that can grow and become . . ."

"Become what?" Dani whispered the words. A tiny seed of hope was sprouting inside her, but fear threatened to quash it.

"Become something amazing." Mark took her hand and caressed the top with his thumb. "I'm not ready to give you up. And I think you're not really ready to go back home, either."

She looked up at the fifth floor, where she'd spent so many nights. "But it's so *hard*."

"I know," he said.

"What if neither of us ever makes it?" Dani didn't realize until the words were out of her mouth that she'd almost agreed to stay. The idea was growing larger in her mind.

"Then we'll take turns waiting tables and working as cashiers and taking tickets. Maybe we can start up a wedding DJ company to pay the bills between auditions. And we can go to the park and spend days busking just to buy a couple of amazing hot dogs and tickets to a play. I don't know all the answers, but I have to believe that we'll figure them out along the way if we give us a shot. Even if *we* work out but the music and dance don't—that would be worth it. And I can't help but think that no matter how miserable all of the hard parts will be, they'll be easier if you're there going through them with me."

Dani imagined coming off a horrible audition, knowing that Mark would be there to hold her and kiss her, then make her laugh, and make sure she had a raspberry smoothie. *So much better than sitting on my bed with a pint of ice cream.* Maybe she could face rejection for longer—a lot longer—if he was with her the whole way. She threaded the fingers of both hands through his and stepped closer. "I don't think we ever did see the African collection, did we?"

Mark's mouth slowly curved in to a wide smile, and his eyes lit up. "Or the Costume Institute, either."

"Hmm. Weren't you going to take me to Chinatown? I think we've got a *lot* of things you still have to make good on, and that'll take a *long* time. Months, probably. Maybe years." She was unable to maintain the banter when her insides were ready to burst.

He brushed a strand of hair from her face. "Years."

ABOUT ANNETTE LYON

Annette Lyon is a Whitney Award winner, a two-time recipient of Utah's Best in State medal for fiction, and a Silver Quill recipient from the League of Utah Writers, as well as a cum laude graduate from Brigham Young University with a degree in English. She writes historical fiction, romance, and women's fiction, and has also published several nonfiction titles, including a grammar guide and a coauthored book on being productive and reaching your goals. When she's not writing, editing, knitting, or eating chocolate, she can be found mothering and avoiding the spots on the kitchen floor.

Sign up for her newsletter at AnnetteLyon.com/contact
Find her online:
Website: AnnetteLyon.com
Blog: Blog.AnnetteLyon.com
Twitter: @AnnetteLyon
Facebook: Facebook.com/AnnetteLyon
Pinterest: Pinterest.com/AnnetteLyon

&

Lisa Mangum

OTHER WORKS BY LISA MANGUM

After Hello

The Hourglass Door Trilogy:

The Hourglass Door
The Golden Spiral
The Forgotten Locket

ONE

"Are you sticky yet?" Devon asked.

"Excuse me?" I looked up from the computer screen, but my fingers kept typing, finishing the last sentence of the last rejection letter I had to send today. *We wish you the best in finding the right home for your manuscript*—fifty rejection letters in thirty minutes; a personal best—*Sincerely, Baker Publishing House.*

Devon scrubbed his hair from his forehead, the ends spiked from the specially ordered coconut-scented gel he used. I wondered if he was still using the bottle I bought him for Christmas, or if he'd picked up another one from the Village by now. With the stuff costing $17.99 an ounce, I hoped he hadn't splurged and used it all at once.

"Sticky," he said again. He sighed and leaned against the doorjamb of my office. "I hate summer in Manhattan.

Everything is so . . . sticky." He examined his fingernails, his mouth turned down in distaste.

"Then leave," I said. My email alert chimed: fifteen new messages. I scanned the names. Nothing from Monica. Yet. But something was coming. It had to be. I'd been in charge of the office since Monday, and I couldn't imagine my boss not contacting me to see how the week had gone.

It had been an hour since I'd checked my phone, forty-four minutes since I'd checked my IM feed, and thirty-nine minutes since I'd checked my text messages. I wanted to believe the extended silence was a sign of her trust, but I couldn't shake the feeling of a shoe hovering nearby, waiting to drop.

"Are you even listening to me?" Devon sighed again.

"Yeah, yeah, Manhattan. Hot. Sticky. You hate it." I spun in my chair, neatly grabbing a red pen, a stack of paper, and my phone all with the same hand. "Have you heard from the Fergusons yet? Danielle said John was going to call back about some revisions—"

My chair swung and almost completed the circle, but stopped as Devon grabbed the armrests and leaned closer to me. I could smell the coconut hair gel and the citrus from his aftershave. Honestly, did the man think he was going to a tropical island somewhere?

With his skin tanned to the perfect caramel hue, he could have been.

"Lucy," he said, his voice low, his eyes intent on mine.

"Devon," I replied, setting the manuscript on my lap and leaning forward to close the distance between us. I couldn't help it. My crush on him had started last fall, during my first week at Baker, and when he asked me out for the first time, I nearly tripped over myself to say yes.

Almost before I knew it, Devon and I had become office

friends, then after-hours friends, then dating friends, then exclusive friends. In the beginning, we talked all the time, and we explored the city together.

And then Christmas happened. And *Unmarked* hit #1 on the *New York Times* list. And I got a promotion, which transformed my internship into a permanent position.

Starting the New Year, I'd thought my life couldn't get any better.

I was right. Somehow, as the year slid into summer, it'd gotten worse. Devon and I still dated, but it was different. He was still suave and professional, but we talked less, and he wasn't interested in exploring the city anymore. At times I felt his distance and wondered if I'd done something wrong. Other times, his arrogance was more than I could handle.

I suspected the expiration date on our relationship was inevitable, but I didn't want to be the one to make the first move to end it.

Still, when I felt his muscles beneath the pull of his shirt, his breath on the side of my neck, I wondered if maybe I was fooling myself. Maybe there was still something worth preserving here.

My office phone rang, and, grateful for the distraction, I shifted to answer it.

He countered my move, blocking access to the desk with his body. "Luce. Put your work away."

"I can't." The phone rang again, shrill and demanding. I glanced at the flashing red light.

"You can." Devon's voice dropped even lower, as though we were sharing a pillow together, or a secret. "I gave Everett the afternoon off—"

"What? He was supposed to show me his cover designs for *Highland Park* today—"

"—and Monica is in California on a business trip—"

"—Monica is probably the one calling—"

"And you are altogether too beautiful a woman to be locked inside a hot, *sticky* office like this on a Friday night. Let down your beautiful blonde hair for once, and let me show those exquisite brown eyes something special."

I swallowed, unable to stop the blush creeping into my cheeks. I curled my fingers tighter around the cell phone. I wavered, nearly succumbing to Devon's charm. But, no. Monica had left me in charge of the office. I needed to stay in charge. Which meant I needed to stay here.

But if I was in charge, why didn't I feel like it?

Devon slid his palms up the armrests, closing the distance between us even more.

I could see the line of his collarbone through the open neck of his shirt. The slight sheen of sweat only accentuated the curve of his body. "Come with me."

The phone stopped ringing, and the silence that remained sounded loud in my ears.

He leaned down, his nose brushing my cheek. His hand found mine and closed around my cell phone. He pulled it away from me the moment it buzzed with an incoming text.

"Come play with me tonight, Lucy," he breathed into the hollow behind my ear.

"Devon, don't." I hated how unsteady my voice sounded. "Give me back my phone."

He shook his head and dropped the phone on the side of my desk next to him. If I reached for it, I'd put myself closer to him. So sneaky. I was tired of his games. He seemed to be playing more of them lately, and they were starting to wear on my nerves.

The heat I'd felt building between us evaporated.

"Devon."

"Lucy," he countered. I could hear the smile in his voice. He thought he'd won. Again.

&

Two could play at this game.

I slipped my arms around his neck. Stretching up, I whispered in his ear, “Not tonight, honey, I have to get my work done.”

My cheek was pressed against his, so I felt the frown that crossed his face. His shoulders tightened, and he jerked back as though I’d burned him. Like a switch had been flipped, he went from charming to bitter. He pulled out of my embrace and glared down at me. “I was trying to be nice.”

I sighed and rolled my shoulders, trying to relieve some of the tension that seemed to accompany all of my conversations with Devon of late. “I know you don’t like it when I say no, but it’s just . . . Tonight isn’t good for me.” I took a deep breath. “I need some time—”

“You need a night out. But if you’d rather stay here . . .” His eyes swept my desk—buried under stacks of paper—with a look of disbelief.

“I’d rather get my work done so that when Monica returns, she’ll know she was right to trust me with the house in her absence.”

Devon gave a quiet laugh, mean and small. “I hate to tell you that you’re out of your depth, sweetheart, but you are. Don’t you know that?” He pointedly didn’t look at the flashing red light on my desk phone, or at my buzzing cell, dutifully collecting incoming messages, or at the stacks of colored Post-it Notes that littered my desk, half of which had my boss’s name scribbled on them. “Last year, you were her intern. Now you think, what? That you’re her heir?”

I folded my arms across my chest, protecting that hidden place where I stashed my fear. What if Devon was right? Was if I was still a nobody, pretending to be somebody? “I found *Unmarked* in the slush pile. That has to count for something.”

Devon shook his head. "You still don't get it." He backed away and paused at the door. "Monica publishes the books. Everett designs them. I sell them. You—do what you're told." He turned on his heel and left without a backward glance.

I listened until I heard the front door close and lock, and then I buried my face in my hands to muffle a scream.

Here I'd thought there might be something worth preserving with Devon. Guess I'd thought wrong.

It wasn't fair. I had worked hard, fought hard, to get the internship at Baker. I'd earned it. I'd wanted it more than anything I'd ever wanted before, and the first thing I did after getting my degree from NYU was to apply to every single publishing house I could find.

I'd told myself that I didn't mind the late nights, the long hours, the endless paperwork, the lack of recognition and praise, because, for me, it was all about the books. The chance to work with words was a chance I couldn't pass up.

And to have Devon, of all people, tell me that I wasn't good at my job just because I wasn't good at being his girlfriend?

I growled low in my throat and pushed my hands through my hair. The low afternoon sun pounded like a hammer against my back. When Monica first gave me this office, she warned me that a westward-facing window wasn't ideal. I didn't care; *I had a window office in a publishing house.* And I wasn't going to let a jerk like Devon intimidate me out of it.

My cell phone buzzed again, and I grabbed it, barking out a sharp, "Hello."

"Lucy?"

My heart spiked. *Why, oh why didn't I check the ID?*

"Yes. Hi, Monica. Sorry, yes, I'm here."

&

"You'll have to speak up. We finally boarded Whittaker's yacht, but I'm afraid the reception here is spotty at best. We've been going over ideas for his next project; several show promise."

I could hear the snapping wind and the purr of a powerful engine in the background.

"How is California?" I asked.

"Bottled—the water and the blondes."

"And Whittaker?"

"Effervescent with an undertone of malaise."

I smiled. That was one of the reasons I loved working for Monica Baker: She had impeccable taste in vocabulary.

"And how is his yacht?"

Monica huffed a sigh—*overindulgent*—and I could imagine the specific way she would twist her wrist. Sometimes my boss didn't need to use any words at all to say what was on her mind.

"I have the revisions on Whittaker's contract for his next book ready for you to review when you return," I reported. "And I've prepped the press release and left messages with—"

"Yes, yes," Monica interrupted, "I'm sure your work will be sufficient. I need you to spearhead another project for me, however."

Grabbing a pen, I uncapped it with my teeth and dropped the lid on my desk. I flipped over the closest piece of paper—*Falling into Deep Water*, page 256—and scratched circles with the pen until the ink started to flow.

"What do you need help with?"

"I need some wedding invitations printed."

I raised my eyebrows in surprise. Monica wasn't dating anyone, as far as I knew. Then again, we weren't exactly the sleepover-and-paint-our-fingernails-together kind of friends.

"And who is the lucky bride?" I asked, a hint of a smile in my voice.

"Why, you are, my dear. The invitations are for you."

TWO

My pen stopped.

Ice filled my fingers, the cold spreading through me and across my back like wings. I pulled the phone away from my ear to make sure it was working properly. "I'm sorry. I think you're breaking up. I thought you said—"

"The invitations are for you," Monica repeated, unruffled by my confusion.

"But . . . but I'm not . . . I mean I'm not engaged—" My dry mouth wasn't helping me stammer out the words. I tried to laugh, but only managed a noise that sounded like a cough. I deliberately didn't look at the wall separating my office from Devon's.

"Of course you're not. The invitations are part of the celebration party I've planned for the success of *Unmarked.* And you, as the one who found that prized diamond, will be attending, of course. Consider yourself the maid of honor, so to speak."

The chill freezing my veins transformed into light, filling me with joy. I gripped my pen tighter in a hand that trembled.

Monica didn't notice my silence. "Draft up copy for the invitations. I've scheduled the reception"—I could hear the quote marks in her voice and knew she meant "party"—"for two weeks from today at the Terrace Ballroom at the Roosevelt. I'll be back in the office by then. Print a hundred and fifty invitations on the company account at Kinko's and send them to everyone on our Gold List. Guest plus one."

"Of course," I whispered, scribbling as fast as I could. "I'm happy to. I know exactly what to do. Anything else?"

But the line had disconnected. I held my phone for a moment, staring at the screen.

This was it—what I'd been dreaming of from the moment I read the first page of *Unmarked* last year, the moment I knew—just *knew*—that I'd found something special. Something that would change my life.

I clicked my phone off and dropped it on my desk. I held page 256 of *Falling into Deep Water* with both hands, cradling it as if it were made of gold.

A laugh bubbled up in my throat, and I let it out with abandon.

I spun my chair toward the filing cabinet. Pulling out a drawer, I maneuvered my way past stacks of old manuscripts, dog-eared and festooned with sticky tabs, until I found my prize.

The original draft of *Unmarked*. The author, Whittaker Jules, had bucked tradition and mailed us a hard copy of the manuscript. Devon would have sent it back unopened, but one day, I started reading it at lunch. I finished it that evening, and it was on Monica's desk the next morning. That was the beginning of everything.

The stack of paper I held in my hands was proof of the journey I'd taken through its pages, the dawning realization that the story Whittaker had written was elegant and timeless and *perfect.* Reading his book had been like falling in love—instantaneous and complete.

And now thousands had fallen in love with the characters and story too. Countless top-ten lists. Enough starred reviews to light up the night sky. Praise from readers all over the world. Nearly six months at #1 on the *Times* list.

I held the pages to my nose and inhaled deeply. This . . . *this* was what I loved best about my job.

I set the manuscript on the edge of my desk in a place of honor and then opened a blank document marked with the company logo and letterhead at the top.

Baker Publishing House formally requests the pleasure of your company at a reception honoring the enduring love of Violet Stevenson and Chester Hammond . . .

It was nearly midnight by the time I finished. I'd gone through a dozen drafts before settling on the exact wording I wanted.

Leaning back in my chair, I stretched my arms above my head and rolled my shoulders. My eyes burned from staring at the computer screen for too long. Hunger rumbled through my stomach.

I printed off the final draft and closed my eyes while the soft hum of the printer filled the room. Did it get any better than this?

Sighing with satisfaction, I checked my inbox one last time—a handful of emails from Monica, but nothing about *Unmarked.* I scanned the other subject lines, grateful that nothing jumped out as urgent. Then I noticed an email from my mother.

I clicked on the note and read the short message.

Why aren't you answering your phone? Call me. We should do lunch tomorrow. It's been forever since I've seen you.

"I saw you last Sunday, Mom," I sighed. Glancing at my phone, I saw a hard red line slashed through the battery icon. *Thank goodness for small miracles,* I thought, then immediately shook my head. It wasn't fair of me to avoid my mom just because she was getting remarried.

But the small, lonely part of me thought it also wasn't fair that she was on her second marriage before I'd even found my first.

I'd been overlooked before. When a girl is average height, average weight, average everything, that tended to happen. Growing up, it didn't bother me—in books, no one cared how I looked—and even after my height inched higher than average, and my weight hovered just below, I still thought of myself as average. Was it too much to ask that just once, I would be first in someone's life? *I* wanted to be the undiscovered diamond.

Always the bridesmaid, never the bride.

There was a time when I thought Devon and I might—

No. I pushed the thought straight out of my mind. Not Devon.

The satisfaction I'd felt from a good day's work faded, and I frowned. I replied to Mom's email.

Lunch would be nice. Tomorrow, 12:30 at Josi's Diner?

I shut down my computer and turned off the monitor.

&

Gathering my purse, my phone, and the printout of the wedding invitation, I headed out of the office.

When I hit the sidewalk, the ever-present energy and heat of the city met me, and I relaxed, letting the buzz surround me. As much as I loved my office, I loved the raw, wild life of the city more. I loved sliding into the flow of people streaming up and down the sidewalks, weaving through the obstacle course of endless construction, avoiding plumes of steam from street vents, and feeling the rumble of the subway underfoot. I loved darting across streets, dodging cabs that might slow down—or might not. I loved how safe I felt in the shadows of the tall buildings towering over me.

I'd never lived anywhere else—and I never would.

I turned the corner, aiming for the 24-hour Kinko's where Baker Publishing House had a standing account. I'd need a fast turnaround for the invitations if I was going to meet Monica's deadline and pull off this party without a hitch.

Yes, I could have emailed the file to the store and picked them up in the morning, but this was for Violet. If I was to be her maid of honor, I wanted to do it right. I felt like I owed it to her to deliver them by hand.

Reaching the store, I pulled on the handle and heard the distinctive clank of a locked deadbolt hitting a metal frame. It was only then that I noticed the dark windows, the closed curtains, and the large sign: *Closed for Remodel. Will Reopen Soon.*

Soon? What? No, I needed it to be open *now*. I didn't dare drop the ball on this reception. If I did, the part of me that felt insecure at work might never go away. I heard Devon's voice in my head again: *You—do what you're told.*

That wasn't true—I knew it wasn't—but tonight, after a long day at work and a missed lunch and dinner, it *felt* the tiniest bit true.

Trust yourself, sweet pea. Grandpa's gruff whisper filled my memory. It had been more than a year since he'd passed, but I still missed him. *You can always find a way to add an "and" to your day.*

I shifted my purse on my shoulder. I didn't need this Kinko's to get the job done. This was Manhattan, for crying out loud. There were probably a hundred Kinko's within walking distance. I could figure this out. All I had to do was add an "and" to my problem to see where the solution would take me.

The store is closed, but I need invitations printed right away . . . and . . .

I looked up and down the street at the storefronts closest to me. A grocery stand. A mom-and-pop Mexican restaurant. Two single, unmarked doorways—one black, one blue. A travel agency. A Starbucks.

Hesitating on the familiar coffee-shop logo, I slid my gaze back a few stops. The black door clearly guarded the entrance to an apartment complex building above me, but the blue door next to it was wedged into a space so narrow that it was practically an alleyway.

. . . and what have we here?

Even after midnight, people were scattered along the sidewalk, and a few couples were finishing drinks and cigarettes at café tables in front of the Mexican restaurant.

Approaching the blue door, I saw a sign in the window, a small square of creamy cardstock with bold, black lettering.

THIS IS A PRINTING OFFICE

Crossroads of civilization

Refuge of all the arts against the ravages of time

Armory of fearless truth against whispering rumor

Incessant trumpet of trade

&

From this place words may fly abroad
Not to perish on waves of sound
Not to vary with the Writer's hand
But fixed in time
Having been verified by proof
Friend, you stand on sacred ground
This is a printing office
—Beatrice L. Warde

My breath caught, my senses tingling. Could it be? How did I not know about this place?

A voice in the back of my head, which sounded like Devon, said, *Because you never stray from your path. If you're sent to Kinko's, you go to Kinko's.*

I stepped back and scanned the blue doorway, looking for a business sign, or even—hope against hope—an open sign.

I couldn't see a shop name anywhere on the door, but at eye level was a wooden ampersand symbol.

Were there supposed to be names on either side of the symbol? Perhaps they'd fallen off. No matter. Below the symbol, but above the printing office sign, was a clock face with two black eyes and a smiling mouth from which the words "Yes, we're open!" floated in a bubble.

That was all I needed.

Oh, Grandpa. I smiled at the unexpected synchronicity. *Thank you.*

THREE

The building was barely larger than my apartment. The room was nearly square, with a dark brown countertop across the front that had a hinged wing on the left-hand side. I counted four bookcases stuffed to the edges with paperback novels. Two vinyl chairs flanked the door.

Hanging on the back wall were framed fragments of paper of various sizes, covered with words in all kinds of fonts, styles, and colors, like a menu board at a restaurant, but here, you ordered words.

The shop felt crowded, but cozy. Worn along the edges, but comfortable and well-cared for. The temperature was a sweltering ten degrees hotter inside than on the street, but I didn't mind. Whoever had hung that sign in the window and owned this place was someone I wanted to meet.

"Hello?" I called to the empty room. "Are you open?"

&

A strange, creaking wheeze emanated from somewhere in the back of the shop. I heard a thunk and a bang. A crack in the back of the wall appeared, revealing a previously hidden door.

"Hello?" I asked again as the door swung open and a man emerged from the back room.

He carried a tray of small metal cubes, which he almost dropped when he saw me. "Whoa, what are you doing here?"

His voice was dark and deep—smoky, like his eyes. Black hair brushed back from his forehead hung nearly to his shoulders, and his five o'clock shadow was closer to seven o'clock this late at night. He filled the small space as if he belonged there.

He set the tray on the counter and dusted off his hands. "We're closed."

"I'm sorry," I stammered, pleasantly distracted by the sight of his muscled arms and chest, covered only by a T-shirt and a brown leather apron. "The sign said you were open?"

He glanced past me to the door, then briefly closed his eyes with a sigh. "Seriously, Pops? Again?" he muttered. He jerked his chin toward the door. "Would you mind?" he asked me. Then he turned his attention to sorting through the chunks of metal on his tray.

I knew a dismissal when I heard one. I looked from him to the door, considering my options. Leaving wasn't one of them. Not now. "Listen, I'm sorry for coming in so late, but I really need your help. I have this invitation and—"

He held up one hand without looking at me, pointing at the door.

"You don't understand. I'm not leaving," I said, clutching my purse and my invitation like a sword and a shield.

He paused in his sorting and frowned at me. "Why would you leave?"

I hesitated, confused. "Because you're closed?"

His frown turned into a half-smile. "Yeah, but we were open when you came in. That makes you my last customer of the night." He glanced at the chunky silver watch on his tanned wrist, and his half-smile turned into a full grin. "Or my first customer of the day. Either way, could you flip the sign for me? Pops always forgets on his way out. I'd hate to have anyone else wander in; shop's a little small for a crowd." The grin reached his eyes, lighting them up.

Relieved, I reached back and flipped the sign to *Closed.* "Only in New York," I murmured. Yet another reason why I loved this city: You could run into an eccentrically helpful person at midnight, and it was not a big deal.

When I turned around, the shopkeeper had his hand extended for me to shake.

"Name's Jesse."

"Lucy." I shook his hand, feeling the smooth callouses on his fingers and the heel of his palm. These were the marks of a man who didn't mind hard work. So different from Devon's hands.

"Nice to meet you, Lucy," he said with a warm smile. "How may I help you today?"

Someone had raised this boy with manners, I thought with appreciation. "I need some wedding invitations, and—"

"Ah!" Jesse interrupted, clapping his hands together once. "My specialty."

So much for his impeccable manners.

"First, tell me about the bride," he continued, brisk and efficient. "What's she like?"

"They're not for me," I clarified quickly. I didn't want Jesse getting the wrong idea. *And what idea is that?* I asked myself. *That you're available?* Was I available? Did I want to be?

"Even better." He grinned, but not in a creepy, I'm-going-to-follow-you-home sort of way. More like as if I'd said my favorite ice cream flavor was butter pecan, and—happy surprise—it was his favorite too.

"You're the maid of honor?" he asked.

"Something like that." I held out my draft of the invitation. "If you could just print this—"

Jesse took the paper and set it aside without looking at it. "We'll get to the words in a minute. Tell me about the bride and groom. How did they meet? How did *you* meet them?"

"Why does it matter?" I asked.

Jesse straightened to his full height. He was *tall.* Taller than I was; probably even taller than Devon. "Because love is an art. And invitations extended to celebrate that love should be a work of art as well. And to understand art, you must first understand the artist. If I know about the bride and groom, I'll know the perfect font for their invitations."

I blinked. Jesse looked like an athlete with his broad shoulders and powerful frame. Could there be the heart of a poet beneath all that muscle?

He might have blushed under my gaze; between his stubble and the shadows, it was hard to tell. "Sorry. Sometimes I get carried away." He offered up an explanation with a half-shrug. "Words are my business."

"Mine, too," I said.

Serious intrigue filled his expression. He pushed aside the tray, the metal bits shaking and rattling, and leaned closer to me. "Writer?" he guessed.

I shook my head. "Publisher." It was almost the truth. For a couple more weeks, at least. Then I'd go back to being Monica's intern-turned-assistant.

Jesse whistled low. “A kindred spirit. Which house?”

“Baker. We’re just down the road from you.” I waved in the general direction of my office. “But I haven’t seen your shop before.”

Jesse shrugged and looked around the space. “We moved in a couple of weeks ago. Still shaking the dust off our boots. How many titles do you publish?”

“Thirteen a year.”

His laugh filled the room. “Baker’s dozen. I like it.”

“We’re a small house, but we pride ourselves on being exclusive. Only the best of the best make it at Baker’s.”

His eyes met mine, held them steady. “I can see that.”

Now it was my turn to blush. And the heat I felt moving up my neck wasn’t all from the summer temperature. How long had it been since Devon had looked at me with such genuine interest?

I cleared my throat. “About the invitations . . . It’s to celebrate one of our books. Maybe you’ve heard of it—*Unmarked*?” I felt like a proud parent. Everyone had heard of my book.

Recognition arrived right on cue. “That’s yours?” Jesse asked, whistling below his breath. “Congratulations.”

“Thanks. Did you like it?”

“Haven’t read it yet,” he confessed, scratching his cheek. He nodded to the nearest bookcase. “Still working through my current list.”

Scanning the spine-out titles, I saw everything from pulpy mystery novels to autobiographies to graphic novels to YA novels to cookbooks. History. Religion. Science. Classic novels for both children and adults. A well-worn and dog-eared edition of my favorite book, *A Wrinkle in Time,* rested in easy reach.

Jealousy and admiration vied for my attention.

&

A hot guy who read—no, *devoured*—books like I did? Devon and I never talked about books. He said he didn't like to bring work home with him, but I wondered if there was another reason.

I touched one corner of the paper, which was still face down on the counter, and pushed it toward Jesse. "Well, see, the bride's name is Violet. And when she met Chester, it was love at first sight."

Jesse stopped the paper with a single touch. His fingers were long, delicate but strong—the hands of a practicing pianist, a working artist. He hadn't stopped looking at me; I found I didn't mind in the least. There was something in his eyes, though, an emotion or expression I couldn't quite identify.

"Cool," he said reverently. "Tell me the rest of the story."

FOUR

"So the book ends with Violet as an old woman standing over Chester's grave, surrounded by their children and grandchildren, and all their friends—everyone who ever loved them, which was practically everyone, and she says—"

"No, don't tell me." Jesse held up a hand. "I don't want to know."

I blinked, sitting up straighter on the vinyl chair I'd pulled closer to the counter. "But it's the best bit of the whole book."

"It's also the last bit of the whole book. I want to be surprised when I read it."

"But I've told you everything else. There are no surprises left."

"Except the ending. Endings should always be a surprise. That's part of what makes the journey so much fun."

&

I grinned and raised my nearly empty water bottle in a toast. “As you wish.” I drank the last swallow. “Can I get another one?”

“At this hour? Will you be safe to drive home?” Jesse teased.

“Ha-ha,” I said. “For your information, officer, I don’t drive, so that’s not a problem. And it’s just water. I can stop anytime I want.”

Jesse laughed, a rumble like distant summer thunder. I liked the sound of it, and the way it rolled through me.

“What time is it, anyway?” I asked, standing up and stretching. I’d settled into the chair around chapter four, kicked off my heels at chapter six, and polished off a sleeve of Ritz crackers that Jesse had found in the back by chapter eleven. It was a good thing *Unmarked* only had a dozen chapters.

Jesse checked his watch. “Five minutes to three.”

“Seriously?” I reached across the counter and grabbed his wrist. “How is that possible?”

“Well, you see, whenever the little hand moves past twelve, the big hand—”

I smacked his forearm, which only made him laugh harder.

“It’s fine. I’m almost done, anyway.” He stepped aside to reveal what he’d been working on for the past couple of hours as I talked.

A beautiful wooden tray rested in front of him on the counter, the edges worn smooth from constant handling and care. Narrow rows were marked out from top to bottom, some thin, some thick, and resting on each row were individual blocks of metal, each one engraved with a letter, a number, or a symbol.

The words were exactly what I had written out for the invitation, but in reverse.

"Impressive," I said, leaning closer to the tray of type. "You do this all the time?"

Jesse shook his head, his hair slicked back with sweat. "Only for special occasions. Mostly it's a hobby, now. Pops taught me how to set type when I was a kid. There's not much call for hand-pressed materials these days, but still . . . I like to design the fonts and make the punches. The press in the back is vintage; still works even though it's ancient. Dad prefers the computer, which is good, because it keeps the business running." He ran his hand over the type, his mouth softening in a smile. "But this . . . this is . . ."

"Art," I whispered. "Magic." I reached out and touched the hard point of the V that started Violet's name.

Jesse traced the curved back of Chester's name. "Exactly."

I resisted the urge to lean my head against Jesse's shoulder. I'd only just met him, but he was a poet, an artist, and a booklover, like me. He made me laugh, easily and with abandon. He listened to me as if he had all the time in the world. So much about him made me feel comfortable.

I hadn't realized how much I *hadn't* felt that way with Devon lately.

Devon was polish and shine; Jesse was earth and wind.

I shook my head at the overly poetic thought.

Maybe it's the fact that he's rocking the tall, dark, and handsome look hard. Or maybe all that water has gone to my head after all, I thought, amused.

"Lucy?"

I got the impression Jesse had said my name more than once.

I blinked, the day's excitement and exhaustion finally catching up to me. "Yeah?"

&

"Are you okay?"

I nodded, but what I said was, "I'm really tired."

He smiled at me. "I can tell. Let me call you a cab."

"Nah," I said. "I'll just go back to my office. It's close enough. And then I can pick up the invites as soon as they're done."

"You're sure?" Jesse asked.

I shrugged. "Wouldn't be the first time I spent a weekend at the office." Inwardly I smiled at his concern. Sometimes it was nice to be fussed over, even by someone you'd just met.

"Must be some book," he said, shaking his head, "to have you go to all this trouble."

"It is," I replied. "It's the best." Before I could stop myself, I trailed my fingernail along the length of his forearm, lightly resting my hand over his. "But the best is always worth the trouble."

Jesse returned my flirty smile with one of his own and nodded. "Isn't that the truth."

A half hour later, I crawled onto the couch in Monica's office, grateful for the lush cushions that cradled me.

What a strange day. My thoughts swirled around Devon, *Unmarked,* and Jesse, until they mixed together into a blend of desire and surprise. Lately, being with Devon had been like nibbling at a hangnail—irritating and hard to ignore. You knew you shouldn't do it, but you did it anyway because it's what you'd always done.

Being with Jesse tonight, though, had been like pushing off on smooth ice. Cool, easy, but with a hint of danger that you might fall off the narrow blade beneath your feet.

I could fall for Jesse if I let myself. I'd already started. What was I thinking, touching his arm like that? Who was that girl, flirting with a stranger after midnight?

Actually, I thought, dreamily, *that would make a great romance novel title: Flirting with a Midnight Stranger.*

I could see the cover now: A navy-blue sky dotted with stars and crowned with a full moon. A swarthy hunk of a man would be holding a swooning woman in his arms. And yeah, so what if the hero looked a little like Jesse? I could swoon with the best of them.

Giggling to myself, I pulled the throw blanket off the back of the couch and up to my chest. I reached up and twisted open the blinds. The hard angles of the neighboring buildings sliced what little sections I could see of the sky into smaller bits and pieces. The stars were nearly invisible, washed out by the electric glow that rose from the streets like mist.

I didn't mind. This was my wilderness, a countryside I understood. Listening to the endless murmur of traffic below, I counted the lit windows from the buildings as if they were stars until I fell asleep.

FIVE

Sun on my face warmed me awake. Feeling deliciously comfortable, I yawned and stretched from my fingers to my toes. The large clock on the wall ticked another minute closer to noon. I'd slept the morning away.

Why hadn't my alarm sounded? I reached for my phone, its black screen reminding me of the dead battery.

A fragment of memory floated through my mind. I was supposed to do something today. *Pick up invitations. Yes, but there was something else . . .*

I sat upright on the couch, the blanket sliding unnoticed to the floor.

Lunch with my mother.

At 12:30.

Across town.

I'd never make it. And then I'd never hear the end of it.

I pressed my hand to my head. So not how I wanted to start my Saturday.

Padding across the hall to my office, I rummaged on my desk for my extra phone charger, waiting for the screen to flicker to life before I made the call.

My mother answered on the first ring.

"You're not coming," she said by way of greeting.

Guilt stabbed through me. "I'm sorry, Mom. I overslept. I'm at the office and—"

"And you have too much work to do," she finished. "No, no. I understand. It's fine. I don't mind eating alone."

I bit back a sigh. "It's not like that. I planned to have lunch with you, but it's not going to work out today. What about next week?"

"I have plans for next Saturday. With Lydia and Carl." Silence filled the line between us. "It's fine," she repeated in an airy tone that still cut. "This way you can spend the day with Devon, which is what I know you'd rather do."

I groaned. I'd been meaning to have this conversation with her for a while now, but there'd never been a good time. And since I didn't think there *would* be a better time coming up, a bad time like this would work just as well.

"I don't think it's going to work out with me and Devon," I said.

She gasped. "Did you get fired? Why didn't you tell me? I warned you that inter-office romances were a bad idea."

"No, Mom, I didn't get fired. I just . . . I feel like maybe Devon and I should see other people."

That was putting the best spin on it. I hadn't told Devon how I felt because he was the kind of man who wanted to do the leaving, not be the one who was left.

"Are you seeing someone else?"

"No." Last night's memory of Jesse's dark hair and

&

Let's see: I didn't go out with Devon last night, and then he finds me alone with another guy? No wonder his face had hardened with disapproval. What a mess. I sighed. I was tired of disappointing Devon, tired of disappointing my mother, tired of worrying about what Monica might want or think or need from me. I wanted to get away from work for a bit.

"*We* were just leaving," I said, picking up the box, my purse, and my phone. I looped my arm around Jesse's and headed for the main door. "Remember to lock up when you leave, darling. I'd hate to have to report your laxness to Monica."

Devon's mouth thinned, and I felt the heat of his glare even after the door closed behind me.

"Did you just use me to get back at a guy?" Jesse asked with a chuckle.

"That obvious?"

"I'm a self-professed student of all languages, both spoken and unspoken." He paused. "Plus, I've seen that same look from other guys when a girl was stolen away."

"I can't imagine any girl wanting to be stolen away from you," I said. *Oh, please,* I chided myself. What was it about this guy that made me say whatever was on my mind?

Jesse's smoky eyes met mine, and he tucked my hand more securely around his arm. "Who said the other guys were the ones doing the stealing? Now, I believe there was some discussion about lunch . . ."

SIX

"Where would you like to go?" Jesse asked as we exited the post office and headed down the sidewalk.

The invitations were safely stamped, mailed, and on their way to the members of our Gold List, and the last of my work commitments were done for the day.

The summer sun had already moved past hot and had tipped toward broiling. The air smelled of exhaust and metal and people and sweat and trash and flowers and urgency. Horns honked and a siren sounded nearby; a second siren picked up the call, echoing a few streets away. The sensory overload was both familiar and intoxicating.

"My treat, my pick," I said. I was on the arm of a hot guy, strolling through the best city in the world. No pressure, no plans beyond lunch. I felt like a truant, and it made me smile. "And I know exactly where we should go."

&

I nudged his shoulder with mine, relishing the sensation of hitting hard muscle under his shirt, and directed him where I wanted to go: the corner of 5th and 40th.

Jesse looked up at the gorgeous stone building on the corner. Lions kept watch over the stairs, which led to a trio of arched entryways.

"Ah, the library." His deep voice held more satisfaction than confusion.

"Actually, we're going to Bryant Park, behind the library. The grill has excellent rooftop views, and their brunch menu is to die for."

"Best Eggs Benedict on the block," Jesse said.

I tilted a look in his direction.

"What? Don't I look like a man who enjoys brunch?"

I think you look like a man who enjoys everything he touches, I thought, grateful that, for once, I was able to keep my thoughts to myself. But that didn't stop a tremor of excitement from snaking through my veins.

"There is one small problem, though," Jesse said with a downward turn of his lips.

It wasn't fair that his frown was as sexy as his smile.

"Our deal was for lunch. *This* is brunch. Totally different meal."

I tightened my grip on his arm as we neared the restaurant. "Rain check?"

He grinned and held the door open for me.

The Eggs Benedict were every bit as good as Jesse had promised they would be. And the view from the garden rooftop was every bit as relaxing as I remembered it being.

Jesse leaned back in his chair, sipping a cup of coffee. A breeze kicked up and ruffled his dark hair. He stretched out his legs.

I scraped the edge of my spoon around the rim of my sorbet glass, savoring the tropical flavors.

"Dessert after brunch. I approve," Jesse said, setting down his cup and picking up a cookie from the small plate.

"Please tell me you didn't work all night on those invitations," I said. "I'd feel bad knowing you had a sleepless night on my account."

Jesse shrugged. "I was up anyway. Night owl."

"So your dad runs the store during the day, and you watch over it at night? And the ampersand on the door is part of a sign that's supposed to read something like 'Dad and Son Family Printing Business'?"

He laughed. "No, the sign is exactly what I intended it to be."

"The name of your shop is 'Ampersand'?" I flipped my spoon upside down and slid more melting sorbet onto my tongue.

"Technically it's 'And.' Most people don't know the proper terminology."

I raised my eyebrows. "Showoff."

"You knew what it meant."

"I'm in words, remember?"

He leaned forward, a playful look in his eye. "Prove it."

I twirled my spoon between my fingers and leaned over the small table. "What did you have in mind?"

"Definitions. I stump you, you have dinner with me tomorrow night."

"Bold." My heart decided to pick up its pace. "And if I stump you?"

"You won't."

&

"Even bolder." I smiled sweetly, but with enough bite that he'd know I was ready to play. "But let's just say you lose . . . What's in it for me?"

"What do you want?" He kept his gaze level with mine.

My sorbet melted in the heat.

"Something more than dinner, that's for sure."

"Deal," he said before I could elaborate on the specifics. "Ubiquitous."

I huffed. "Please. Ubiquitous, u-b-i-q-u-i-t-o-u-s. It means existing everywhere at once." I shrugged a shoulder and took another bite of sorbet. "Junior high spelling bee champion two years in a row. Defenestration."

Appreciation lit a spark in Jesse's eyes, and he scratched at the stubble along his jaw with one hand. "Throwing a person out of a window. I love that it's apparently happened enough that a word had to be invented to describe it. Serendipitous."

"Finding something valuable that you weren't necessarily looking for." *Like today.* I stole one of the cookies off his plate. "Lasciviousness."

"Who taught you such a dirty word?" he teased. "It means being filled with desire—as I'm sure you know. Sesquipedalian."

I laughed. "You made that up!"

Jesse stole the cookie from my fingers, crunching it in one bite. "And that, my friends, is the sound of you admitting defeat."

"Never. Give me a minute." I turned the word over in my head, thinking out loud. "*Sesqui* could be a hundred and fifty. And *ped* is *foot.*" I bit my lower lip, ready to hazard a guess but unsure if I still wanted to win. Dinner with Jesse sounded like a worthy prize. "Something with a hundred and fifty feet?"

I knew it was wrong even before Jesse's mouth split in a grin. Shaking my head, I scooped the last of the sorbet into the hollow of my spoon. I raised it in a toast. "I surrender. Now tell me what it means."

"Sesquipedalian: characterized by the use of long words."

This time Jesse joined my laughter, and we made so much noise that the couple at the next table gave us disapproving frowns.

We laughed all the way to the green lawn of the park. Collapsing on a bench in the shade of the library, I kicked off my shoes and buried my toes in the grass.

"So why 'And'?" I asked. "What does it mean?"

"No wonder you lost at Definitions if you don't know what *and* means."

I smacked him on the leg. "I'll win next time." Would there be a next time? Without a doubt. In a single afternoon, Jesse had managed to secure a future lunch *and* dinner date with me. It felt nice to be desired. To feel like I mattered to someone.

Devon had liked being with me, but I suspected that he liked being *seen* with me more. He liked the idea of being with a tall, blonde woman who complemented his suave style and polished charm. I wasn't interested in that scenario anymore; I wanted to be the one who was seen, the one who was wanted.

Jesse reached his arm around the back of the bench. Not quite close enough to touch me, but close enough that I knew he was there. "Calvin and Hobbes. Laurel and Hardy. Ben and Jerry's." He held up a finger for each duo.

I matched his move. "Sonny and Cher. Romeo and Juliet. Peanut butter and jelly. What are we playing now?"

"What do they have in common?"

"They're pairs. You usually don't think of one without thinking of the other. Adam and Eve. Bonnie and Clyde. David and Goliath. I've got a million of them."

"I'll bet you do." Jesse suppressed a chuckle. "It's the *and* that makes them a unit, a team. What would Sherlock be without Watson? Batman without Robin?"

"Personally, I think Batman is better *without* Robin, but go on."

"The *and* makes them inseparable."

I rested against the back of the bench, feeling the solid pressure of his arm around my shoulders.

"There's even more to it than that, though." Jesse fell silent for a moment, his eyes searching the faraway clouds as though he could see letters in the wispy threads. "When my dad proposed to my mom, he said she cried so hard that she couldn't say anything for two whole minutes. There he was, down on one knee, ring in hand, having just asked her to marry him, and she's incoherent. So Dad looks up at her and says, 'And?' You know, prompting her for an answer. And she says, 'Yes.'

"Mom's been gone a dozen years now, but I named the shop in her honor. To me, the symbol on the door means togetherness. Completeness. The joining of two halves into a whole. Inseparable." He looked down at his hand resting on his thigh. "It means *yes.*"

"My grandfather believed something similar. 'Look for the good, sweet pea,' he used to tell me all the time. 'Add something positive to your life every day.' Then he'd draw an ampersand on my hand." Drawing on my leg, I made a sweeping swirl with my finger: up, around, down, loop, and hook. "It was our own secret symbol."

"He sounds like a good man."

"The best." I paused. "Is that why you helped me last

night? Because you like to say yes?" I asked quietly. Our flirting had mellowed into something more intimate.

When he looked at me, another shiver spiked through me. "I think I could get used to saying yes to a girl like you."

Another breeze blew through us, carrying with it the never-ending sounds of life moving in fast motion. But for that moment, I felt the world narrow down to just me and Jesse.

He held out his hand to me, and I took it without hesitation.

&

"Damn right I was. And it's a good thing, too. Do you know what Monica would have done to you if you had actually gone through with this insanity?"

I looked up at Devon, feeling fire in my eyes. "I know what she did the last time I championed a book."

Devon shook his head. "When are you going to realize the truth? *Unmarked* wasn't your victory. Monica was the one who made the decision. If she hadn't liked it, it wouldn't have been published."

Stepping away from Devon, I set the paper on the table by the couch. "She liked it because she read it. And she read it because *I* gave it to her. Tell me, Devon, have *you* read it yet?"

He clamped down on his jaw. "That's beside the point."

"No, it *is* the point. You're in sales. How can you sell something if you don't even know what it is?"

"Books are books. They're widgets. I can sell one as easily as another."

I blew out my breath, frustrated, and ran my hands through my hair. "Why are you really here, Devon? Surely you didn't come all this way to pick an old fight about our differing views on books."

He stepped towards me, his energy suddenly shifting from anger to something less confrontational, but still dangerous. I eyed him warily.

"Luce." He lowered his voice, but his stance remained tense, coiled. "My Lucy."

"What?" I crossed my arms, squaring my shoulders and trying to look as imposing as I could. I wished I were back in my business suit instead of yoga pants and a faded T-shirt.

"You're right," he said softly. "I didn't come here to talk about books, or Posey what's-her-name, or any of it. I came because . . . when I saw you with that guy, I realized something. I still care about you."

"You have a funny way of showing it."

He reached out to touch my hair, but I moved away. "Look, I know I haven't been the best boyfriend lately. And I'm sorry I stormed in here—I could have handled that better—but you've got to see that going down this path will bring you nothing but trouble."

"Which path is that? The one where I find another book, or the one where I find another *guy*?"

"You're not going to find another guy, Lucy." He scoffed as if the idea were absurd. "You belong with me. We're a team."

I rubbed my thumb across my fingers, remembering all the pairs I had rattled off with Jesse. That was the root of the problem. I'd never felt a part of the "Lucy and Devon" team. I had been his girlfriend, but he hadn't necessarily been my boyfriend. I curled my hand into a fist and narrowed my eyes, unsure how to respond.

"I'm trying to look out for you. Help you. It's important to stay on Monica's good side, you know that, right?"

"I'm just trying to do my job."

A muscle tightened along Devon's jaw. The glare in his eyes sharpened to a point. "It's like you're not even listening to me."

I stilled. Actually, I was hearing him clearly for the first time. How had I never seen this side of him before? All of those weeks and months when the only talk in the office was about *Unmarked* and then about my promotion. Those were the same weeks and months our relationship had started to flounder, then falter.

Until today, when we clearly reached the breaking point.

"Oh, I see," I said softly. "That's what this is about. What it's always been about. You wanted my job."

&

A wall went up between us. Devon crossed his arms and took a step back.

"But why?" I asked, baffled. "You don't even like to read."

He blew out an irritated breath and turned away. "It's not rocket science. You pick the good ones and reject the bad ones."

Now it was my turn to laugh. "There is so much more to it than that. No," I said, following my thoughts out loud, "it wasn't the job. It was the *promotion.* The reward. You wanted the recognition."

"Five years," he said. "I've been there five years, and some fresh-outta-college intern swoops in and—" He shook his head and wouldn't look at me. "You were an *intern.* You were supposed to be in and out, three months, tops. You weren't supposed to stay. It's not like those kinds of jobs open up all the time. Yeah, I wanted the salary. So what? Does that make me the bad guy? We all worked on that damn book, but only you got the reward."

"And you thought that dating the new girl—the girl who had the boss's favor—would put you in the limelight? Is that all I was to you? A stepping-stone for your own career? Even now, you're here only so that when I find the next million-dollar book, you can catch some of the glory."

I felt deep, bone-searing anger. But I also knew exactly how he felt. Too many times *I* had felt adrift in a sea of people, struggling with everyone else, trying to stand out, to be noticed, to be chosen. When Monica offered me the job, I swore the heavens opened and a shaft of light had beamed down on me.

But knowing how Devon felt didn't mean I approved of what he'd done. It wasn't right to use a person's heart to get what you wanted. A person's heart was sacred and special. I hated myself that I'd ever given any part of mine to someone who didn't appreciate it.

Devon said nothing, but his silence told me I was right. He looked me up and down, as if trying to decide if I had been worth it. After a moment, he shook his head, gave a half-laugh, and picked up the page from *Falling into Deep Water,* crumpling it in his fist. "First rule of publishing: They can't all be winners."

Pain stabbed my heart. How had I ever found him attractive? I shuddered at my own bad judgment. There was no *and* to be had with Devon. No teamwork or togetherness. No positive additions to be made. He wasn't interested in any kind of *yes* unless it furthered his own career.

"Get out."

"Gladly." He flashed me a winter-cold smile. "See you Monday."

I rubbed my hands over my arms as though I could wash away Devon's lingering presence. The nerve of the man. The ugliness in his soul. Thinking back to those evenings when we went dancing after work, the nights with his hands on my skin, his lips on mine—I wanted to throw up.

Devon's pride wouldn't let my insult stand. He'd have to make a power move soon if he wanted to secure his position in the office—but what would he do? Whatever it was, it would be bad for me.

Would he tell Monica about Posey's book? That I had considered making an offer without her? If so, what would Monica do? If she heard it from Devon, she'd probably fire me. Did Devon have that kind of cruel streak in him?

I remembered his cold eyes, and shivered again.

If it meant making my position vacant, I wouldn't put it past him.

After sweeping back the curtains, I leaned against the window and gazed over the rooftops of the city. *What do I do next, Grandpa?* I thought to myself. *How do I turn this mess into something positive?*

I took a deep breath and tried to clear my thoughts. The sun was setting, the light catching the corners of the buildings, the windows reflecting the sheen like gold. Was there a person like me behind each of those windows? Someone struggling to find her own way, her own happiness? Someone who had made mistakes, who had faced heartache and fear, and who had learned to reach for something more?

Exhaling, I fogged up the glass with my breath. I drew an ampersand in the mist and smiled. My heart filled with courage at the familiar symbol. It made me think of my grandpa; it made me think of Jesse. In a city of more than eight million people, I knew how easy it was to get lost, but I'd also learned how easy it was to find a friend.

If Devon tells Monica, that's a problem. And the best way to solve a problem is to stop it before it starts. What if . . .

I tapped my finger to my lips. No. It was a terrible idea. A crazy, dangerous idea.

On the other hand, it could be the best idea in the world.

I could wait for Devon to make the first move, or I could take action and claim the prize for myself.

Was I brave enough? Did I believe in myself enough?

That was the real question.

Being with Jesse, even briefly, had shown me a side of myself that was a sassy, flirty, bold girl who spoke her mind and wasn't shy about what she wanted. That girl must have always been inside me, but my mother hadn't seen her. Devon certainly had never seen her. I hadn't ever, really. I suspected my grandfather had, though.

And Jesse.

That was what I'd seen in his eyes but couldn't identify—my own reflection. The bravery and confidence that had occasionally surfaced in me, like when I applied for all of those jobs, or when I gave Monica the draft of *Unmarked,* and today when I stood up for myself with Devon—that was, in reality, a part of me that finally got a chance to shine.

It took a stranger seeing the truth in me to help me see it for myself.

If I could summon that girl now, push past the sting of having been used by Devon, perhaps I could still add something positive to my life.

Another of my grandfather's favorite words came to mind: *Moxie. Definition: Courage, determination, know-how.*

It certainly wouldn't win me another round of Definitions against Jesse, but I held on to the word like a lifeline.

I padded over to the couch and picked up my phone then returned to my spot by my window. I wanted to see the entire view of the world in front of me while I made this leap.

Opening my text messages, I composed a simple note to Monica:

Falling into Deep Water *is a winner. Would love to have you read it when you return. Perhaps we could make an offer?*

Fear ran up my spine at the same time that elation spread to my fingers. Before I could stop myself, I hit send.

If Monica was going to hear about Posey's book, it would be from me, not from Devon.

All that was left to do was wait for Monday.

EIGHT

"Good morning, Everett," I said as I passed his office on Monday. "Did you have a nice weekend?"

He gave me the thumbs-up sign but never broke concentration from his computer screen.

"Glad to hear it," I said, stepping into my office and closing the door. I took my time settling in for the workweek. Checked my messages, returned a few emails. Found myself humming under my breath.

What a glorious Monday it had turned out to be.

I checked my text messages one more time—just to be sure—then picked up my office phone and pressed three buttons.

"Devon, could you come to my office, please?" I didn't bother waiting for his answer.

It took him five minutes to come next door and knock.

He didn't bother waiting for me to answer. He pushed open the door and stood in the entryway, arms folded, feet spread for stability. He probably thought he looked intimidating.

"We need to finish our conversation from Saturday," I started without preamble.

"I thought we said all that needed to be said." Devon shifted his weight, frowning.

"We did. But Monica wanted to add a postscript." I tapped a few buttons on my phone and held it out for Devon to read.

Six words. Monica preferred precision.

I trust you. Make the offer.

Smiling at Devon, I said, "That'll be all, Mr. White. Thank you."

He didn't say anything. I wasn't sure if he could speak; the muscles in his face and jaw had locked tight. His eyes frosted over, and he turned and left, pulling my door closed in a near slam.

I looked at the message again, still pinching myself every time I read the words. When my phone had buzzed during my dinner with Jesse on Sunday evening, I knew everything would be okay.

Monica and Lucy. We were going to make a great team.

I wasn't so foolish as to believe there wouldn't still be an *and* connecting me to Devon. I doubted this would be the last time I'd clash with him over a book. But that was all right. Batman had Robin, yes, but he also had the Joker. At least now I knew I had the strength to stand behind my convictions and go after exactly what I wanted.

And what I wanted was to be part of the "Jesse and Lucy" team.

Picking up where I'd left off humming a tune, I turned

to my computer and began composing an email to Ms. Posey Phillips, welcoming her to the Baker Publishing House family.

Two weeks later, the reception for Whittaker Jules and his world-renowned novel *Unmarked,* held by the staff of Baker Publishing House in the legendary Roosevelt Hotel's Terrace Ballroom, was nothing short of a smashing success. The room was decorated in brown and gold silk, with original Tiffany chandeliers and arched, floor-to-ceiling windows that overlooked 45th Street.

All three hundred guests arrived, and nearly everyone commented on the beauty of the handmade invitations.

I made sure to direct each compliment to Jesse, who hovered all night by the far wall, champagne flute in hand, positioned perfectly to snag an hors d'oeuvre from each tray as it passed. If even half of the people who accepted one of the business cards he handed out contacted him, Jesse would have enough work to last him a year.

Monica worked the room like a queen reigning over her subjects. Her presence was a gravitational force, and a line of people trailed behind her like a comet's tail. She greeted every guest by name and commented on a personal detail she knew about them. She even kissed my mother's cheek when I introduced them to each other.

"Your daughter is a treasure," Monica said, bestowing a benevolent smile on me.

My mother beamed and squeezed my hand. "Thank you for inviting me. This is so exciting."

"Enjoy the party, Mom," I said before leaving her to dance with Everett.

Devon was not in attendance.

Lifting a champagne flute for myself from a nearby tray, I sauntered over to join Jesse. His eyes followed my every step and sway.

"The belle of the ball," he said with appreciation and delight.

I twirled for him, showing off my shimmering gold dress with the low neckline and woven straps in the back. With diamonds at my throat and ears, I felt like I had stepped out of a storybook.

"How are things with your mom?" Jesse asked, gesturing with his flute.

"Better," I said. "I'm taking her to lunch tomorrow, where I hope we will *not* talk about my work. She's writing her memoirs, did I tell you that? I think she thinks I'll publish it and make it a bestseller."

"Ah, the power of having friends in high places."

"I don't have that much power. But I'm still interested in reading it. She hasn't always been an easy person to get to know. Maybe this will help."

I watched my mother on the dance floor, and I realized that ours was another relationship where the *and* was there to stay, and that I had a responsibility to make it better.

"Do you think she'll like me?" Jesse asked, following my gaze.

"Of course she will. Everyone likes you. Especially me." I leaned against his side and ran my hand up the lapel of his jacket. I could feel his heart beating strong and sure beneath my touch. "You look nice tonight."

He'd slicked back his dark hair, the ends skimming his collar, and he'd allowed his stubble to grow into a neatly trimmed beard. With the bowtie and pocket handkerchief, he looked every inch how I imagined Chester Hammond might have.

&

"Hey, when you're the honored guest on the arm of the most beautiful woman in the room, you do what you can to make an impression. And this is some party. At the Roosevelt, no less."

"Monica picked it because it's the original building from 1924, the year—"

"*Unmarked* is set. Your boss has a nice flair for the dramatic."

"You read it? I thought you had all those other books to read first."

Jesse shrugged. "You've probably heard this a lot, but I couldn't put it down."

Smiling, I took another drink of champagne. "Welcome to the club."

"You were right, you know. About the last line. I'm glad you didn't tell me what it was. It was better to read it for myself."

"'He saw the diamond inside me,'" I quoted from Violet's last speech. "'He knew I was capable of strength and clarity and light before I knew it myself. I will love him forever for showing myself to me.'"

Jesse's eyes sparkled. It had been those eyes—that saw art in the words that surrounded him, that saw beauty in unexpected places, that saw the diamond inside of me—that I had fallen in love with first. Instantaneously and completely.

"That Violet is quite the captivating narrator."

I touched his cheek and turned his face towards mine. "Thank you," I said, knowing the words weren't strong enough to express my gratitude at having found Jesse, and at having been found by him. "I'm glad you're here with me."

"I couldn't pass up an invitation to the party of the century. Especially not since I printed them myself."

"Oh, certainly not the century," I demurred with a wicked lift to my grin. I took a final sip of champagne. "Perhaps the decade."

He slipped his hand around my waist, and a spark flared to life deep inside me. He leaned closer. "Does that mean I'll need to come to more of these parties with you? I don't know if I can handle seeing you in all those beautiful dresses all the time."

"What's wrong with my dress?" I asked.

"It's still on you," he husked, lifting my hand to his lips and pressing a kiss to my wrist where my pulse throbbed.

What had started as a spark transformed into a rolling heat. I parted my lips; the air I breathed in was heavy and sweet.

He pulled back, meeting my eyes. "There wouldn't happen to be some place private at this party, would there?"

I wove my fingers through his. "Follow me," I managed.

Weaving through the crowd, I headed for the back of the ballroom. We deposited our flutes on an end table before stepping into the cool shadows. People milled around the main floor, visiting with Monica and Whittaker, or grouped around the tall windows, enjoying the view of the city, but lucky for me, the alcove was empty, and when I pulled Jesse around the corner we were suddenly and completely alone.

He pressed me against the wall, his hands resting on either side of my face. He was close enough that I could feel the heat from his body next to mine. Close enough to cling to. To kiss.

His desire was palpable, demanding. But he didn't move. He looked at me with his dark artist's eyes as though he could read my emotions as they crossed my face. He probably could. I felt each one of them surging through me—satisfaction, anticipation, joy, desire.

&

"You are an amazing woman, Lucy," he said, touching his forehead to mine. "A diamond to rival the stars."

I lifted my face to him, relishing the nearness of his skin to mine. I had once thought of him as earth and wind, but I was wrong. He was fire and steel.

"And?" I whispered. My lips could barely form the word.

"And every day with you has been a revelation." His right hand slipped around the back of my neck, holding me steady.

I needed the support. My breathing quickened. "And?"

"And every day I'm more grateful that the open sign was still up when you came to my shop." His other hand slipped down my shoulder, my arm, to rest in the curve of my waist above my hip.

"And?"

He hesitated. "And?" he repeated.

I couldn't wait any longer. I wrapped my arms around his neck, threading my fingers through his hair and arching my body to meet his. "And, are you going to kiss me?"

He grinned, then lowered his mouth to mine, his lips soft and sure at first, but then he deepened the kiss. His fingers tightened on my waist, and at the back of my head, holding me steady, keeping me close.

I matched his passion with my own, determined to never let him go. I smiled beneath his lips, flushed with the knowledge that I had been chosen.

He kissed me until all I could do was surrender.

And all I could think was *Yes.*

ABOUT LISA MANGUM

Lisa Mangum has worked with books ever since elementary school, when she volunteered at the school library during recess. Her first paying job was shelving books at the Sandy Library. She worked for five years at Waldenbooks while she attended the University of Utah, graduating with honors with a degree in English. She has worked in the publishing industry since 1997. In 2014 she was named the Editorial Manager for Shadow Mountain.

Besides books, Lisa loves movies, spending time with her family, trips to Disneyland, and vanilla ice cream topped with fresh raspberries. She lives in Taylorsville, Utah, with her husband, Tracy.

She is the author of four award-winning books: the *Hourglass Door* trilogy and *After Hello*.

Follow Lisa on Twitter: @LisaMangum

Dear Timeless Romance Anthology Reader,

Thank you for reading this anthology. We hoped you loved the sweet romance novellas! Heather B. Moore, Annette Lyon, and Sarah M. Eden have been indie publishing this series since 2012 through the Mirror Press imprint. For each anthology, we carefully select three guest authors. Our goal is to offer a way for our readers to discover new, favorite authors by reading these romance novellas written exclusively for our anthologies . . . all for one great price.

If you enjoyed this anthology, please consider leaving a review on Goodreads or Amazon or any other e-book store you purchase through. Reviews and word-of-mouth is what helps us continue this fun project. For updates and notifications of sales and giveaways, please sign up for our monthly newsletter here on our blog:

TimelessRomanceAnthologies.blogspot.com.

Also, if you're interested in become a regular reviewer of the anthologies and would like access to advance copies, please email Heather Moore: heather@hbmoore.com

Find us on Facebook for our latest updates.

Thank you!

The Timeless Romance Authors

MORE TIMELESS ROMANCE ANTHOLOGIES

Made in the USA
Middletown, DE
21 October 2022

13187002R00179